THE WAR STORIES OF THE SEVEN TROUBLESOME SISTERS BOOK 4

SHE'S THE ONE

WHO DOESN'T SAY MUCH

S. R. CRONIN

For Kevin, because he understands.

Warning: You Are About to Enter Ilari

Welcome to the thirteenth century in a universe almost identical to your own. The one major difference here is the existence of Ilari.

Ilari (el ARE ee) is a small hidden coalition of principalities in far eastern Europe. It has never been conquered thanks to its natural protection and the magic of its people. The lack of outside influence means that much will be new to you. But fear not, you have tools to help.

A map of Ilari is located at the front and back of this book. The back also contains a description of the twelve nichnas (tiny principalities) that comprise Ilari.

Ilarians do not use any variation of the Roman Calendar, as Rome never invaded their realm. Each chapter starts with a picture of the Ilarian calendar. The darkened area is when that chapter takes place.

Ilarians use nine-day anks instead of seven-day weeks. They use forty-five-day eighths of the year instead of 30-day months. Each eighth begins with one of their eight seasonal holidays. They call the holiday and the eighth that follows it by the same name. Details are at the back of the book.

They have some unique words with no English translation. Those words are also provided in the back. On the last page, you will find a list of the characters you are about to meet.

Ilarians of the 1200s have some contact with the outside even though legend says interaction with others used to be far more rare. Ilarian scholars know facts about world history and the current events beyond their borders. What they know matches what you know because the world outside of Ilari is like the one in which we live.

However, the world inside is filled with surprises.

Enjoy your visit!

The Map of Ilari

The Year of Immense Concern

~ 1 ~

An Unexpected Scrudite

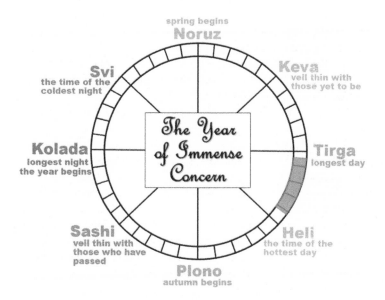

"What's your name?"

His calm face told me he meant to be polite, nothing more, but such a direct question from a Scrudite made me nervous. Yes, I needed his help, but I'd been taught to use caution when dealing with these people.

"Must you know my name in order to tend to my injured horse?" I asked. I stood tall, willing my slight frame into all the bulkiness I could.

He laughed, but his shoulders slumped as he turned away from me.

"No, I'll help you no matter how disagreeable you are."

Bold words from one such as him. "I'm not disagreeable."

"Perhaps not," he said. "Maybe you're frightened. I have trouble telling the difference."

His words froze the response on my lips. I *was* scared of him and his people. Most Vinxites, especially those from families like mine, had never spoken to a Scrudite.

I turned my artist's eye upon him. Despite his weathered skin, he was young, like me. Unlike me, he had muscles from a life of strenuous work. The sun had added glints of gold to his brown hair and his clothes were the usual mishmash of tattered rags worn by Scrudites.

"It's just a sprain," he said as felt around my horse's front right ankle. The mare stood still, unusually cooperative around a stranger. He massaged her leg gently.

"I'll get a poultice on it. Let her rest overnight; she'll be able to walk on it tomorrow and carry your things, though you shouldn't ride her yet. Not for a few days."

"She can't possibly rest here for the night. I've no place to stay."

I had to pass through a small piece of Scrud to get from my parents' farm to the art studios in K'ba where my friends lived. I knew our poorest nichna lacked the inns found throughout the rest of the realm, but I hadn't worried. My journey was short, and I didn't intend to stop. Who knew *what* a stranded traveler did here.

"No Scrudite would expect a stranger to sleep alone in the desolation." He seemed offended at the thought as he pointed out toward the dusty openness. "Our wolves are far too bold. You'll sleep with me."

"I'll do no such thing!"

Another laugh, this one more amused.

"That's not what I meant. The people of Scrud do not force themselves on each other, much less on those passing through. One of my sisters will be glad to share my hut to put you at ease. I've room for three. I'd prefer to send you to *her* hut, but your horse needs to remain still, and I suspect she'll only do so if you stay nearby."

This man, this Scrudite, was doing his best with me. It wasn't his fault my horse had managed to step into a hole only paces from where he made his pitiful life. Despite his situation, he'd offered me as much courtesy as any gentleman in Pilk would have. Perhaps more.

"Thank you. If your sister is as kind as you, I look forward to meeting her."

I looked around. He and his family had to be part of the clan of Scrudites whose tiny huts hugged the forest's scraggly edge. These people made their meager living carving the beautiful hardwoods that grew at the margins of their nichna. Our entire realm valued the products they produced, and some thought his clan accessed ancient magic to infuse into their creations.

I'd always considered that last bit to be wishful thinking. Some Ilarians imagined they saw the old magic everywhere they looked.

As he turned to fetch his sister, I reached out for his arm to stop him. He seemed startled at my touch.

"Olivine," I said. "My name is Olivine."

"Odd name. Mine's Bohdan."

"Thank you for helping a traveler, Bohdan."

The next day I walked to K'ba, leading my mare along the dusty road. Despite the long days of Tirga, nightfall nipped at my heels by the time I arrived. I must have looked pitiful, hobbling with aching feet into the main street in my grimy dress with my limping horse behind me.

I'd come to meet five artist friends for a reunion we'd planned on our last day of school. We'd all finished our studies a few anks ago; three men and three women, all unattached. For two years we'd shared dedication to our art and those poignant first experiences away from home. I felt we were friends in the truest sense of the word. Only I and one other in the group had the misfortune to live outside of K'ba.

I found all five of them in the tavern owned by one of their parents. They looked like they'd been enjoying free ale for a while.

"Olivine!"

A young man shouted to me as I came through the door, his deep voice carrying across the room. Large in body and personality, Magomet covered the distance between us and had his arms around me in a friendly hug before I could say a word. I tried to squirm out of it, but for a heartbeat he held me tighter as I did. Then he let go.

Back in school, he and I had celebrated a few holidays together the way unmarried tidzys do. I'd backed off, fearing he would develop an interest in marrying me. I liked him and admired his talent, but I tired of the way he filled every room while I, with my quiet ways and slender frame, melted into nothingness next to him.

Despite my clear message, though, he always managed to remind me that he remained interested.

After I wiggled out of his embrace I hugged the other men and women around the table then gulped down an entire ale while they shouted over the noise in the tavern to get caught up on our lives.

"Now that we've finished school, we need to do this a lot more," one said.

"How about we form an artists' group?" another suggested. "Olivine and Arek can come over to K'ba, and we'll paint together and critique each other and share ideas like we did when we were in class."

"Brilliant," Magomet agreed. His artist parents had allowed us to use their huge studio when school went on break. "We'll meet when my parents are gone so they won't mind us painting in the studio."

"I bet mine will still give us supplies," said the friend whose parents ran an art supply store and had been giving us surplus items for free.

"Mine will help with food and drink," said the one whose parents owned the tavern we drank in.

"Mine too," added Zoya, my closest friend in the group. Her parents had already agreed to put me up that night at their inn.

Arek and I smiled the hardest. We'd both worried about how we'd pursue our art alone, back in our home nichnas, with no one to encourage us.

I stayed for three more days, soaking up the joy of sharing my life's passion with those who felt as I did, and giving my horse enough time so she could be ridden home. I didn't wish to make that hot dusty walk twice.

As I got ready to leave, I remembered the surprisingly kind Scrudite who'd helped me. Funny, I'd told my friends all about my horse's injury but I'd largely left Bohdan out of my story. Did I think my well-off friends wouldn't be sympathetic to a kind Scrudite? Of course they would be. It just wasn't my way to tell everyone everything, like so many others seemed compelled to do.

Yet, I wanted to thank Bohdan for the supper I'd shared with him and his sister, for the blankets and straw they'd lent me, and for the way they'd entertained me with their stories of other travelers. So, I found an artists' stall selling items to those who sculpted.

"I'd like to see your better knives," I said.

"For you?" True, few women were sculptors.

"No, for a friend." The man nodded, more comfortable with that request. "How adept is your friend?"

I had no idea, so I guessed. "He lacks formal training but is quite skilled for the self-taught. He works with wood not stone." I didn't offer the information that my friend carved practical items, not artistic ones.

The man produced his best suggestion. It cost more coins than I wanted to spend, and almost more than I had with me. Yet, what would I have done without Bohdan's help?

"I'll take it."

****

"I couldn't possibly take this."

Bohdan had been easy to find because he lived in the shack closest to the road. I wondered why. Perhaps his group viewed him as some sort of guard?

"Please. It's my thank you."

"Scrudites do not accept presents as thanks for acting like decent human beings," he said.

I'm sure I rolled my eyes. "Could you use this knife?"

"Yes. It looks excellent and is something I could never afford."

"Then take it as a gift of … friendship."

"Oh. We're friends now?"

I sighed loud enough for him to hear,

5

"I'm going to be passing this way often. It's on the direct path between my parents' home and the art studio I'll be using. I could use a friend along my route. Yes, I know." I held up a hand to stop him. "I'm sure Scrudites do not require gifts in order to be nice to passing strangers. Will you take it to please me?"

"Only if you'll say hello whenever you pass through. When you do, I'll show you the things I've made with this wonderful knife."

He smiled. I smiled. And I realized that yes, the Scrudite and I could become friends.

****

As the long days of Tirga moved towards the intense heat of Heli, I traveled to K'ba every ank to meet the other artists, usually spending four or five of the nine days there. My parents didn't complain, as long as I did my share of chores and I asked them for only a few coins to support my travel.

The ride over to K'ba took over half a day, so I usually left well before dawn, knowing my eyes dealt with faint light better than most. Even so, sweat poured down my face by the time I arrived. But the heat of the summer didn't deter me.

Bohdan often worked outside when I passed and I wondered if it was deliberate or not. He always insisted on giving me a drink, and perhaps some fruit, maybe berries he'd found ripening in the forest earlier that morning. I began bringing baked goods with me, so I could offer him a pastry in return. I didn't think the Scrudites did much in the way of baking, but he sure seemed to have developed a taste for it.

Sometimes I got off my horse as we exchanged these gifts, and we'd talk about our work as we ate. I learned a little about carving; he liked knowing more about my paints. It broke up the ride, and before long, I looked forward to our visits.

Most of the artists I met in school grew up in K'ba. K'ba had once been as poor as Scrud, before musicians and poets began moving to its northeast boundary along the Canyon River. Over many decades, actors and playwrights followed. Eventually, the wealthiest began to make the trek through the desolation to be entertained. Now, taverns and eating places employed imaginative cooks while lavish lodging catered to their desires for a memorable experience.

Artists had made their home in K'ba for generations, and my friends' talents had been encouraged since birth. Seldom did a daughter of farmers become one of them. Yet, I had.

So over the next few anks, I made a plan, a most unusual plan. I would produce enough sellable art to be able to move to K'ba, pursue my passion, and be with my friends all the time. Unmarried daughters seldom left home like that, and I worried about the dowry I'd be cheating my family out of by leaving. I figured I needed to sell enough to offer them some compensation and still be able to rent a room with the space to work. After that, I'd live off of my art as I enjoyed the life of my dreams.

I settled onto the front porch of our farmhouse early one morning, hoping to sketch before the day got too hot. I knew of a bird's nest in a tree a hundred paces away, tilted so I could see the eggs from the porch.

I enjoyed the morning breeze on my face as the world blurred around the edges and my eyes focused on the tree in the distance. I turned the force of my stare onto its branches as the small nest filled my field of vision and the leaves around it smeared into an indistinguishable green haze. I stared harder as I studied how the light reflected off of the tiny eggs, preparing to draw.

"Put that sketchbook down and do something useful." My mother's voice pulled me back with words she'd said a thousand times before. "You're wasting your life with those drawings. How will you find a husband if you never get out there and talk to anyone?"

I don't want a husband. He'll expect me to cook and clean instead of draw and paint. Why would I want that?

But I knew to keep such an answer to myself.

"Just let me finish this one thing," I replied for the thousandth time. Then I picked up my charcoal as she shook her head and walked back into the house.

~ 2 ~

Celibate in K'ba

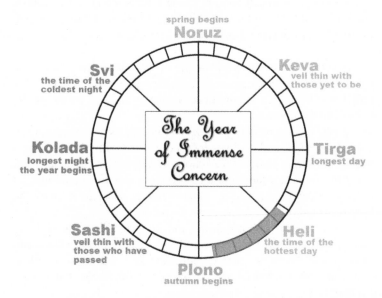

Most young people embraced the freedom offered to them on the holidays with enthusiasm. But not all, and certainly not every one of *my* sisters. Our oldest, Ryalgar, charged ahead with confidence in most arenas but hesitated in this one. Coral, only a year behind her, claimed to enjoy the holidays quite a lot while Sulphur, the sister that followed a year later, acted as if it was all a nuisance.

Celestine, my twin, had beautiful features and a warm personality people loved. Even when we were children, boys paid more attention to her than me. Another sister might have felt

8

jealous, but I considered it a gift. Being left alone between holidays gave me more time to paint.

As to my enthusiasm in this regard, I resembled Coral. I found boys' bodies intriguing and once I discovered the pleasure they could provide, I saw no reason to hold back.

Until Magomet.

He and I celebrated Svi together during our first year of advanced studies. I'd already observed several holidays with others and didn't hesitate when he asked me to enjoy Noruz with him, too. But after Noruz, he looked at me differently. He tried to touch me all the time. No matter what I did, he was always around. I had second thoughts about celebrating Keva with him, but no clear reason to say no.

His passion that night exceeded anything I'd encountered, and the next day he begged me to return to his bed and never leave. That's when I knew I had a problem. I didn't want Magomet for a lover or a husband. Yet, he was my friend, my benefactor in the sense of letting me use his parents' studio, and a close buddy to every other friend I had. What to do?

So, I came up with a creative solution. I would put all of my sexual energy into my art. Better to live without sex, than to have a lover I didn't want or to lose my closest friends and, along with them, the future I craved. How hard could being celibate be? At least two of my older sisters had largely managed it, and they seemed fine.

When I declared to everyone at school that I would begin directing my sexual energy to my painting, I meant it. My announcement caused curiosity and some admiration, but Magomet's reaction differed. I saw his disappointment and hints of anger. Then, within a few days, I saw his acceptance. He could wait. I'd come around, and he'd be there with open arms.

Thus, he and I began the strange dance we still did over a year later. He pretended to be a staunch supporter of my lifestyle, and I pretended I didn't notice his touches and the longing in his eyes. Our friends ignored it all.

The problem with my brilliant solution was that I still wanted to have sex, only with *other* people besides Magomet. Worse yet, once intimacy wasn't an option, I craved it in a way I never had.

So, I tried celebrating holidays at my parents' farm. I snuck off to gatherings of other tidzys from Vinx and engaged in discreet encounters with local boys, hoping word of my behavior would never make it back to those I knew from K'ba.

However, I couldn't hide my actions from Celestine. We shared the same friends growing up. She reminded me that many our age knew others elsewhere, and eventually people talked. She made a good point. So when my second year of advanced studies started, I returned to being as celibate as I claimed to be, and far more frustrated than my fellow artists realized.

The morning of Heli I helped my mother with chores, thinking I'd leave for K'ba the next day, after my usual quiet holiday night at home. As we polished the silverware, I thought ... why not leave today instead? Maybe I'd see Bohdan on the way. Maybe .... My insides responded unexpectedly to the thought of a proper holiday celebration.

Oh my. Did I find Bohdan that appealing?

Honestly, the more I got to know him, the sexier he was. I knew he didn't have a wife or a girlfriend, because he'd joked about how his mother referred to him as the oldest single man she knew. I couldn't imagine why the girls of Scrud hadn't fallen all over him, but that was another matter.

Who would hear about anything that happened in Scrud? No one.

Did he have plans for Heli? Quite possibly. But I'd never know unless I rode through, would I? And if he did, I'd just move on and spend an evening alone in K'ba. What was the difference?

My mother and I sat at our dining table, polishing the eating utensils. As I told her of my change in plans, she laid down her cloth and looked at me.

"Remember, it's just as easy to fall in love with a prince," she said.

I dropped a spoon on the floor.

"You've been saying that to me since I was six. What if I don't want a prince?"

"Oh, don't be so defensive. I'd think a young woman like *you* would want a husband with all the means possible."

"What do you mean like *me*?"

"You know. One who wants to paint. You must realize the arts are the prerogative of women with rich husbands. Anything less than a house full of servants, and you'll be too busy with your chores to have a hobby."

Did she suspect I planned to live on my own?

"You spend a lot of time over in K'ba," she said with a knowing smile. "I understand the place is full of free spirits who probably appeal to you, but think twice. An artist husband won't give you the life you want. He'll expect you to take care of him while *he* paints."

No. She suspected I'd fallen in love with another artist.

"There's nothing wrong with trying out possibilities, dear. That's what being a tidzy is for. But you're outgrowing your time. Consider being more friendly. I'm told the boys here thought you didn't like them because you kept to yourself so much as you grew up."

"I liked the boys fine, Mom. They were all busy paying attention to Celestine. She saved me from a lot of stupid conversations."

"Well, there aren't many men who can give you the future you want. Remember that."

She had no idea of the future I wanted, and it was probably best kept that way.

I didn't get to Scrud until midday, and then I didn't see Bohdan anywhere. Scrudites lived in tiny huts meant only for sleeping. I'd learned they did most of their cooking and socializing in communal areas. Bohdan could be having a midday meal.

I tethered my horse and walked into the shade of the sparse trees, looking for the common area I'd visited before. Several Scrudite men of all ages sat together on the ground under a canopy, laughing and eating soup. I had no idea where the women had gone.

Bohdan looked up and it was the first time he appeared less than pleased to see me. I turned to go. I had walked into his home uninvited, and I had no wish to cause him trouble.

He jumped up and followed me.

"I didn't mean to intrude," I said.

"It's okay. You surprised me. You've never come through here so late in the day."

I knew it was more than that.

"What was going on back there?"

"Pfft." He made a dismissive sound with his lips. "The old men. They've nothing better to do than tease us unmarried ones on the holidays."

"They think you should be celebrating more?"

He laughed. "It's complicated. I suppose they get satisfaction from talking about what they once did. They particularly like to pick on me."

"Hmmm. I left my parents' farm after getting a similar lecture from my mother. According to her, I need to be more friendly."

I looked him in the eye.

"Really?" he said. "You're thinking of being more friendly with me?"

Was I?

He cocked his head to one side and smiled.

"It seems your horse is tired from the heat and needs to rest overnight."

"My horse is fine."

He ignored me. "The wolves are fierce after dark in this part of the realm. A man from Scrud would never let a woman sleep alone out here."

"My horse doesn't need to rest."

"But, alas, my sister, who would normally serve as a chaperone, is busy tonight."

Was he playing with me?

"She's not one to let a holiday go by unobserved. Not her. You'll have to stay with me all alone."

He looked me in the eye to see if I'd finally caught on. I had, and to be sure he knew I had, I put my arms around his neck and kissed him. I could tell by the way he kissed back that he liked where this was going.

"What about the old men back at your pavilion?" I managed to ask.

"Pfft. Let them have their fun imagining what we're doing. We'll be the ones doing it."

Of all the decisions I'd made recently, the one to follow Bohdan into his tiny shack felt like one of my better ones.

The next morning I rode on to K'ba, feeling like I owned the world. I stopped first at Zoya's parents' tavern. I'd grown the closest to Zoya and had confided in her about Magomet. She looked at me as I walked in and raised an eyebrow.

"You seem unusually happy."

I shrugged but said nothing.

"Is it possible someone broke her vow of celibacy on this hot Heli holiday?" Her voice teased, but I knew she meant well. "Olivine, you can't stay away from men forever…"

"Okay. Maybe I haven't. Completely. But let's keep that between us now, please. Until … until later."

"Of course." Zoya didn't push, and I liked that about her.

"Our inn is full, what with the holiday, but let's go over to Pasha's place. I think they have a room for you."

"I can pay for my room, you know. I've sold a little, and my father gave me coins, too."

"None of us want your money, not if we have space. Come on, we're all happy to have you here."

"I hope to paint more this time. My mother is making me crazy. I can't wait to move."

She took my hand and held it in both of hers. "I can't wait to have you living here, either."

I do remember that Bohdan was the first person who asked me to worry about the Mongols.

I stopped off to see him on my way home after Heli, telling myself I wanted to ensure there was no awkwardness between us. The holiday was over, after all, and I hoped he and I would continue to be friends.

He sat outside his shack, tending to something as I rode by. His wave and shout assured me he wanted to see me. Good news.

I rode over and as I grew close I saw the same longing in his eyes I'd seen in Magomet's.

My first thought was *horse scump, not this again.*

My second thought took a different turn.

It is still kind of close to a holiday. I could get off this horse right now, and he'd have sex with me, and it would probably be every bit as good as it was four days ago.

My third thought was to get off my horse and see if I was right.

I did. And I was.

We lay together afterward, talking as people do. I shared my ideas of living on my own in K'ba, and he shared what he'd worked on recently. I'd already seen a set of beautiful bowls he'd carved with the knife I'd bought him. Now, he turned to a bin near his mat and pulled out a handful of small shivs, sized to fit in a skirt pocket.

"Our leaders in Scrud worry about these Mongols, too," he said. "They worry the army won't bother to defend the likes of us. But I've been thinking about the women in Ilari. We've heard what happens to females in an invasion. The idea of … my mother, my aunts, my sisters. It just makes me sick."

"Women face added risks," I said. "When conquered, we endure things men generally don't."

"I know. I thought I could make these, and give them to women to carry. Here, hold this." He put one of the shivs in my hand. "What do you think? Could you defend yourself if you had this?"

I held the tiny weapon tight. Perhaps I imagined it, but the wood felt poised to defend me.

"I could do some damage, if it was up close and personal, which I guess it would be. Then maybe once they discovered how dangerous Ilarian women are, they'd think twice before assaulting us."

He nodded. "That's what I'd hope for. I'm going to start making as many of these as I can. Give one to every woman I meet."

I looked around at his meager belongings. There were no comforts. None. "Bohdan, don't you think you should sell them? At least for a little something?"

"How could I do that? Come on, Olivine. No woman should have to pay me to keep herself safe."

Then he looked at me and his face softened. He reached out and took a piece of my long bronze hair between his fingers and looked into my eyes. He'd already told me how much he loved their intense green color. I expected him to compliment them again, but instead he said, "I wish you were more of a fighter."

I raised an eyebrow. "I rather thought you liked me the way I was."

He looked down, embarrassed. "Oh, I do. I mean I wish you had more ways to look out for yourself. You're just not that physical, and I think force is all these monsters will understand."

"I have physical skills."

"Yes, so you've demonstrated. I don't mean those, you're great in that area."

"I don't mean in that area. They made me learn stuff in school, told me I had to develop my body to be well rounded."

Right away I regretted saying it. The Royals of each nichna prided themselves on sponsoring basic education for children, everywhere but Scrud. If Scrud even *had* Royals, which I wasn't sure they did. I'd already learned Bohdan was embarrassed he'd never been to school, although an older sister had taught him to read and write some.

"So what did they make you learn?" he asked.

"How to shoot an arrow with a bow."

"Seriously? Are you any good?"

"I used to be. Surprised everyone, most of all me." I paused. I hesitated to talk too much about the many things I'd gotten to do over the years because Bohdan had been offered so few opportunities.

"I do this thing, it's hard to explain, but if I concentrate on something small that's far away, like a flower or a bee or a leaf, it looks bigger and it comes into clear focus while everything else goes blurry."

"Sounds useful for an artist."

"Oh, it is. I used to think everyone could do it. I mean, who talks about how their eyes work, right? But when I was in Pilk I found out it's called being a long eye, and it's uncommon. Some artists have it but most don't. Anyway, it helped me with archery, too. Not so much the seeing far part, but more the ability to focus on something so intently. I got a kick out of being good at a physical activity for once."

He'd gone back to worrying. "If I asked you to pick up a bow again and practice, would you? For me?"

"Of course, but why? You know I'm trying to make as much art as I can so I can move to K'ba. There are only so many hours of light in a day."

"True. But it could be a way to defend your home. I think Ilari will need all the fighters it can get, and all the *kinds* of fighters it can get."

He just wasn't going to stop fretting about the Mongols. I rolled my eyes.

"Okay. A little archery every day, I promise. The sunshine will do me good."

~ 3 ~

An Inappropriate Choice

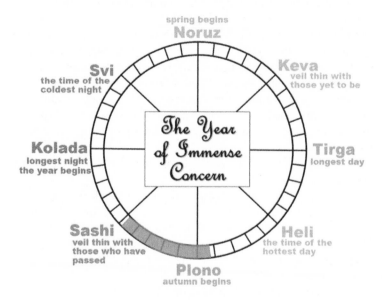

Soon, I looked forward to the rides back and forth as much as I looked forward to my time in K'ba. Bohdan knew my schedule and never failed to be near the road on the days I came and went. His family and friends mostly left us alone, but when someone curious found an excuse to come by, he introduced me as if Scrudites often entertained travelers from Vinx. I wondered if perhaps they did, and Vinxites were the ones who didn't mention it.

We usually exchanged small gifts, typically food and drink, until I gave him one of my paintings. A tiny thing done on wood, it showed a green bird alighting on a branch. He held it against his heart like something precious, then he hung it in his hut. I couldn't have been more pleased.

As Plono approached, I suspected he hoped we'd celebrate it together, but I explained that my sister Coral was with child and would be married that day. Obviously, I needed and wanted to be at her wedding.

Had Bohdan been from Vinx, or another nichna, I'd have invited him to the festivities as my guest. No one would have raised an eyebrow. But a woman from Vinx didn't show up at her sister's wedding with a Scrudite guest.

After getting to know Bohdan, I questioned why this was so. But I also knew a Scrudite's presence would generate a lot of attention. Was it fair to Coral to turn my growing qualms about social status into a centerpiece of her wedding? No. So I avoided the topic with Bohdan. If he was offended, he didn't show it.

On my last visit before Plono, I felt out of sorts. I got off my horse only to exchange a few words before I rode on. As I turned to mount my horse, he touched my arm to stop me. I expected trouble, maybe an argument about not inviting him to my sister's wedding.

"I almost forgot," he said. "Look what I did to the painting you gave me."

He disappeared into his hut and came out with my tiny green bird. He'd put attractive sticks of wood around all four sides of it.

"See. I carved them to look nice, and then I attached them to the edges to protect your work. If you like it, I can do this to other paintings, to keep them from getting damaged when you cart them around."

I thought the decorative border did more than protect. The wood seemed to murmur "Look at this. Isn't it beautiful?"

"It improves the painting," I said. "Makes it bigger, too. I think people will prefer to hang them with these good-looking pieces of wood. I'll sell more."

"That's even better."

He put his arms around my waist. When he drew me in to kiss me, I realized I'd lost my desire to kiss anyone else. Had I found a man who understood me, after years of thinking such a thing didn't exist?

If so, given the circumstances, what could I possibly do about it?

As I helped my family get ready for the big event, I thought about my predicament. Before meeting Bohdan, I assumed I'd be one of those women who never married. I'd spend my life painting, supporting myself with my art. I'd enjoy the pleasures of being a tidzy for as long as was reasonable, then once I got too old, I'd do without.

But Bohdan had complicated my life. I still liked my plan, a lot, except for the act like a tidzy part. I didn't want different men. I wanted Bohdan. Once couples got to that point they usually wed.

But I didn't want a husband.

Even if I did, a life with this one would be an uphill battle. My parents preached tolerance and never specifically forbade courtship with anyone. They preferred to focus on the sort of man they favored. Or rather on the sort my mother favored. To be honest, my father said little on the subject, acting as if matchmaking was best handled by women.

Scrud was the poorest nichna in Ilari, followed by Eds, I supposed, and maybe Faroo. People from all three tended to marry their own, though exceptions happened. They seldom happened, though, with families like mine. Those with less education and little social standing faced this situation.

Yet, my parents were reasonable people. Perhaps if they understood how much I cared for Bohdan, and what a good man he was, they'd welcome him into their lives. I'd never know unless I made some gentle inquiries. And what better day to do it than on a day already centered around love?

The more I thought about it, the more I felt certain Coral's wedding would be the perfect day to learn more about Mom's flexibility when it came to selecting a mate. She'd be in her glory, having orchestrated the marriage of one daughter to an honorary prince. My question about finding love in an unexpected place would be as well received then as it could ever be.

Then once I confirmed she was as open-minded as I hoped, Bohdan and I could face the question of whether we wanted a future together, and what that future would look like.

A few days before the wedding, Sulphur brought Ryalgar from her new home in the forest. I'd missed my oldest sister, a dark-haired woman with my mother's strong build and with a mind of her own. Growing up, she'd loved her studies as much as

I loved my art; I'd always felt a strong unspoken bond existed between us.

Yet, she was one of the Velka now. These mysterious women tended to our health and reproductive needs and handled other assorted requests involving potions and, occasionally, spells. People argued about what the Velka could and couldn't do, but no matter what anyone thought, plenty of others would always dispute those theories with their own stories.

I tried to get her alone, to tell her about Bohdan and see if she had any advice on how to approach Mom, but she remained too busy with Coral and wedding preparations. Oh well. I'd find a way to win Mom over.

When the big day came, I sat with Sulphur and Celestine and tried to hide my qualms about the conversation I planned to have. Sulphur, normally sunny and confident, kept running her hands through her oddly cropped blonde hair as if she was more anxious than me. Seeing Sulphur agitated made me more nervous.

Celestine had spent a lot of time writing a song to perform for Coral. Because my beautiful twin worked hard at her appearance, others considered her self-absorbed. I knew better. Celestine lived for her music and considered her looks to be part of the package she delivered to her audience. I felt lucky that my passion could be pursued in the privacy of my home, where no one cared in the least how I looked.

I waited until the ceremony ended, Celestine sang, and the dinner was eaten. Then I waited longer while the bride and groom observed the little traditions. I didn't want to take away from anything that mattered to Mom. By the time it all ended, she looked exhausted, but I charged ahead. I followed her when she wandered off to the outhouse.

"Why are you following me, dear? I'm fine. I can find my way in the dark."

"Of course you can, Mom." Enough lanterns hung everywhere that it hadn't occurred to me she'd need help. "But let me walk with you anyway."

"Well, you're unusually caring tonight." She gave me that hopeful smile. "So, any young men here who interest you? I do think Davor's younger brother is nearly your age, and he *is* unattached."

"He's not a prince," I pointed out. "His older brother is a Royal by decree." I don't know why I said it. I guess she irritated me by suggesting the young brat.

"In your case, dear, I've rather given up on the idea of a prince. Your father and I would be happy if you merely found a suitable man."

That annoyed me more.

"Well, Davor's little brother is hardly suitable. He's still a child, and spoiled and full of himself."

She gave me a pleading look but said nothing.

"How about if I found a genuinely caring man, instead? One I loved?"

"As long as he's an appropriate choice, love would be nice. I'd wish that for you."

"And what if he isn't? What if he's an inappropriate choice? Not proper, or seemly or fitting? Just a wonderful man, one I'm in love with?"

"Don't be childish. You're my least starry-eyed daughter, and that's saying something. You'd never go for some ne'er-do-well out of a misplaced sense of romanticism."

"And what if I did, Mom? What if I did?"

She stopped and stared at me, as if she were seeing something she'd never noticed before and, now that she'd seen it, she did not like it.

"Perhaps all this time in K'ba is encouraging a level of rebellion in you that needs to be addressed," she said in a deceptively soft tone.

I knew the tone. I stared back.

"What do you mean? You wouldn't dare keep me from going to K'ba."

"If I thought your friends there poisoned your mind with silly notions about what is seemly for a young woman, I'd not only prevent you, I'd lock you in the root cellar myself and guard the key until you came to your senses," she said in the same low sweet voice.

I froze. If she found out about Bohdan, she might be so upset that she'd take away my freedom. I could lose my life as an artist and my secret time alone with him. I could lose everything in the world that mattered to me.

"My friends are doing no such thing," I said. "They all come from fine families that share your outlook. Now if you'll pardon me, I'm going to go seek out some boys to dance with."

I turned and walked back to the dance floor before she could say another word.

I stayed home for the rest of the ank, avoiding conversation with my mother and spending time with my younger sisters who were usually off at school. Under other circumstances, I would have confided my newly discovered love for Bohdan to one or more of them, but now I feared that any innocent comment they made back to Mom could wreck my life. So I said even less than usual as the others all talked.

****

Vinx borders Scrud but the two nichnas don't interact much. Ours sits high on the ridge emerging from the mountains and is half surrounded by cliffs. The grasslands of Bisu run along most of our north and east borders, and only at our northwest corner do we touch the barren nichna of Scrud. The only reason to travel to this spot is to go to K'ba.

To compound the situation, most of Scrud's sparse population lives at the other end of their nichna where their flimsy huts hug the Canyon River. Those who live where Scrud meets K'ba provide cheap labor for the establishments there. The other group lives by the border with Bisu, where they find work tending Bisu's herds. Only the carvers of Scrud cluster near the forest, seeking out the finer wood to make items from this rare bit of bounty.

For the rest of the ank, I puzzled over my insolvable situation. Mom's response made it clear I'd never receive her blessing to marry Bohdan if he and I chose such a path. Yet, I loved him too much to live without him and too much to marry another.

Then I realized the brilliance of my original plan to move to K'ba. For in that less traditional nichna, a man and woman could live together *unmarried*, and neighbors would leave them be. Who needed a wedding? My friends wouldn't care, and my family wouldn't know. Bohdan and I could make a life together, and I could sell enough of my work to support us both. Surely he'd be happy with such an arrangement. I just needed to move there, and it would all be okay.

Plono heralded the start of autumn, but the days were still long and the weather mild enough to favor the outdoor paintings I did best. I knew that would change by Sashi, so I spent most of that eighth painting and making sketches to use through the winter. At home, I worked on our porch, enjoying those bright blue skies only autumn brings.

I had made a promise to Bohdan to practice archery daily, so I did. Every morning I ignored the raised eyebrows, muttered something about needing exercise, and walked far behind the barn with my bow. Once there, I assumed an archer's stance, nocked an arrow, and then took a deep breath. You have to relax to shoot well. Then I'd fire arrows at a small black circle I painted on the back of the barn long ago. I didn't stop until my arms began to tire.

To my surprise, the workouts helped my painting. I suspected the deep breathing and relaxing played a role. All that eighth, I honed a skill not common among women like me.

As the eighth came to a close, Bohdan and I made plans to celebrate our first holiday together as proper lovers. On the morning of Sashi, I would pretend to make a sudden decision to go see my friends, much as I'd done on Heli. Only this time he'd be waiting for me. We both looked forward to it.

Then the morning before Sashi my mom declared she wanted a special family celebration this year with Celestine and me. Why?

Celestine spent more time away from home than I did, giving us little chance to share private information. I'd noticed that over the past eighth a certain fear had replaced our exchange of confidences. I guessed she had a lover now, too, probably a musician in Pilk. I couldn't imagine why, but he must have made her as nervous as Bohdan made me.

"I can't stay. I'm leaving this morning," she told Mom, defiance in her voice and her stance.

"No. You're not." Mom's voice rang out as firm as Celestine's. "We've been more than tolerant about the way you two girls come and go; I can't imagine other parents putting up with such. But not today. This means a lot to me, and you will stay."

Celestine and I exchanged a look. Sashi celebrated those who'd passed from this world into the next. Was Mom dying? Was Dad? We both knew we couldn't leave until we found out.

~ 4 ~

The Problem With Plans

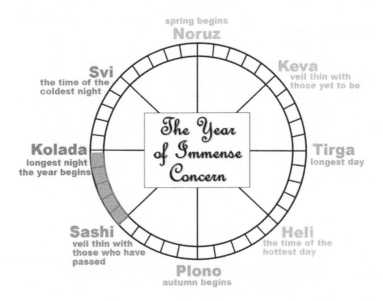

On Sashi Eve mom charged ahead, pouring full glasses of her best dinner wine for all of us. Dad stared at his food, avoiding eye contact and giving us a view of his thinning grey hair as we ate.

I tried to appear festive, but I could see Celestine's sorrow at missing something, or more probably someone. When the conversation lagged, Mom prodded us to talk. She wanted to know more about our friends. Our pursuits. Our prospects.

It took a while for me to realize no one was dying, at least not anytime soon. And this wasn't a celebration. It was a well-disguised interrogation of two older unmarried daughters who were making insufficient efforts to remedy their situation.

25

I wondered if Mom had any idea how she'd terrified me with her remark about locking me in the root cellar. Celestine appeared as spooked as me, saying little and barely touching her wine. I followed Celestine's lead. Drink little, say less.

The next day Mom kept up her relentless attempts to engage us, and the evening brought more food, more wine, and more questions. Dad looked tired but played along. Once again, Celestine and I did not.

The worst part was having no way to tell Bohdan of my predicament. The idea of him thinking I'd abandoned him on Sashi for a night with another nearly brought me to tears. Well, tomorrow I'd make my way to Scrud and explain the bizarre family incident.

The next morning when I asked Dad about it, he shrugged.

"Your mother thinks she's losing touch with you twins. She persuaded me we needed to spend more time together, to get reacquainted."

"Do you agree?" He didn't sound like he did.

"You can't make people share what they don't wish to." Another shrug. "It didn't hurt you girls to spend a holiday with us, though."

I gathered that was all the sympathy I'd get.

Bohdan's bafflement at my explanation told me nothing similar would happen in Scrud. I assumed the idea of marrying well wasn't part of his world, but maybe I was wrong. I didn't understand Scrudites any better than he understood my kin.

The two of us sat on the bench outside of his hut, drinking the afternoon wine I'd brought and eating the holiday honey cakes I'd stuffed in my bag.

"Why aren't you married?" I hoped I didn't sound rude.

He nodded as if he'd expected the question.

"I'm the seed of fertile people on both sides and the recipient of unfortunate timing."

My puzzled look must have told him I didn't understand.

"Ahhh… of course this would confuse you. Where to start? Scrudites prefer to marry our own, for many reasons, but this preference requires us to pay attention to lineage."

"You worry about incest?"

"Bluntly put, but yes. We try to avoid having even more distant relatives ….what I'm trying to say is that while my sisters have several men to choose from, I'm too closely related to every unmarried woman in my clan."

"Oh. So you're …"

"Celibate. By custom and choice, except when I travel and I don't leave often. I can't and won't leave the carvers for good and that's the real problem."

"You won't leave for good?" *Had he just said he'd never leave the forest's edge? Like never go live in K'ba with a woman he loves?*

I sucked in a breath of air to keep from speaking.

"When my situation happens, the man goes elsewhere in Scrud to seek a wife. You know. Because a woman stays near her mother all her life. So another in my situation would go to one of the two clans along the Canyon River to marry. But I can't."

"Why not?" The wonderful vision of the two of us happily living together in K'ba dissolved as I listened.

"I'm too attached to the wood here," he said. "They say I'm one of the best carvers in generations, that I have a strong feel for the heart of what the trees provide."

"You can't carve from elsewhere?"

"It's not possible. Transported wood would lose its essence before it understood its purpose."

"Okay…"

Why hadn't it occurred to me this man could be as dedicated to his art as I was to mine?

"So you will never marry?"

"No, I may. I have pressure on me to do so."

"Why?"

He hesitated. I guessed I asked delicate questions.

Finally, he spoke. "We Scrudites are few, so we are all expected to marry and have families. Some girls among the carvers will be possibilities soon. Everyone wishes for me to court them when they are ready and to wed one."

He watched my face. I worked to keep all emotion out of it.

"Yet whether I do so *will* be my choice."

The full folly of my plan sunk in. "So you and I …."

"…would have to give up much to make a future together, if we wanted one. When I met you, Olivine, I hoped we might have fun, of a type lacking in my life. I never intended to feel for you the way I do ... or for you to feel for me the way I think you might..."

"Perhaps we should end this now ..."

"No!" Then softer. "Why? We make each other so happy. Please. Give us time to learn more about each other, time to decide if we want to make the sacrifices a life together would take."

Easier on the heart to end things now, my mind said. But my mind wasn't in charge of this situation. My heart found wisdom in his words. We didn't know enough yet to decide.

Then I had to laugh as another realization sunk in. No wonder he'd been as anxious to bed me last Heli as I was him. We could have been the two most sexually frustrated tidzys in Ilari.

"I'm so glad we found each other."

"Me, too."

After our conversation, my spirits improved. Perhaps knowing more about Bohdan helped, or finding out he had hurdles of his own to face. He *had* told me he cared for me and we'd shared a sense of facing our problems together. I hoped they were problems we could solve.

When I returned home, Celestine stood in the kitchen in her usual evening dress, scrubbing the insides of the cupboards with a vigor I'd never seen her put into housework. Did she hope to stave off further inquisitions? I grabbed a wet cloth and joined her. She smiled a knowing smile.

A brisk autumn wind blew the fallen leaves around the next day as three Svadlu rode up to our farm. My heart raced when I saw them approaching. Had they come to warn us that the dreaded Mongols crossed our borders? Or had they come to take my father, forcing a gentle intellectual into our desperate army?

In normal times, the Svadlu were an elite peacekeeping force. More people wanted to join than were admitted, and my father would have been turned away if he'd tried. But all the talk of invasion had forced our Svadlu to lower their standards. I'd heard their encouragement efforts had grown more aggressive as winter approached.

A third fearful possibility lurked. They seldom admitted women; females had to be uncommonly adept at fighting to get in.

My twin sister and I wouldn't meet their lowest standards, but Sulphur would. She was physically strong and fierce inside. As the third of seven girls, she'd often stepped in as our protector, serving as the brother we lacked.

Dad or Sulphur? I didn't know what possibility was worse.

Then my dad and the three Svadlu looked at Sulphur and I knew. They *had* come to take my sister. My heart froze with fear for her.

"Did you girls know the Svadlu want to double their numbers before winter comes?" my dad said.

"I heard about that in the market," Celestine replied.

The man who appeared to be in charge spoke. "We targeted your farm because we've heard there's a daughter here with fighting skills." The soldier barely glanced at me and Celestine before he turned to our older sister. "Would you come with us?"

This couldn't be happening! It was awful for Sulphur, and with her gone Celestine and I would struggle even harder for the freedom to set up the lives we wanted.

"Are you going somewhere I wish to go?" she answered them with a grin. I looked closer. She was about to be forcibly conscripted and she looked as happy as I'd ever seen her. My fear made its way to understanding.

Oh, no. She wanted *to join the army.*

What could I do but be happy for her?

****

As Kolada neared I felt winter's approach. Less daylight and the need for warmth cut into my time to paint. During Coral's wedding, Ryalgar had invited me to visit her before winter, but no word had come. I knew my sister wouldn't forget me, though. We'd always been close despite the nearly four-year age difference. It was a familiarity born of being serious women, people who threw themselves into the projects we loved.

Finally, an ank before Kolada, a Velka in the marketplace confirmed my invitation. Dad took me to the forest's edge and I clawed my way through the thick underbrush as I'd been instructed. The smell of decaying leaves and damp earth filled my nose while the strong vines and thorny plants fought my entrance. I feared I wouldn't make it through, but after a little more frustrated wriggling, a woman in men's pants reached out to grab my hand. She gave me the reins of a small donkey and we rode further into the forest.

Although my sister lived in a magnificent lodge, the Velka seemed so ordinary. Many weren't that friendly, and some ignored Ryalgar. I felt offended on my sister's behalf.

She and I sat together on one of the many small porches on my last afternoon there, sipping fizzy green wine in the sun. I'd decided not to confide in her about Bohdan until I knew whether he'd be part of my future. So instead, I listened as Ryalgar told me of how she learned to better use her talents to move objects with her mind. Everyone in my family knew Ryalgar could nudge smoke and keep away small insects; she'd always been that way. It surprised me to learn others with the same talent used it more effectively, and the Velka sought them out and trained them.

"They call it oomrush here," she said. "Honestly, learning more about it was one of the things that drew me to the Velka. Other women here have their unusual talents, too."

Well, maybe some of the rumors of the Velka's powers weren't unfounded. Greatly exaggerated perhaps, but not entirely made up.

"Like what sorts of unusual talents?" I asked.

"The biggest one is making plants do amazing things. We have a lot of women with close connections to all that grows."

"Like that horrible perimeter around the forest?" I asked.

"Exactly."

It gave me an idea.

"Do the Velka ever teach people who can do unusual things, even if they *aren't* Velka?"

"Not really."

Too bad. Ever since I'd learned from my artist friends that being a long eye was uncommon, I'd been eager to discover more about the skill. I'd hoped some of the Velka were long eyes and could teach me about it. I described my peculiar vision to Ryalgar.

"Can it be used for anything else but art?" she asked.

"Of course. I use it for lots of other things." I spoke of finding my way in near darkness, and my archery and how I'd picked up my bow again to practice.

"How far can you shoot an arrow?" she asked me.

"At best I use a medium weight bow, so maybe a hundred paces. I can see much farther than I can shoot. If my arrows traveled further, being a long eye would be more useful."

She stared at me, then started babbling about how she could make twigs fly further than she could throw them.

"What are you talking about?"

"This could be important, Olivine. Listen. Could you stay a day or two more while we look into this?"

Normally, I'd have been happy to collaborate with Ryalgar on anything, much less something so exciting. But Kolada approached and I planned to split the celebration between my family and a stop in Scrud on the way to see my friends. A stop during which Bohdan and I could celebrate the holiday the way proper couples did.

This time, I wouldn't break my promise to him.

She gave me a pleading look. "My idea would be amazing if it worked. I just need a day or two more of your time. Please?"

"Of course. As long as I'm back at the farm by Kolada."

"That shouldn't be a problem."

The Year of Extreme Distress

~ 5 ~

Kolada Surprises

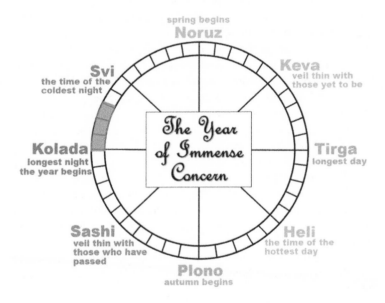

The small group of oomrushers made up Ryalgar's closest friends in the Velka. I liked them all, especially Joli, her best friend. Once these women learned of my skills as a long eye they wanted to include me in their plans. From what I understood, they worried the Svadlu couldn't defend our realm, and they wanted to provide additional options for Ilari's defense.

The idea of the Svadlu being insufficient scared me. The idea that the likes of me and Ryalgar could be our last hope for safety horrified me. Nonetheless, I agreed to participate in a bizarre test involving archery before I left the forest. They wanted me to stand at one end of the clearing and shoot arrows as hard as I could. Half the time, Ryalgar would try to oomrush the arrows further, and we'd see if she made a difference. I was told it would be just our little group, so no need to feel self-conscious. Ryalgar only wanted to know if her idea of pushing my arrows had merit.

It took us a while to get set up. By the time I nocked my first arrow, several dozen Velka had come outside to watch. *Great.* When I noticed how large the crowd had grown, my hands started shaking. Unlike my crowd-loving twin, I froze up when I tried to do things in front of a lot of others.

I pushed the butt of my left hand hard against the grip of my bow, forcing it into stillness. I took my right hand, curled the uppermost knuckles of the middle three fingers, and hooked them around the string. The familiar pose calmed me.

You're all alone. Look straight ahead. No one is here.

I aimed into the distance and made a steady shot. The crowd made no sound. I picked up another arrow and did it again.

After I nocked the third arrow, I let it fly exactly as the first two. It took off with no noticeable difference, but where the other arrows began to slow and drop to the earth, this one did not. It flew as if it had developed an eerie mind of its own, moving until it was so far into the trees I didn't see it fall.

I couldn't ignore the hooting and cheering that followed.

The fourth arrow fell as the first, but the fifth one followed the third into the forest. The crowd gasped and applauded again. I guessed Ryalgar had pushed, as she called it, on arrows three and five and she'd had more effect than she expected.

I shot five more times, with arrows six, eight, and ten going into the woods and eliciting more hoots and cheers. I was so glad when it ended.

When it did, Ryalgar only said "I have to go," as she hurried off with a group of women who seemed to be in charge. I stood alone holding my bow and wondering what to do next. As the crowd dissipated, I wandered onto the porch. Joli found me there in a rocking chair looking lost and asked if she could join me.

"What you and Ryalgar did? It worked far better than anyone expected."

I nodded. I'd figured that much out, but I didn't know if I felt happy about it or not.

"Your sister is an up-and-coming force around here," she said. "She's off securing permission for us to take this idea further. You up for it?"

I didn't get the chance to answer. Ryalgar came out to the porch with a grim determination in her eyes. She'd always been purposeful. Now she looked like the weight of the world sat on her shoulders as she begged me to stay for a couple of more nights.

I couldn't. If I didn't make it to Scrud, Bohdan would have no way of knowing why and I could *not* do that to him again.

Ryalgar saw my reticence. She sat down in the rocking chair next to me and talked. She spoke of the fierceness of the Mongols, the inexperience of our soldiers, and of the possibility that they would forfeit Vinx to make the rest of Ilari easier to defend. Slowly she convinced me of the importance of our discovery. I realized I had to do this and then find a way to get Bohdan to understand.

So the next day, I went back in the clearing, shooting while others took measurements. The day after was Kolada Eve and I did it again, so we could verify the measured results.

"That was some impressive shooting," a familiar voice said. I turned around to see thick short blond hair that could only belong to Sulphur. What was she doing here? Behind her stood a very pregnant Coral.

"I'm here to have my baby. Sulphur brought me."

Mom had mentioned this; I just hadn't realized it would happen so soon.

"The baby isn't due for another eighth yet," I said.

"No, but Davor wanted me safe before winter. They say the Mongols can attack any time once it's cold."

"Why in the world do the Velka have you practicing archery?" Sulphur asked.

Coral answered for me. "I think they're working on a way to defend Vinx."

Sulphur gave her a baffled look. "With Olivine?"

Then she looked at me. "No offense, but that's the job of the Svadlu."

I happened to agree.

Coral would move into a cottage of her own soon, but it wasn't ready so we gave her the extra bed in Ryalgar's room and I moved my bedding to the floor. Sulphur found her own corner and put her bedding down. There was no point in trying to leave now; it was already Kolada Eve. At least I had three sisters to spend the holiday with. I'd go home once the celebrations were over.

On our first night together, Sulphur became angry.

"Why not just train more Svadlu?" she said. "Even poorly trained fighters are better than farmers. And they're surely better than anything you and the Velka can do!"

"No, they aren't." Ryalgar's hands were on her hips, her feet far apart in a fighter's stance as she spoke. "We're not to going to go into battle, which is what more Svadlu would do. We're going to chip away at the Mongol forces, in ways they don't expect. We're going to use skills they don't know we have."

"And you've thought of ways to use such powers against an invading army?" Sulphur asked.

"I'm working on it."

The next day we split our time between the Velka's Kolada festivities and brainstorming in Ryalgar's room. Joli joined us, and other oomrushers came and went. Ryalgar also brought in women with different talents or more knowledge. We talked about horses. Poisons. Fires. Insects. Shrubbery? Yes, shrubbery. Ryalgar had a lot of ideas, and she wanted our help with the complicated schemes she wove. We all understood a simple approach wouldn't be enough.

Sulphur remained dubious, but she contributed her expertise and by the end of our third day together Ryalgar had a rough outline of what she planned. It was a true sisterly collaboration.

"You've still got a lot of unanswered questions," Sulphur said as we were about to fall asleep on the third night. She was right.

"Do you think the younger sisters could help?" I asked. I knew the small age difference between me and my twin didn't matter, but I'd always considered myself one of the older girls, and Celestine not. It was more about personality than the timing of birth.

"Maybe...." Coral said.

"Don't be ridiculous," Sulphur said at the same time

We all laughed. They were both right.

Back on the farm, my mother surprised me when she didn't complain about my being away for Kolada.

"Celestine performed over in K'ba for the holiday, but both Iolite and Gypsum came home and we had a lovely time. I'm sorry you missed them, but it's important for you girls to spend time together too," she said as she put a loaf of fresh bread on the table and poured us both a small mug of light citrusy breakfast wine.

I cut into the bread, savoring its smell as I reached for the jam.

So. Mom didn't care about my not being on the farm as much as she objected to where else I usually was.

Then that evening, as dusk came, Celestine surprised me by suggesting we bundle up in our cloaks and hats and go for a walk in the falling snow. As children, we both loved the first snowfall of the season, sharing a sense of magic in those initial huge flakes as they fell from the sky. We'd often used that time to share secrets best told far from the house and its many prying ears.

"You're in love," she said as we walked. It wasn't a question.

I'd hesitated to share my dangerous secret with Celestine after my mother's threat, but the snow drifting down around us held special meaning. So I told her the story of how I'd fallen for a man who would never be considered marriage material by my family.

"That *is* tough," she said.

"No one knows this yet, but I'm saving coins, hoping to live on my own in K'ba. Then I hope he and I can be together more."

We approached the house in near darkness and I realized I'd talked too long.

"What's happened with you? There is something different about you as well."

I hoped to learn at least a little of her situation before our walk ended. I could still see but I noticed she stepped with care in the fading light and she stumbled as I asked my question.

"It's a conversation for our next walk," she promised

But a second walk never happened. She left the next morning.

Bohdan surprised me by being more upset than I expected after I failed to spend some of the holiday with him.

"We agreed to be a proper couple. Does this mean we are one *only* when you don't have anything better to do?"

"Don't say things like that. You know it's not true."

"Do I?"

Perhaps I'd taken his understanding nature for granted. I didn't know how to respond. Would I always be having to prove to him he mattered? I hoped not.

Once I explained my reasons for staying in the forest, however, he surprised me again. After learning how Ryalgar wanted to ensure Ilari's safety, he went from frustrated to delighted.

"It's *exactly* what we need," he said. "Those Svadlu, so full of themselves, they think they can do anything. We've heard how these Mongols have overrun realms far larger and fiercer."

"Well, her plan is for both the Velka and the Svadlu to play a role in our defense, as well as any Ilarians who are willing."

"It's brilliant."

"Complicated would be a better word. Her ideas will take a lot of people, a ridiculous amount of coordination, and a giant helping of luck. And yet, I agree. It's better than waiting to get slaughtered. So, I'll be part of her initial wave of defense, the piece that peels off the first part of their army."

"What else does this initial wave need?"

"Well, mostly long eyes who've become capable archers. I don't know how many of those we can find. And oomrushers, of course, but the Velka will provide those. I think that's it."

"No." He shook his head. "You need bows, which you have. And you need arrows, but not just any arrows. You need the best my people can make for you."

"We have plenty of arrows. I don't think they can be made better."

"Of course they can. We'll make arrows with wood that understands the need for a longer flight."

Understands? I thought maybe I hadn't heard him right, but I didn't want to say anything to dampen his enthusiasm.

The final and perhaps best surprise came once I returned home and my father asked me for help in the barn. I suspected he wanted to talk. He did, but it was more than that. He had a gift for me.

We stood at the bench where he made his repairs, where the smell of sawdust overcame the odors of hay and animals.

"I know how much your painting means to you, Olivine. Your mother and I were so proud when your school asked if they could sell your work to buy more supplies and you were only twelve years old! Ever since, we've known what a unique gift you have, but, well, I don't feel like she and I have made that clear lately. I want you to know how proud I am of you, and how much I want you to do what you love."

"Thanks, Dad." He'd always been more supportive of my art than Mom, but I didn't think he'd ever been so blunt about it. Perhaps her recent behavior irritated him, too.

"I was thinking. I mean, I don't want to speak out of turn, your paintings are gorgeous."

"I'm happy to get feedback, Dad. It's okay."

"Well. Sometimes, they're a little, I don't know, washed out. Faint? They could use a jab of boldness now and then."

"I agree. It's hard to do with the colors I can afford. I'd love richer paints, but only those commissioned to paint for Royals can afford them."

"That's what I guessed. Thus my idea. You know they mostly pay me to look at dirt, right? I figure out why some soil grows one plant better than another and how to make the rest of the dirt do better. But the part of my job I love isn't that. I love learning about metals. The sparkly rocks."

"Like gold? And silver?" I'd never known this about my father.

"Those of course, but there are so many more. Did you know some of them can be ground into a fine powder? I've been playing around a little." He looked embarrassed. "Trying to find ways to mix the powders with oils. I've had a few successes. More failures. But I thought you might, you know, give a little of this metal paint a try. It takes forever to make even a tiny bit so ..."

"So I just use it for accents. To add a jab of boldness to a piece of art."

"Exactly."

He brought three small vials out of his tool cupboard. Two were silver and one had a coppery sheen like my hair. I uncorked one and touched the top of the silver paint with my little finger. My skin glistened in the sunlight as I held it up and examined it.

"It's beautiful. I can do a lot with this."

"I hope you do. Let me know when you run low. I can make more."

~ 6 ~

A Jab of Boldness

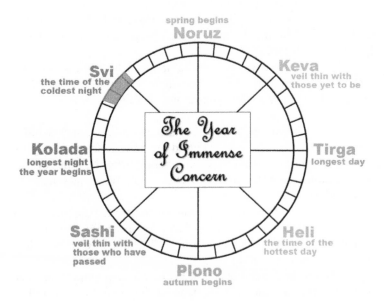

spring begins
Noruz

Svi
the time of the
coldest night

Keva
veil thin with
those yet to be

*The Year
of Immense
Concern*

Kolada
longest night
the year begins

Tirga
longest day

Sashi
veil thin with
those who have
passed

Heli
the time of the
hottest day

Plono
autumn begins

Ryalgar's concerns about Ilari's survival hung heavy on me as we moved into the coldest part of winter. Every Ilarian knew of this pending invasion, but many preferred to pretend everything would be okay. I wanted to pretend, too, but I believed my sister. So I continued to sneak out of the house each morning, even in the wind and snow, to practice with my bow.

I'm sure Celestine saw me and wondered why, but she never asked. Mom and Dad ignored my practice sessions, too. Maybe they all understood the fears behind them.

I vowed to get back to K'ba as soon as the temperatures allowed, so I could start recruiting more long eyes for Ryalgar's plan.

An ank after Dad gave me the new paints, the weather warmed. Dad used the pleasant day to escort Celestine to the forest so she could be there with Coral as she gave birth. I gathered my things to make a rare winter trip over to K'ba.

"You're going over there now? The weather could turn cold again at any time," my mother said. "You could be stuck there for days before you can get back."

"There'll be a nice day sooner or later, and I'll travel home then," I said. "Besides, I have to go; I promised some people I'd help them with some things."

I'm sure my cavalier attitude annoyed her. She shook her head. "Your time for finding a suitable match won't last much longer. Think on *that* while you're over there having fun."

Of course I stopped to see Bohdan as I rode through Scrud. I found him carving an arrow. He told me he experimented to get a sense of what this endeavor would entail. So far, he'd discovered that crafting these to his satisfaction took far longer than he expected. How many did I need?

Before I could answer, he brought two of my paintings out of his hut. He'd made beautiful borders for them too and he now called these wooden devices "frames." Did I like them? How many more frames could I use?

I sat on the bench outside of his hut, overwhelmed. He came and sat next to me and held my hand, saying no more. How did he know to do that?

After a while we kissed, then we ate from the pot of food his mother brought over most days. I'd noticed adult Scrudites tended to live alone, or as a couple, or with small children in a one or two-room hut meant mostly for sleeping. Floors were of dirt, walls were made from sticks and animal skins, and there was little furniture other than mats. These sleeping huts were small and closer together than homes elsewhere.

However, most Scrudites spent their days in the large shared spaces meant for living, cooking, and eating. These were partially outdoors, filled with chairs and tables, and utilized pelts that could be raised or lowered to take advantage of breezes or provide protection from the elements. Family members and friendly neighbors lived in clusters around these areas, sharing chores and taking care of each other as if they lived in a big house. It was an odd arrangement to a Vinxite, but it seemed to work for them.

The next morning before I left, I showed him one of the tiny vials of metallic paint my father made.

"It's like liquid silver," he marveled as I took the cork out. "Try it on one of your paintings."

"The ones here are all finished," I said, but he handed me a small framed one of spring flowers. I saw what he meant. It needed something more.

I got my tiniest brush and moved the painting and the little precious vial into better light. Sitting in the dirt, I added a stroke here. Three dots there. A bolder stroke on the left. Yes, that was it. Now it was finished.

"It's perfect," he said. "But my frame is not."

He took the brush from my hand. I started to complain, but curiosity stopped me.

Using a bit more of the paint, he extended the one silver stroke out onto the wood. He added more dots on the frame, near the ones I'd made, and then he put a smaller bold stroke over on the wood to the right.

"Look. Now the frame and painting go together. Like me and you."

If he hadn't had such a satisfied smile on his face I think I would have complained, and my life would have gone differently. Instead, I looked again and realized what he'd done was nice. Not art really, but creative and attractive. The entire piece would now sell for more.

"We make a good team," I said. "Let's try another one."

"We should let this dry first and make sure we like it. I'll keep it safe until you come back."

Of us six artist friends, four were long eyes, and the four of us sat in a tavern laughing and drinking. Delia and Pasha, the two that lacked our gift, were becoming a couple and they spent less time with us.

I took a hard look at the other three long eyes. Who should I approach first?

Zoya was the easiest, because she and I had grown close, and her parents owned the tavern where we sat. After the others left, she showed me to a vacant room, insisting it was no trouble at all. I asked what she knew about the upcoming dangers to our realm.

I got a bigger earful than I expected. Turns out tavern owners hear all sorts of stories from those passing through, and often after their tongues have been loosened by drink. Zoya not only knew about the Mongols, but she also had information on several other sources of doom I'd never heard about.

"You learn not to take any story too seriously," she assured me as my eyes widened at her tales of vampires moving down from the north, and werewolves living off to our west. "But I will tell you this. The stories of horsemen from the east have come from so many, I think they're probably real."

I suppose I felt relief knowing she thought our biggest threat came from other humans.

She settled onto the foot of my bed and we talked of my oldest sister who lived with the Velka, and my next sister who had married a Mozdol, and the third one, newly inducted into the Svadlu as a fighter. She'd heard about my family already, but I needed to convince her I was a credible source of information before I described Ryalgar's plan for using long eyes.

Zoya sat up and listened, interested to discover our shared skill could have some use, but her face fell when I mentioned archery. I kept talking anyway and finally she looked at me with tears in her eyes. Then she pulled down her blouse and turned away from me. I saw deep purple scars twisting along her back and her upper arms, and burrowing well into the soft tissue of her armpits. She'd kept these scars hidden under the modest clothing she always wore. What could have caused such injuries?

"Did you ever wonder why I, of all my siblings, never carry the heavy trays to clear the tables? I don't serve large orders; I don't even clean the rooms. Why? I can't lift anything much heavier than a paintbrush for long enough to be of any help."

"Zoya. I'm so sorry. I had no idea. What happened?"

She shook her head as she put her blouse back on. "No questions. I only showed you so you'd believe me, and not think I made up an excuse. I'd do anything to help your cause, but archery is well beyond what I could manage."

I believed her. "Maybe Ryalgar could use your long eyes in other ways. Is it okay if I tell her and …."

"Yes, because I want to help. But no one else, please."

"Of course. Zoya …" My mind raced. Zoya's avoidance of intimacy and the way her parents had always treated her as if she were fragile suddenly made more sense.

"I'm sorry I never noticed. I had no idea."

"You fool. Not noticing is the nicest thing you could have done. Now be my friend again by pretending you never saw this."

The scars were horrible. I wished I never had.

Arek was the only member of our group who liked to rise early and paint in the morning light. I knew he still lived with his family in Gruen, but, like me, he spent most of his time in K'ba. I forced myself out of my warm bed at dawn and headed over to the studio to find him.

He preferred to paint people, and this morning a model posed nude for him. The young man, named Nikolo, appeared to be a close friend, or maybe more. No matter what their relationship, I didn't want to make my inquiries in front of anyone.

I fooled around with my paints, hoping the model would take a break, if for no other reason than to relieve himself. Finally, Nikolo wandered off, and I took my opportunity.

I gave Arek much the same information I gave Zoya, but I may have been less persuasive. I felt rushed. At any rate, he reacted differently. The idea of Ilari forfeiting any of its nichnas made him indignant, and he argued with me. Such a thing would never happen.

His friend came back in the middle of our conversation and I tried to end it, but Nikolo had overheard too much. He offered his opinion and, to my surprise, *he* agreed with me. He had a cousin in the Svadlu who'd expressed many of the same worries and it had weighed on him since.

"Arek, is this lady asking you to help with some sort of underground defense for K'ba?"

"I'm not sure what she's asking of me, exactly. We hadn't gotten that far." Arek seemed annoyed at Nikolo's interjecting his opinions into our conversation. Nikolo reached out and took his hand.

"You and I couldn't live the way we do here if we were back in Gruen. We both know that. If K'ba gets turned over to these Mongols, our life together is over. We need to defend what we have."

Nikolo turned to me. "Can *I* help?"

"I don't think so, but …" *What the Heli.* I felt I could trust this man, so I told him about my sister's schemes.

"You're on the right track," he said before I'd barely begun. "From what we've heard, traditional armies won't stand a chance. We need to throw things at them they don't expect."

"Exactly." As soon as I started talking about long eyes and oomrushers he got more excited and turned to Arek.

"This long eye thing? It's what you and I both have, isn't it?" he asked. "See? We *can* help her."

"Wait. You're a long eye too?" I asked Nikolo.

"I've never picked up a bow and arrow in my life," Arek interjected. "I wouldn't know where to begin."

"And I've never painted," his boyfriend said. "But I'm a good marksman. You know I still teach archery to kids in their basic studies. How about I show you as much as I can? We'll see if you've got latent talents you don't realize."

Nikolo grinned at me, and I understood I'd done more than meet another long eye. I'd made an ally.

"Try it," I said to Arek, "and let me know afterward if you want to be part of this or not." Then to Nikolo. "If you've got experience teaching archery, maybe you'd train all of us? We could use a coach."

He took a deep breath. "There's nothing I'd like more."

Later in the day, I found Magomet. Despite his problematic infatuation with me, Magomet was a friend. His parents were both well-known artists who owned the spacious studio in which we all often worked, and they treated us with generosity, sharing not only their place but also their supplies. I got the impression they enjoyed encouraging the next generation of artists.

As soon as I started my conversation with Magomet, his eyes widened and he pointed towards the supply closet. I looked inside. His mother Jasia sorted through jars of paint in there. He walked out of the room and I followed him outside.

"Please be more careful," he said as we began walking down the street. "My parents have strong beliefs about this invasion."

"Beliefs? How can you have beliefs about an invasion?"

"We K'basta pride ourselves on being better informed than most. My parents have listened to many stories and have decided they don't want any of us to fight. At all."

"But how do you defend yourself if you don't fight?" I said. "What else do they think we should do?"

"Nothing. They believe the only way Ilari survives is if we all agree to whatever demands the Mongols make of us. Resistance will bring our demise. I believe this too, Olivine. You should know that before you say anything more to me."

"But ... but what if all the invaders want is for us to die?"

"That's highly unlikely, from what we've heard. They prefer servitude. But if that's the way it goes, we accept that fate," Magomet said. "Fighting will only result in more suffering for us first."

I studied his face. He was serious.

"That's absurd."

"Look, if you can't be tolerant about my family's beliefs...."

I cut him off. I hardly wanted to sever my relationship with these kind people. "I'm sorry. I didn't mean to insult your parents. But, come on. Just die?"

"None of us want our lives to end. We believe the invaders will only take some of what we have and move on. If we don't fight them, we'll be fine. I'm only saying we're willing to suffer the consequences if we're wrong."

"Then I'm fairly sure you're not going to want to help me with a plan to fight them off, are you?"

He laughed. "Safe assumption. Olivine, my parents think a lot of you and they also think your paintings are lovely. I've heard them say you have a real future as an artist. But, understand. They wouldn't hesitate to ask you to leave the studio if they found out you were recruiting fighters to resist the Mongols. Am I clear?"

"You are. I won't bring it up again. Anything I do, I'll keep far away from your parents."

He didn't look entirely happy with my promise, but he nodded. "I wish you didn't feel like this was something you had to do. There are some here in K'ba, including powerful people, who will do their best to make sure our ideas prevail. Please don't get in their way."

I couldn't guarantee I wouldn't, but I'd do my best to make sure Magomet and his family never knew about it if I did.

~ 7 ~

Art Sensations

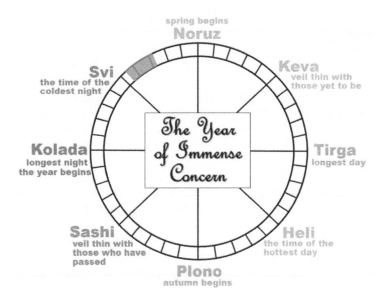

When the next day began warm and clear, I decided to ride back to the farm. My recruiting mission was a mixed success at best. Zoya wanted to help but couldn't. Magomet wouldn't, and he and his family would complicate my life if I didn't hide all this from them. Arek might help after he picked up a bow to see how difficult archery was. The only enthused recruit I'd found was Nikolo, who wasn't even an artist. But, I'd gained him as a coach, and that counted for something.

I'd come across a few other long eyes when I studied art in Pilk, though neither the older nor the younger classes had as many as ours. I'd track them down once spring made travel easier.

As I rode, I worried about the time needed to turn this nutty idea into a reality. It seemed our lives depended on this invasion not taking place until next winter.

I arrived in Scrud by midday, hoping to spend the night. A warm greeting from Bohdan conveyed his delight with my plan. I thought I could use the light of the afternoon to sketch while he tended to his things, but the sky had clouded over as I rode and now a cold wind blew. By the time I set my supplies on his bench, a light drizzle started, too.

So. I could sketch outside his hovel as well as anywhere else in pleasant weather. But in harsh conditions, I needed a well-lit room with large glass windows. My friendship with the son of well-off studio owners had solved that problem for me until now and would continue to do so if my benefactors didn't learn of my beliefs.

Much as I hated to admit it, my mother had a point. Art during the winter required a certain amount of wealth on somebody's part. I settled into the pile of blankets and furs and took nap instead.

The next morning Bohdan showed me how the dried metallic paint looked on the picture of the spring flowers. It didn't sparkle like when it was wet, but it still improved the painting. I'd use the technique on the other pieces he'd framed.

Next time I came through, I'd bring those creations to the shop in K'ba that sold my wares. They looked different than anything I'd seen there and I felt they'd sell well. I needed to ask my father to make more of the amazing metallic paint.

I hoped I wouldn't have to stay in Vinx much longer. Life would be so much easier once I could paint all the time, see Bohdan whenever I wanted, and have my place in the nichna I loved.

The ank after I dropped my new creations off at the shop, I stopped in to see if they'd sold. All three of the paintings had gone for twice what I'd hoped, and the shopkeeper had taken orders for five more done in a similar style.

Zoya came with me that day to check on my sales. She knew how much I wanted to move to K'ba, and she knew why.

"How soon can you get me the five more?" the shopkeeper asked. "Wait. Let's *not* do it that way. Make me five more and we'll hang the best one, so more people will place orders. We'll use two to fill existing orders, and then I'll let customers place bids on the other two. I'm sure they'll sell for more that way, now that you're becoming fashionable. The others who ordered will understand; it can take time to get a painting from someone in demand."

"It's okay to do that?"

He laughed. "It's better than okay. They'll love telling everyone how they're waiting for work from someone so popular. Trust me. You're about to become the new darling of art collectors." He hesitated. "You *can* keep making these, can't you?"

I nodded. "Sure. People who place new orders can tell me the size they want and let me know if there are special colors or subjects they like. I only do plants and animals, but I'll try to accommodate them."

"Oh, that is going to be hugely popular. Can you get another artist to help you with these?"

"No." It came out harsh, but really, this shopkeeper ought to know better. Making a painting wasn't like making shoes, where more cobblers could up the production.

I tried to soften my response.

"I do have someone who carves the wooden edges for me, and he helps me apply the metallic paint to the wood. I'll get him more involved, and that will speed things up a little."

This seemed to be exactly the news he wanted to hear.

"A partner. How wonderful. My patrons will *love* learning that these beautiful creations are a collaboration between two ...." he gave me a sly smile "can I say between two lovers?"

I shrugged. I wasn't anxious to have my work marketed that way, but people were such romantics. I'd probably sell more and at a higher price.

"You could say that."

"Then I will."

"Why not move now," Zoya said as we walked back to her parent's tavern. "Get a place. Tell your family. Make it happen."

"I *could* do this with the coins he gave me today."

"So, let's ask around. Someone may know of a perfect place for you. Or is it for you and Bohdan?"

Zoya was the only friend who knew about Bohdan, and she'd kept my secret. I hadn't felt ready to ask the others to accept that one of their own was dating a man from Scrud. Maybe once I became a K'basta like them, they'd be more open.

"I wanted the two of us to live together, but Bohdan tells me he needs to keep his place in Scrud and spend time there because of his carving. So I need a place for me and my painting, with enough room for a visitor."

"It will be easier for you to settle in here by yourself," Zoya agreed.

She didn't know half of it. I hadn't told my parents I wanted to move here, and they wouldn't be happy when I did. Now I could break it to them gently, tell them it was because of my new success. Once they'd accepted my unconventional life, then I'd mention Bohdan. All Heli would break loose but by then my mother would realize she couldn't lock a well-known artist in her root cellar.

Even though Zoya's parents were so different than mine, she understood without my having to explain.

"Sometimes it's better to do things one step at a time," she said. "I'll start asking about space for a single artist who needs room to paint and occasionally have a visitor."

Nikolo came to see me later that day.

"Arek practiced with me and he did okay. We both want to work with you and the oomrushers. When can we start?"

"Are you sure Arek agrees?" I didn't want to drag my friend into a risky situation unless he felt as enthused as his boyfriend, and his absence at the moment was not a good sign.

"He does. He and I went back to Gruen last ank, and we got out my equipment. Arek's not bad, and he'll get better. That's not why I came alone today."

He leaned in closer to me and lowered his voice. "Have you heard about the wall the Svadlu are building between Gruen and Pilk? We rode over to it and it's huge, taller than most trees. The Svadlu try to keep people back but it's easy enough to get close if you know Gruen well. Olivine, listen. That wall is not meant to slow down an invasion. It's meant to stop one. And it's not stopping anything that hasn't already run over Gruen!"

I nodded. I'd heard about this wall when I spent time with my sisters in the forest. It had been upsetting news then because it implied the Svadlu might give up other nichnas besides Vinx. I hadn't considered how particularly upsetting it would be to Gruenites, however.

Gruen has richer soil and gets more rain than Vinx, so they grow more crops including coveted fruits and vegetables. The Pilkese and the western nichnas rely on Gruen for many of their favorite delicacies. The people of Gruen must have believed they'd be protected, even if the Svadlu sacrificed others. To be honest, I would have thought so too.

"Those rantillions aren't even going to try to defend us!" Nikolo said.

"Probably not. I don't understand why."

"It's unacceptable. We're not going to let this happen. I'd organize my own army of Gruenites except I think it makes more sense to work with you and the Vinxites. Who else are they planning to sacrifice? Scrud? Biru?"

"Probably. We're making plans with both nichnas and with the Velka too. Please, don't try to start your own army. Work with us. My sister says K'ba and Eds could be forfeited too if the Svadlu have their way. She's going to try to involve them as well. All six nichnas may be sparsely populated, but we've still plenty of people to work with."

"Oh no, not the Edsers!" His eyes widened and he took a step back from me. "I mean, everybody knows the people in Eds despise the K'basta. Heli, the Edsers don't like anyone."

I had to agree. The Edsers were a cranky lot at best and I wasn't anxious to work with them either, but this was no time to be picky about our allies. We needed all of us.

"We have a worse problem though," he said. "And one closer to home. We have to be careful in K'ba because we *all* have too much to lose. That's why Arek didn't come with me today. He thought it would be safer if I spoke with you alone."

I had a sinking feeling I knew where this was going.

"Is this about Magomet's parents and their plan to surrender?"

"Oh, it's way more than a plan, now, Olivine. Many of the powerful families in K'ba are involved and they see complete capitulation as the only way to survive. Arek thinks we could be asked to leave K'ba simply for discussing what your sister is doing."

"Oh come now. It's hard to imagine people in K'ba being so intolerant of anything."

He laughed as he shook his head. "Fear of annihilation is a powerful incentive for them not to tolerate our views."

I remembered how anxious Magomet had been to keep his mother from overhearing me. Icy bits of fear were beginning to work their way upward from my knees to my gut.

"Arek and I value the life we have together in K'ba. We don't want to lose it. And, he wants to be an artist and he can't be if he's associated with any resistance to the invasion. All of the planning and training we do with you *has* to be in Vinx or Gruen or somewhere far from here. For your sake too."

That's when I realized my problems had grown in a whole new direction.

Much as I yearned to become a full-fledged K'basta, it couldn't happen now, or any time before this invasion. I needed a home elsewhere to practice archery and help Ryalgar. My life in Vinx would cloak behavior the K'basta found objectionable and allow me to fight for those I loved. What choice did I have?

The irony wasn't lost on me. On the same day I finally got the means to move off of my parents' farm, reach for my dreams as an artist, and make a life that could include the man I cared for, I also learned I wouldn't be able to do those things. Not for a while.

I painted as much as I could over the next few days, anxious to meet some of my obligations with the shopkeeper before I went back to the farm to set up formal archery training with Nikolo and Arek. I told Zoya of my decision to delay my move and the reasons, but I kept conversations with everyone else centered on art or the weather. Having chosen my path, I wanted to remain above suspicion.

Then I rode back to Scrud, hoping to enlist Bohdan in my plans. First, I had to explain to him why I wouldn't be living in K'ba anytime soon. I expected him to be disappointed.

"The idea of spending time with you in K'ba seemed more like a dream, not like something that would really happen. Scrudites don't leave Scrud. Not often."

"Maybe that needs to change," I said. I wasn't sure if I thought it needed to change for him or me, but either way, how could we envision a future together when we'd never spent the night anywhere but in his hut?

I hadn't wanted to ask Zoya's parents to lodge Bohdan with me. I knew they wouldn't be bothered by our co-habitation on a non-holiday, and I thought they were open-minded enough to not mind a Scrudite at their inn. But they catered to Ilari's wealthiest families, and undoubtedly some of their paying customers *would* mind. They could ill afford the trouble.

Today, I had more than enough coins to purchase us a room in a lower-class establishment with a less picky clientele.

"Come with me to K'ba tomorrow," I said to Bohdan. "I want you to see my world or at least the place I hope I'll live someday. We can work on the paintings where they won't have to be transported far. It will be easier and faster."

He knew what I was doing, and he liked it. I thought he might be nervous about the trip, but no. He grinned in anticipation of the adventure.

~ 8 ~

New Scrudite Chic

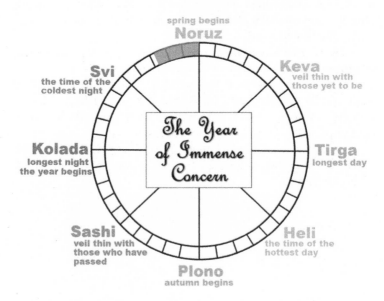

When we brought my new paintings into the shop, I walked in first and the owner's eyes sparkled. Then his glance moved to Bohdan, who carried the larger of the two paintings. Skunk scump. I'd meant to get Bohdan different clothes to wear in K'ba, but we'd gotten so involved in finishing our project I forgot.

"A Scrudite?" the shopkeeper said.

"I am." Scrudites' ill-matched clothes strung together from rags were the butt of many unkind jokes but Bohdan was not the least ashamed of who he was. I was the one who'd hoped to disguise his origins.

"Interesting," the shopkeeper said, his tone softening. "It could *possibly* be spun favorably. There's more tolerance these days for those born into less fortunate circumstances. Perhaps even an ironic kind of glamour."

Bohdan raised an eyebrow and turned to me.

"I told him you helped me with these," I explained.

Bohdan laughed. "I didn't do much. But okay, if having a poor Scrudite involved helps you sell more paintings, I'm happy to contribute my unfortunate life story to the cause."

The shopkeeper seemed impressed by my lover's practical side. "Excellent. Could we consider you two to be common law man and wife then? It would, uh, make the publicity easier."

I balked at this. I hoped to someday live with Bohdan as much of the time as we could manage, but we didn't live together yet.

"I'd rather not call us that," I said.

"Please reconsider. What I mean is, if you can stretch things a little, I've got great news for you."

"Like what?"

"Like one of your originals made its way to Pilk and caught the eye of a prominent merchant who runs a large art fair every year at Noruz."

I knew of this man and his art fair, of course. The inclusion of my work in his spring equinox exhibit would ensure my place in the art world. I absolutely wanted to be part of his show.

"I'm honored beyond belief," I said. "But he seldom includes the works of young people: it's always the old masters. I'm surprised he wants to include me."

"Well, that's the thing. He's been accused of being stodgy, so this year he's trying to appear more trendy. However, there are limits to his flexibility. At least for now."

"What do you mean?"

"He's never exhibited work by a woman before. Don't get me wrong, he's all for women artists. He just doesn't think they produce at the same high level as the top men, and he only exhibits the best. However, he's been persuaded to accept your paintings because, uh, I assured him the product was done by a couple. A married couple." The shopkeeper actually looked embarrassed. "He prefers that kind. I didn't mention it was common law marriage because, you know, details ...."

Bohdan got the point. "You want her to pretend I did half the work on these so some old fart will agree to show them?"

I put my hand on his arm. "Later, we could tell people the truth."

"You shouldn't have to do that," Bohdan said. "It's stupid."

"You walk away from a lot if you say no," the shopkeeper warned me. "I tried to persuade him to exhibit your work without involving your paramour, but he wouldn't budge until I mentioned your, uh, husband's contributions. Then, he saw a way out and took it. He really wants to show one of yours, without obligating himself to show other women's work in the future. You understand?"

"I'll do it," I said. "That exhibit is filled with nothing but rich people from Pilk, Kir, and Lev. Nobody I know goes there, so nobody in Vinx has to know."

I turned to Bohdan. "If I do this, I'll be able to sell paintings for the rest of my life."

He sighed. "I don't like it, but if it makes you happy, I'll go along with it."

"What a fine fellow," the shopkeeper said to me. "I see why you care for him."

He looked at Bohdan. "You'll both need to be at the exhibit of course. I'm sure you'll get lots of questions. Uh, vague is good." He looked at me. "Perhaps a newer, cleaner version of normal Scrudite attire?"

I nodded.

"What's wrong with my clothes?" Bohdan said.

"Nothing, but we're marketing *me* as your creative wife and *you* as the embodiment of the new Scrudite chic. And we're both going to be as nice about it as we can."

"Got it," he said.

I let my mother know I'd be celebrating Noruz in K'ba. She said nothing; I think she expected it.

"I'll be back after the holiday. Then I'll probably be around here a lot more. I hope that's okay."

She smiled. "Problems with your young artist?"

"Something like that." At least the lie sliding out of my mouth was partly true. "We're going to take a bit of a break from each other after the holiday."

"That's so wise, dear. Make time to get out there and socialize. Consider those other options." She reached out and took both of my hands in hers and looked into my eyes. "Remember. It's just as easy to fall in love with a prince."

The best I could manage was a slight nod as I disengaged my hands and walked outside.

I found my father in the barn and asked him if he had any objection to my conducting archery practices on the farm with a few boys from Gruen.

"Of course you can practice here. We've plenty of room." He gave me a questioning look. "Are *all* you girls involved in this thing Ryalgar is doing?"

"Probably. I don't know how the others see it, but I can't imagine life without this farm, or without Vinx to always come home to."

He turned away as I said the last part, but when he turned back to face me, I saw the tear in his eye.

"Neither can I. I'm proud of every one of you." He said it fast, in a quiet tone, so I wasn't sure I heard him right. I started to say something back, but he walked out of the barn before I could.

Several days before Noruz, Celestine and I rode away from the farm together. My parents thought we headed to K'ba in each other's company, me to say good-bye to an artist boyfriend who didn't exist, and her to perform her music for the holiday crowds.

In fact, she turned left before we reached the forest, following the main road into Gruen to go to Pilk. She had finally admitted to me she had a lover there, though she'd balked at giving details. I guessed she'd been invited to celebrate Noruz with him and this invite had made my sister happier than I'd seen her in a long time. I understood her being closed-mouthed about the details.

I turned right, taking the smaller road into Scrud where I'd meet Bohdan. He'd borrowed a horse from his father and a cart from his uncle, so we could transport my painting in the safest way possible.

His mother came out to greet me, and she took my hands in hers, much the way my own mother had done.

"I've cleaned and mended his clothes as best I can," she told me. "I hope you'll be proud to be with him."

"I always am."

We exchanged a look. Hers said *I like you, but don't you dare break his heart.*

Mine said *I have no intention of doing so.*

We left for Pilk at dawn a few days later. I rode my mare, and Bohdan took on the more difficult job of riding the horse pulling the cart. I'd asked for the cart to protect my painting in case of rain or snow, but the day stayed cold and clear while the cart slowed us down. I'd hoped to be hanging my painting in the exhibit tent by noon but we didn't arrive in Pilk Central until late in the day.

Crowds of revelers packed the streets, making me thankful the merchant in K'ba had secured sleeping quarters for us in advance. Bohdan wanted to go there first, but the exhibit only lasted three days, and I'd already missed much of today. So we tethered our animals in one of Pilk's many public stables and set off on foot for the exhibit tent.

As we pushed our way past the people looking at the other art, a tall man, more elegantly dressed than most, waved to us across the crowd.

"Over here!" he called. Then as we got closer he added, "I'm so glad you finally made it. You must be Bohdan. Welcome. The place for your work is prepared and waiting."

He gestured to one side of the tent, the one with fewer people. It was devoted to the younger artists, I supposed.

"Let's get that masterpiece on display," he said to Bohdan. His eyes didn't flicker towards me once.

"Thank you for displaying this," I said it more loudly than I usually spoke.

He turned to me as if he'd just noticed me. "Of course. It's my pleasure to include some of what our fine young people produce. Let me know if you need anything." His eyes lingered on my bosom. "Anything at all."

Bohdan carried the painting and hurried towards the indicated spot, as anxious to get away from this patron of the arts as I was. We found the place to hang the painting easily, as every other spot was taken. As he moved to put it in place, I read the label under it.

Two Birds Alight on a Single Branch, with metallic highlights

by

Bohdan Avtandil Ukleba of Scrud, and wife

"And wife? They don't even say my name!"

"What?" Bohdan squinted at it. His reading skills were poor, but he figured out the essentials quickly enough.

"I made this," I said. "It's one of the best things I've ever done. And it doesn't even have my name on it!"

He shook his head in disbelief. "I can tell you Bohdan Avtandil Ukleba of Scrud did *not* do this work, and he sure as Heli won't claim he did. A man from Scrud does not do that. Come on. Let's take your painting and go. Maybe there's another place around here that will display it properly."

I hesitated and put my hand on his arm. "We should think about this. Our lodging was paid for by someone who stuck his neck out for me, trying to give me an opportunity. Is it fair to do this to him?"

"I don't think it's fair for him to have done this to you. Do you think he knew how this would be presented?"

I never got to answer because two things happened.

First, I saw Magomet's large body on the other side of the tent. Of course *he'd* be here, given how well connected his family was to Ilari's art scene. He'd seen me too, because he hurried towards us, giving Bohdan's clothes a quick wrinkle of his nose.

"Who is this?" he asked me, not even looking at Bohdan. "And what are you doing here? Your father rode over to K'ba yesterday and looked everywhere for you and your sister."

"Why would he do that?"

"He'd gotten news about another sister of yours receiving some sort of honor here, and he thought you and Celestine would want to come. He couldn't find Celestine either. I think your parents are in Pilk today and they are worried about both you and your twin."

Oh dear. If my parents were here and saw me with Bohdan, or even heard about me being here with Bohdan, this would not go well. I couldn't imagine how I could explain my presence to them.

Then I noticed a ripple of activity out of the corner of my eye. The agitated movement began by the door of the tent and worked its way in. Someone yelled "Get out! Take Cover! The Mongols are here!"

Bohdan grabbed my painting with one hand and my arm with the other and pulled me towards the nearest tent wall, away from the door where everyone else headed. He lifted the loosest part of the tent wall. I crawled under it, took the painting from him and he followed.

Once we were out in the street we saw frightened people everywhere. Some yelled for help, others pleaded for safety and a few started looting abandoned merchants' stands. The only thing missing from the chaotic scene was an actual Mongol.

"Where are they?" I asked.

"In Pilk center," a man yelled to me as he ran by. "They are outside the Palace."

Most people headed away from the Pilk Center, fleeing towards their homes. Bohdan and I looked at each other and neither of us said a word. We headed towards where we'd left our horses and cart, hoping to get to our lodging without seeing anyone else I knew.

~ 9 ~

The Worst Timing

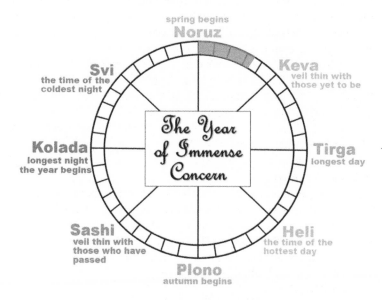

We spent the evening in our room, eating the rest of the stale bread and smoked cheese we'd brought and wondering what the fate of our realm would be. We heard no sounds of battle or any kind of distress, so we fell into an exhausted slumber in the middle of the night.

The next morning, the actual day of Noruz, we ventured out. Pilk Center appeared unharmed. The mood in the streets had transformed from panic to jubilation as word spread that the Mongols numbered only ten and had brought us nothing worse than an ultimatum. The envoys demanded a once-a-year tribute of the products of our realm – smoked meats, fine cheeses, wines, grains, fruits, and vegetables. In exchange, they would allow us to live.

I thought our Royals showed unexpected good sense by sending these messengers off believing we considered their ridiculous offer. After the party had ridden on, we learned that our leaders had assured the masses that Ilari paid tribute to no one, and the Mongols would taste the sharp points of our swords and arrows if they tried to make good on their threat.

Bohdan and I made our way around Pilk Center on foot that morning, taking in the sights and watching the drunken crowds in the street celebrate the courage of our leaders. It puzzled me. Making boasts took little bravery, and telling our people we'd do something we could not bordered on foolish.

I trusted Ryalgar's research. Ilari couldn't fend off these Mongols with five hundred Svadlu and maybe not with five thousand. Perhaps cunning, a little magic and a lot of luck would even the odds. Maybe it wouldn't.

As that realization sunk in, I finally understood what Magomet and his parents saw. They didn't believe in peace, no matter what words they used to describe their philosophy. They believed in survival.

They had thought through what I had, similarly removing the bravado filling the hearts of most Ilarians. They didn't know of Ryalgar's plans, of course, but even if they did, they wouldn't place enough faith in them. They wanted to live. They knew of only one sure way. Do the unthinkable and pay the tribute. Do it year after year, no matter how much gets taken, because as long as you are alive, there is hope.

I didn't agree with them, but I understood.

Bohdan and I tired of pushing our way through the holiday crowd and decided to treat ourselves to a real supper in a tavern. We ended up in a place filled with people talking about how wonderful our Svadlu were. I didn't pay much attention to their prattle.

The exhibit had left me disappointed, and as I walked I'd begun to wonder if my art would ever be appreciated the way a man's was. Maybe I should sign my paintings with a man's name? Maybe I should simply go ahead and use Bohdan's full name all the time? But why should my creations be better received if people thought a man's body did the work? It made no sense.

I knew my bitter mood carried over to my treatment of Bohdan. He'd been nothing but considerate, yet through no fault of either of ours, he possessed the genitals needed for respect in the art world and I did not. Yet I possessed the talent. It was an impasse neither of us could do much about.

I barely spoke to him as we ate, and he left me to my sour thoughts, perhaps knowing anything he said would only make things worse. In my heart, I gave him a silent thank you for his insight.

Because of the nature of my dark mood, my ears caught a conversation about women fighters.

"Fifty or more of those Svadlu are women, you know," a man was saying. "They only count as a half a fighter each, so we *don't* really have five-hundred."

"I wouldn't count 'em as less," a woman rebuked him. "That one that became a Mozdol yesterday…."

"You mean the blonde with the short hair like a man's? Are you *sure* she's a girl?" a different male said, following the question with a rather ugly laugh.

"She's female all right," the woman replied "and I hear she fights like a wildcat. Saved a whole town up in the mountains. That's why they made her a Mozdol."

I stopped listening. There was only one woman in Ilari they could be talking about, and she was my sister.

How could Sulphur possibly have been made a Mozdol and I not know about it? Wait, maybe *that* was why my parents were searching for me in K'ba. Could they have wanted me and Celestine to attend Sulphur's Mozdolo with them? I had to find out.

Bohdan and I turned in early, barely touching each other as we lay. I tossed around so much I finally rose before dawn, moving with a little noise as possible so as not to wake him.

I left word with the innkeeper so Bohdan wouldn't worry, then I walked through the early morning mist to the part of Pilk Central where the Svadlu lived. I didn't know exactly why I went, only that I had to talk to Sulphur and find out the truth. I wanted to tell her how I admired what she'd achieved, despite what others thought.

It took me a long while to get there, but once I did I got directions to the women's quarters. No one stood guard at the entry to permit me to come inside, but that meant no one was there to stop me, either. I walked through the door and found Sulphur alone, packing her things.

"I'm so proud of you, Sulphur," I said. I startled her with my words and she looked up at me in disbelief. I came and sat next to her on her bunk. "Tell me how this happened?"

The two of us had as little in common as two sisters could, yet that morning I watched her fight back tears as she shared her pain at not having any of her family at her Mozdolo. I understood. I'd felt much the same, having to hide my painting's selection for an honor because I needed Bohdan's male name to qualify for the exhibit.

Every one of us had been there for Coral, cheering her on as she married a prince. But then again, marrying a prince was what we were *supposed* to do, right?

Try doing something different, and all the subtle nudges to behave as expected kicked in.

"Oh, could the timing of those varmin Mongols have been worse?" The shopkeeper threw up his hands and rolled his eyes as we entered his store with my painting. "I felt so bad for you when I heard. But why didn't you two stay? They opened the exhibit back up the next day. You still could have shown it."

"This is the best painting I've ever done," I said as I thrust it at him. "It's the one I want you to display in the store, for getting more orders. And I want *my* name on it."

Something in my intonation bothered him.

"For Heli's sake, who else's name would I use?" He laughed at the absurdity.

"Mine," said Bohdan. "That's what the rantallion did in Pilk, and I was nearly as upset about it as she was."

I put a hand on Bohdan's arm. I had enough anger for the both of us, I didn't need his.

"I see," the storekeeper said. "Well, that's unfortunate. It's not what he told *me* he'd do, but then again ... I never did trust him that much."

Now he told us.

"I'm sorry, Olivine. No wonder you left. I don't blame you."

He walked over and placed the painting at the center of the far wall.

"There it will stay. Now, how many of these lovely items do you expect to produce for me during Noruz?"

"One. Maybe two."

His head tilted to one side, in puzzlement. "Why so few?"

"I've learned I can't move to K'ba, so my need for funds has greatly diminished."

"I'm sorry to hear that."

"I'll be focusing on other things, but of course I'll paint too."

He winced. "Please tell me you're not part of these crazy ideas involving farmers and herders taking up arms. What a sure way to get us all killed."

"These are dangerous times," I agreed, my eyes begging Bohdan to keep silent.

"Most of the wealthy around here strongly oppose the idea of resisting at all, you know," he said. "I'm told they hope to persuade the Svadlu to stand down and the Royals to pay the tribute." He gave me a cautious look.

"I'm an artist with no political opinions," I said.

That earned me a smile. "The best kind. Get me as many paintings as you can while you tend to your other things. Please."

We rode to Scrud before dark and spent the night in Bohdan's hut. The warmth of spring crept into the night air, and we tied his curtains back so the breeze could blow through as we cuddled together under his covers.

I'd been a tidzy now for three years and, until Magomet's infatuation forced me into celibacy, I had happily spent every holiday with a boy. I'd learned a good bit from various males, and I felt comfortable pleasing myself and them in just about every way that was practical.

Bohdan had traveled around Scrud enough to have celebrated the holidays with several women, yet I'd noticed a difference with him. Bohdan's tastes were ... limited. He liked to get on top of me and do it. Lucky for me, he liked it a lot, and it nearly always made me as happy. I sometimes tried to gently move us into a variety of other positions or activities, but my efforts met with minimal interest. I wondered if this was peculiar to Bohdan, or a trait of Scrudite men in general. Too bad I hadn't had sex with another Scrudite before I met him, so I could compare.

As we lay together that night after Noruz, I craved sexual release. I wanted the joy to wash away all the bad feelings inside of me, and those between the two of us as well. But I didn't want to do it the way we always did. So after the kissing and touching that proceeded, I became more aggressive. I pushed him on his back, with some force, and then straddled his stomach, positioning myself to be on top for once. Of course, he could easily have pushed me back off and we both knew it. But he didn't.

Maybe a man from Scrud didn't behave that way. Or maybe he was being smart, or kind. Or maybe he really was up for variety. Whatever the combination, he gave me a knowing grin, and tilted his head back to enjoy the new sensation of the vigor of my movements. The result was a cleansing tidal wave of joy, for me at least, and likely for him, if the sounds he made were any indication.

We curled back into sleeping positions without saying a word and I realized that on some deep level, this man understood me. Anyone who thought marrying a prince would be better didn't know much about love.

Over the anks of Noruz, I turned my attention to the battle I'd soon be part of. The Mongols had done us a favor with their ultimatum. We knew we had six eighths of a year to prepare, and we could plan. I supposed they thought we were too naïve to do so.

I practiced a lot of archery with my friend and fellow artist Arek and his boyfriend Nikolo. Nikolo knew so much more about using a bow than I did, and he shared techniques with us I'd never heard of.

"You puff your chest out when you shoot," he told me.

"I do?"

He imitated me and I had to laugh.

"I guess I'm trying to look strong. To feel strong."

"Strong is good but strength for *this* activity comes from a different posture. Pull your chest down. Make your stomach strong."

I tried it and felt what he meant. Strength, from a different place. Then I smiled when I caught the admiration in Arek's eyes as he watched Nikolo imparting this knowledge.

Each ank, Arek and I grew in our skills and our confidence. Sometimes, when the three of us only had an hour or two to practice, we traveled to Scrud because the ride was shorter than going all the way to Vinx. Bohdan liked our visits, and his family and friends often came out to watch us.

He started asking Nikolo a lot of specifics about the arrows and what changes to them would best serve our needs. I had a fairly good idea of where his questions led.

Sure enough, the next time I rode over to visit, Bohdan had a new arrow he wanted me to try.

"I think I've got the perfect design now," he said.

"Really, you don't have to do this."

"Yes I do. You need our arrows because we can tell the wood how others will make it fly farther than it thinks it can go. Once it knows, the wood will help you."

I raised an eyebrow. "Do you really believe that?"

Bohdan smiled, not the least offended. "No, I don't *believe* it. I know it. The things we carve are happy knowing what they are meant to do."

I laughed. How could I argue with such certainty? I hadn't brought my bow with me, but I tucked the arrow into my saddlebag to try it later.

~ 10 ~

Candor Versus Caution

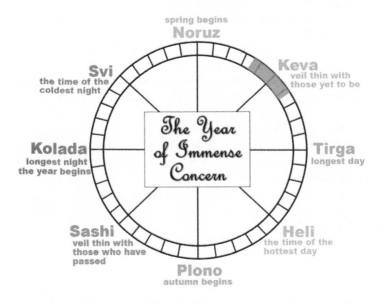

spring begins
Noruz

Svi
the time of the
coldest night

Keva
veil thin with
those yet to be

Kolada
longest night
the year begins

The Year of Immense Concern

Tirga
longest day

Sashi
veil thin with
those who have
passed

Heli
the time of the
hottest day

Plono
autumn begins

After Noruz the weather turned warm, so Arek, Nikolo, and I visited the larger settlements around the edges of the realm, seeking artists, archers, or anyone else who used the ability to see far. We found fewer long eyes than we expected, but the ones we talked to listened to our pleas. Most agreed to train and help. I noted their names and locations to pass the information on to Joli as I'd been asked.

Then as Keva approached, spring storms began and we decided to get off the road during the rains. I returned to K'ba to paint, hoping to raise enough income to support my wanderings as I did my part to get ready for our battle.

As usual, Zoya's parents insisted I stay at their tavern. I made my way over to Magomet's parents' studio hoping they'd welcome me, too.

Magomet gave me an uncomfortable look when I came to the door. I hoped my smile and my eyes assured him I wanted trouble less than he did.

"You poor dear," his mother called to me from down the hall as she came towards us. "We heard all about what that stodgy old art dealer did to you, not even putting your name on your work. How unconscionable."

"How'd you know?" I asked Jasia as she motioned me inside.

Magomet answered. "After everyone else ran outside to see the invaders, I read the inscription for your painting. How did you manage it? Did you pay that guy from Scrud to *fake* being your husband to get your work displayed?" He gave me a hopeful smile. "Very clever."

Jasia pursed her lips and shook her head. "The things women have to do to get by in this world."

I held up a hand to stop the conversation. While I accepted the need to hide my involvement with Ryalgar's plans, I didn't wish to lie to this nice woman about everything.

"No. He really is my boyfriend, and he helped with the painting. Somewhat. He's a woodworker, and he made the borders for it."

"Boyfriend?" Magomet said. "I thought you forsook relationships with men?"

Rat scump. With everything else going on, I'd forgotten the other reason I hadn't acknowledged Bohdan.

"I'm … rethinking my approach. Hadn't, uh, hadn't had the chance yet to tell anyone about it."

Magomet shook his head. "You're joking, right? There is no way a pretty girl like you has a boyfriend from Scrud."

His mother gave him a pointed look. "Their woodworkers are highly skilled," she said, more to her son than to me.

"The shopkeeper asked if he could put both of our names on it, and I agreed to it. I thought it was worth it to have it shown. I had no idea…"

Magomet appeared less concerned with my art and more concerned with my new boyfriend. "You're not really planning on marrying him, are you?"

"Magomet." His mother eyed him with concern, but her tone was sharp.

"It's okay," I said to her, not him. "I understand. My own family will have problems with it as well."

"They don't know?" That seemed to make her sad.

"I've been waiting for the right time. So far I've only told Zoya …. I'm sorry. I didn't mean to burden you with my personal problems."

"Magomet tells me you hope to move to K'ba someday soon." She changed the subject with the grace I'd often seen the K'basta exhibit.

"I did. I even thought Bohdan and I might live together here. But, well, for family reasons I may delay for a while. We'll see."

Her face softened. "Please consider telling your parents about the man you love. Truth is always so much better." She patted my arm. The best I could do was give her a half-hearted nod of agreement. If only she knew.

I left K'ba for a quick Keva celebration with Bohdan. I knew it mattered to him that we spend holidays together like a proper couple, and blossom-filled Keva invited two lovers to be together more than any other holiday.

That night, as we lay in his bed ready for sleep, I spoke of my love for him and he spoke of his love for me.

"Once Ilari is safe, nothing will be more important to me than finding a way for us to make a future together." He played with my hair as he said it, and something inside of me relaxed at his words.

Keva isn't only about lust, it is also about fertility. I suppose that prompted us to speak of a topic we'd never discussed. For most couples it's a given, but Bohdan knew me better than that.

"Do you want children someday?" he asked.

I sighed. "It's the rare woman who uses herbs to see she never has them, but …"

"But I've given your situation some thought. You'd have to give up painting for years to be a mother."

I exhaled in relief. He understood.

"Maybe one child, a long time from now," I said. I didn't want to close the door on the possibility. "But maybe not."

He kept stroking my hair and said no more as I snuggled into his arms.

Back in K'ba, I went to the market for personal items, hoping to paint for a few more days before I returned to the farm. As I gathered a piece of fruit here, a bit of soap there, the lone Velka yelled to me from her small stall.

The Velka had a large presence at other markets, but they were less important here. K'ba's own artisans made many of the same products, albeit without the rumored touches of magic. Many K'basta showed outright disdain for the bits of earth magic thought to remain deep within the forest. Besides, the settlements in K'ba were so far from the forest that the Velka had to ride through much desolation to reach our market. Some said they didn't like being far from greenery for so long.

The sound of my name startled me and once I realized its source, I became more alarmed. The last thing I needed was to be seen receiving a message from Ryalgar. I hurried towards the woman, hushing her as I walked.

"Yes, I want to hear your message, but please. Lower your voice." I hoped I looked embarrassed by the attention. "Don't say anything," I hissed under my breath once I stood close enough to take her by the arm.

"But your sis ..." I pinched her arm.

"Ouch!"

"Shh. Sorry. Didn't mean to hurt you but stop talking. Let's walk down to the Canyon River. It's not far."

"But my booth ..."

"Put up your sign saying you'll be right back. I mean it. We cannot talk here."

She looked at me like I was crazy, but she did as I asked.

Once we were out of earshot of the curious, I held her arm tight as we walked, as if we were old friends.

"Stay right next to me. Change the subject if anyone comes close to us," I instructed.

"You're even weirder than your sister says."

"My sister doesn't understand my situation. No one here can know I'm working with her. Convey it back. All communication with me has to be done in Vinx from now on. This can't happen again."

"We tried to get a hold of you over there, but you haven't been in Vinx for days."

Had I been in K'ba that long? I did lose track of time when no one interrupted my work.

"I'll go home soon. What's your message for me?"

"It's from Joli. Ryalgar put her in charge of the oomrushers and the long eyes. She plans to have all the long eyes meet at the forest's edge in Vinx, near the market, the morning after next. You must be there."

"I guess I go back to Vinx tomorrow then."

"That was my point. I *had* to talk to you today."

I rode back to Vinx the next morning, disappointed Ryalgar wouldn't be at this gathering. When she and I proved the merit of this idea, I assumed we'd be partners, taking on the invaders as a team. It made me sad to learn otherwise. But Joli did a fine job of getting not only Nikolo, Arek, and me there, she also brought in five of the other long eyes we'd found around the realm.

"Eight of you. Better than we thought!" She was in high spirits. "Today we figure out which of you, how many of you, can realistically be trained to shoot a bow well and grow strong enough to shoot sixty times without pausing. That's a tall order and there is no failure in, uh, failing." She laughed. "What I mean is, we have other, important needs for long eyes who can't shoot. Scouts will be vital and you all will have a role."

With that she had us demonstrate our current aptitude while Nikolo walked around making suggestions.

"Raise your right elbow higher. There, that's better."

"Keep your hands parallel to the ground. No, now you're pointing up a little. Keep them flat."

A second Velka, who called herself a recorder, followed him making notes and asking questions.

"How old were you when you first picked up a bow? What are the most arrows you've ever shot in succession? How much time each day can you spend practicing?"

After this went on for half the morning, Joli stopped us. "Beautiful. Well done. We'll confer and get back to everyone. Go to the markets often, and ask the Velka for messages. We'll start formal sessions soon, but keep practicing on your own.

Joli had mounted her horse when I realized Bohdan's new arrow remained tucked in my saddlebag.

"Wait. Take this with you. It was made by a carver in Scrud who claims these will go further, and we should use them."

She reached for it with a shrug. "Maybe they will. I've heard odd things about the work they do. We'll test it out next time."

Good thing Joli didn't ask me why Scrudites had made an arrow for me. I have no idea what I would have told her.

I spent an ank at home after that, helping Mom plant the garden and clean the house. We always did these things when the weather turned warm and I knew my parents missed the help of the oldest three. Iolite and Gypsum would both finish school in several anks, and once they returned home Mom would have more help again. However, when I asked my mother about the two of them, she gave a long sigh.

"I wondered when you'd ask. Iolite barely sends us letters to say she is okay. We don't know when she'll be home. Meanwhile, Gypsum ran away from school and joined the … the reczavy." Mom winced as she said it.

"That's …." I struggled for the right word. *Horrible? Amazing? Confusing?*

"We don't know why," she interrupted me. "And of course Ryalgar and Sulphur have new allegiances now and Coral has responsibilities as a mother. So, we only have two daughters really. You and Celestine, and to be frank, your father and I aren't sure if we have you two, either. You both seem to lead lives away from home, lives that matter more to you."

I didn't know what to say, but before I could think of anything, an unwanted memory pushed its way into my brain.

My family celebrated a holiday together, I think in Pilk. Mom led the way, holding Celestine's hand on one side and mine on the other as she pulled us into the path of some drunkard who stumbled and fell, then yelled at her.

"Get out of my way, you stupid pruska," he'd said. Then he pointed to me and Celestine. "And take your little pruskas with you." He waved his hands at the rest of my sisters. "Pruskas, every varmin one!"

I don't remember much else. I had no idea what a pruska was, but then again, I was six. There were a lot of words I didn't know.

A few days later my mother told me she needed to talk with me. I remember she sat me in a chair and stood over me. My mother is a tall woman with a formidable build, but she looked huge to me back then.

"All your sisters have already asked me. Aren't you curious, too?"

"About what?"

"What a pruska is."

"It sounds like a bad word. I don't need to know bad words."

"Yes, you do, Olivine. You need to pay more attention to things around you. How can you respond if you don't know what a word means?"

"Okay. What's it mean?"

"It means a girl who isn't friendly. One who doesn't smile or talk to people. You don't want to be one of those girls, do you?"

"No, Mother." Even at six years old, I knew better than to argue when she got like that.

"Well?"

My mother's voice brought me back to the present. She expected a response to her tirade about my sisters. She wanted reassurance that she had my loyalty and my love. Perhaps she wanted reassurance that she had my sisters' love as well.

Only now I was an adult, and this time I was standing. It was easy for me to make an excuse and leave the room, so I did.

We all ran to Coral when we were upset, we always had. She knew how to soothe every one of us.

The information about Iolite and Gypsum, and the whole conversation with my mother, left me unsettled. I already felt on edge because I dared not move to K'ba until this invasion happened and yet I wanted to be there. I hated hiding my plans to help with the uprising, I missed seeing Bohdan when I wanted, and only three people in my life even knew about the man I loved. And two of those were Magomet, who was jealous, and his mother, who'd have hated me if she knew what else I was doing.

Enough. The next morning I announced my plans to visit Coral.

"She doesn't have room for guests," my mother said. "She lives in a very small cottage."

"I'll make do." I began filling my saddlebags with the things I needed.

"Here. I made some extra honey cakes for our Keva celebration. Take them to her, please. And here's an extra jug of afternoon wine. You girls can have it while you visit."

I knew my mother well enough to know it was her way of saying she regretted being demanding. She wished she knew how to be less so, but she didn't.

Coral was teaching 1 when I arrived, so I got comfortable on her little porch and enjoyed the spring afternoon. A few flowers grew amongst her weeds, but they needed care. I thought about tending to them but before I got the chance, she arrived with little Votto bundled to her. She sure made motherhood look easy.

She poured the wine I'd brought and I put out the honey cakes as we exchanged family news. Then I played with Votto and I asked her about Davor and her life as a teacher. She gave me plenty of time before she finally said "So. What's bothering you?"

Out it came, the way it always did with her.

"A Scrudite? Oh my. Could you have chosen anyone further from being a prince?"

"Probably not. I didn't try to fall in love with him, though. It just happened."

Coral chuckled. "You love him?"

"Very much..."

"And he loves you?"

"I'm sure of it."

"Then," Coral said, "you're one of the luckiest women alive."

I didn't think she took my situation seriously enough but, given her troubles with Davor, it seemed insensitive to argue the point.

~ 11 ~

No Reason to Look Close

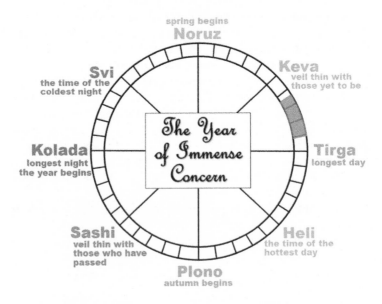

spring begins
Noruz

Svi
the time of the
coldest night

Keva
veil thin with
those yet to be

Kolada
longest night
the year begins

*The Year
of Immense
Concern*

Tirga
longest day

Sashi
veil thin with
those who have
passed

Heli
the time of the
hottest day

Plono
autumn begins

After a day at Coral's house, I rode over to see Bohdan before going on to K'ba. He met me with a question.

"Have the Velka tried out my latest arrow yet?"

"I don't know." I'd expected a more affectionate greeting, but ... "I gave it to Joli the last time we met."

I saw the disappointment in his narrowed eyes.

"I didn't realize you were in a hurry."

"Come. I'll show you why I am."

He walked me to the trees' edge, where I saw the Scrudites had erected a short roofless stall made of blankets hung from ropes. He pulled one back and stepped inside. I followed him.

78

Nothing but a large wooden chair sat inside. The back of the chair snuggled against an amazing tree with the widest trunk I'd ever seen. The blankets hung only neck high, so the inside received direct sunlight most of the day.

A Scrudite woman sat in the chair with her legs curled up under her, humming as she carved with slow meticulous strokes. She never looked up.

"Having not heard back, we decided to start," Bohdan whispered. "Making our most powerful creations requires a consecrated space, and contact with our most ancient tree. Only a handful of us are strong enough for this task, and only one carver can work at a time. We're investing our precious wood and our hearts in this. I need to know if we should keep going."

I felt bad. I hadn't seen an urgency to testing the arrows, but I also hadn't known it took this kind of effort.

"I used the information you told me to decide you need 500 arrows," he said. "A hundred for each long eye. We carve with extreme slowness, so every bit of the wood understands. That means we can make two, at best three a day. Do you know how many days we have until Kolada?"

"A little over half a year. About two hundred days?"

"That's right. Just enough time. So let's go try these out now."

We walked to a place where we wouldn't bother anyone, and I could easily retrieve the arrows.

"I'll shoot three of mine, three of yours," I said.

I nocked an arrow, then stared out into the open wasteland that was Scrud. Bits of grass grew here in the spring, short tuffs of yellow-green sprouting randomly out of the tan dirt. I focused on one I knew to be about the distance my arrows usually went. All else went blurry as the little patch of chartreuse took on a clarity so sharp I could see the individual blades blowing in the breeze. I uncurled the tips of my three middle fingers and the simple movement in my right hand sent my arrow flying into the clump.

"That will be our marker."

I shot two more. They both fell a few paces past the first.

"Now yours. Remember, this is just me, with no oomrusher helping."

"I know. The wood will respond more, I think, with an oomrusher involved."

As I nocked the arrow, it felt different. A little lighter, yes, but also as if it were made out of something other than wood. No, something more than wood. I turned to him and saw the hopefulness in his eyes. He wanted this to work. So did I.

I let my focus settle on the small clump of grass I'd chosen and I aimed beyond it. The arrow took off with a zing missing from my other shots. It flew over the initial clump of grass, over the two other arrows on the ground, and traveled for many more paces.

"Again," he said.

I complied. The second stopped just short of the first. The third went much further than the other two.

"No doubt. Yours are better," I said.

"I thought they would be."

"Bohdan, I'm sorry…"

"It's okay. Get these three arrows to the Velka and let them see for themselves. They must factor this into their planning."

"Of course. I'll take care of it on my way home."

That night, I told Bohdan of my time with Coral.

"I'm glad you told someone in your family about me. I'd like to meet this sister of yours."

"Oh, you will. I think you two will like each other. And Bohdan? You'll meet all of my sisters sooner or later." I wanted to add *and my parents too* but I feared that might not be a promise I could keep.

Then something occurred to me, something I'd never asked about but probably should have.

"What does *your* family think of me?"

I'd met his mother many times and his father twice. I liked his mom. His father seemed to travel a lot and hadn't shown much interest in me. I'd also met three of his sisters and some of the young men he'd grown up with. They all seemed nice.

"Opinions vary. My mother knows I'm in love with you. She's worried you'll hurt me but hopes you won't. Other than that she likes you."

"I'm glad she does."

"My situation with others is complicated. Some of us, all of us really, hold positions in our clan and we depend on each other.

Scrudites who marry outside usually move away because outsiders don't adjust well to our way of life."

I hadn't thought about the angle of our love causing a loss for them. "But you told me you'll always live here part-time so you can remain a carver of Scrud."

"And I will, but it's about more than my carving talents. My people don't want to lose my heart, my commitment to them. But Scrudites are realistic. If my heart is with you anyway, few if any will expect me to deny that."

"I'm surprised they're as nice to me as they are."

He paused. The scrunch of wrinkles between his eyes told me the worst had yet to be said.

"There is one more thing, Olivine. Since you asked. Some think you're not friendly because you don't say much to them. A few have asked me why you don't like them."

Ouch. My life had been cursed by that misunderstanding.

"I like them all fine," I said. "I'm just not much for talking, especially with strangers."

"I know. I told them that. Maybe, I don't know, once in a while…."

"Of course. I'll try harder."

Joli's comments at practice about needing long eyed scouts left me thinking about my friend Zoya. She couldn't take up archery, but she wanted to help. Should I enlist her as a scout?

The answer would have been an obvious yes if not for the growing movement in K'ba. I now had to watch my every word when I was there, giving no one – not a waiter, nor a customer, nor a passerby on the street – reason to suspect I sympathized with the people referred to as "those reckless fools." I'd learned it was short for "those reckless fools who would get us all killed."

Did I want to put Zoya in the same uncomfortable predicament? No, I didn't. But the real question was what did Zoya want?

I rode from Bohdan's place over to her parents' inn in K'ba and invited her to go for a ride with me.

"We need to have a picnic today somewhere along the Canyon River."

"That sounds like a lot of work. Why not just visit in a tavern?" she asked. Then she looked at my face.

"Oh. Okay. I'll get them to make us a picnic dinner in the kitchen. Do we need to go far?"

"Not at all. Past the market on the west edge of town will do. I just need a place where I know we won't be overheard."

Zoya had decided I wanted to talk to her about either Bohdan or my sister Ryalgar, and she seemed disappointed when she found out it was the latter. But as I described the progress of my sister's plans and the long eyes and archers growing involvement, her eyes lit up. She wanted to be part of it, too.

"What do your parents think about all this?" I asked. "Would you have to hide what you're doing from them?"

"Good question." She unpacked a loaf of bread and a crock of soft cheese from her saddle bag as she spoke. A crock of strawberry jam followed.

"I think at first they wanted us to fight the Mongols because they thought Ilari had too much to lose. But they knew they'd have a tough time in the community if they spoke up, so they kept quiet."

I removed the jug of afternoon wine from my bag and filled two small cups.

"And now?" I asked.

"All they've heard since Noruz is how resistance of any kind is a death sentence. You hear something often enough, you start to believe it, especially if everyone you know believes it already. I think they've bought into the Sage Coalition's position now."

"The what? Sage like the stuff growing out here in the drylands?"

She laughed. "No, sage as in wise. The K'basta think they're the wise ones, and everyone else talks like a fool. They make a strong argument. I don't think my parents would be happy now if they found out I worked with your sister."

"Can you do this without them finding out?"

"Sure. They won't go out of their way to check on me. They don't want trouble in our family. They don't want trouble at all."

I nodded. I suspected a desire for no trouble protected me also.

"Plenty of K'basta probably wonder about me, given my family," I said. "My strategy is not to give anyone a reason to look too close."

"Exactly. Luckily, neither of us has enemies. As long as we avoid the real zealots, we should be fine."

"Not having enemies is a good thing." I laughed as I said it, thinking I didn't have an enemy in the world. Then I realized perhaps I did.

"I ought to tell you about something else," I said and I poured out the story of my mistake in telling Magomet's mother about Bohdan. "It made him angry."

She shook her head. "I can't believe you hurt him like that."

I wasn't surprised to discover she felt sorry for Magomet. He was her friend, after all. Heli, he was still kind of my friend, too.

"I didn't mean to. I got so caught up in not telling his nice mother anything about being part of Ryalgar's plans that I forgot about everything else. So now what do I do?"

"Give him some time. I'm sure he'll get over it."

I couldn't think of a better plan, even though I already knew Magomet didn't exactly excel at getting over things.

Over the next few days I finished two paintings to give to Bohdan for framing, and I completed the metallic touches on a third. I took it to the little shop that sold my work. The proprietor greeted me with less warmth than usual. Perhaps other problems preoccupied him. Perhaps not.

"How's business?" I asked, hoping to dredge up information.

"Not bad. Always better in the summer when we have more tourists passing through. Most of them won't buy something as high-end as your work, of course. You now have a more select clientele."

"I guess that's good. Mostly Pilkese?" I asked.

"That, and Kirians and Levish. Your, uh, your sister is becoming more well-known throughout the realm. I think she's seen as a bit of a hero by some over there, and it may be helping your sales a little." His shrug reminded me that this man liked to increase his sales with anyone for any reason. "Not to take anything away from the beauty of your creations, of course," he added.

I chuckled. The idea of Ryalgar increasing my sales didn't offend me, but it did make me curious about the locals.

"How are my sales doing with the K'basta then?"

He shook his head. "I'd say those sales have probably ended. It's not personal, Olivine, but the strength of the Sage Coalition has grown considerably in the last eighth. You've been a little out of touch. Even I, who the Goddess knows avoids anything political like a pox, even I have to admit they make some good points. Have you listened, really listened, to their arguments? You should, you know."

My suspicion was right. The shopkeeper had been converted to the cause.

"I'm trying hard to stay out of this," I said. "Surely you can appreciate …."

"Of course." He returned to his gracious way without skipping a beat. "We'll sell as many as we can to whomever we can. That's what this is all about, right?"

He held up the one I'd just delivered and squinted at it.

"Hmm. This one isn't quite up to your usual standards, huh? A little less detail than most." He turned to face me, concern in his eyes. "Don't be rushing through these on my account. Some orders have been canceled, so we've got breathing room. Take your time and do them right."

It would have been good advice except I knew this painting had no less detail than the others. Was the shopkeeper scheming to lay the groundwork to sell my work for less? Or to sell less of it?

Or maybe he did believe the quality of my work had slipped. Perhaps as he became more attached to this cause, he'd see my paintings as less attractive. Was art that subjective? The idea made me shudder.

I heard my own voice in my head, telling Zoya "Don't give anyone a reason to look too close."

"I'll make sure I give each one all the time it needs," I said. "You'll like the next one better."

"I'm sure I will." He was all polite smiles as he saw me out.

On my way back to the farm I stopped at the Velka's tent in the main Vinx market. I didn't know the woman there, but it didn't matter. I'd learned they all would deliver a discreet message to any of their members. The reliability of their services gave them added power in Ilari. I wondered if others noticed that, too.

This woman agreed to pass along word of my having found an eager long eyed scout and of my need to meet with Joli or Ryalgar soon concerning arrows.

"Arrows?" she confirmed. "Do you need to speak with both of them together about these arrows? And if not, which person do you prefer?"

Well of course I preferred my sister, but perhaps I'd have an easier time keeping my relationship with Bohdan out of this if I spoke with Joli. And, Ryalgar had delegated this part to Joli, making her technically the person in charge of the arrows.

"Joli would be best. I know she's busy so tell her I can meet her here at the market and it won't take long, but she needs to see this."

~ 12 ~

An Unusually Hot Tirga

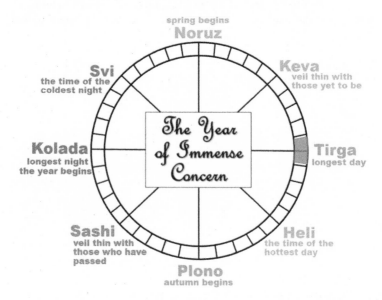

Within a few days Joli and I met near the market. Tirga hadn't yet arrived but the day simmered with heat. Some summers brought an oppressive warmth before Tirga and it settled in and made everyone irritable and lethargic for the next two eighths. Given Ilari's need to prepare for war, I hoped this summer wouldn't be one of those.

Joli offered to buy us a midday meal from vendors selling ready-to-eat food. We settled onto a quilt with a pile of roasted chicken legs and small egg tarts between us.

"I'm told you have something urgent to speak of. You've recruited more long eyes?" she guessed. "Or did those you found all quit?"

"Neither. I, well, I have good news, but it's complicated."

She laughed. "I've yet to learn anything about your family that isn't." She waited.

That morning I'd decided I needed to tell Joli the full story of how I'd come by the arrows. But now that I faced doing the telling, I couldn't get my mouth to form the words. I just sat there. Her faced moved into a mild grimace.

"You've something to share with me that you don't want Ryalgar to know?"

I nodded.

I should leave Bohdan out of this. Even if Joli meant to keep her mouth shut, she could tell Ryalgar, and once Ryalgar knew ... Perhaps Mom would never *lock me up to keep me away from bad influences. But what if she would?*

So I sat, saying nothing, trying to make up a believable story about my involvement with these arrows that didn't include Bohdan.

I finished two chicken legs before Joli finally spoke again.

"Okay, Olivine," she said. "I've heard you're not much of a talker, and I respect that. You probably have good reasons for your silence. So let me ask you one yes or no question. You answer it, and we'll decide how to proceed. Okay?"

That seemed reasonable. Yes or no couldn't get me into much trouble, could it?

"Okay."

"Does the information you don't want to tell me have a good chance of affecting the outcome of our battle with the Mongols?"

She stared hard at me. I knew she was Zurian, the daughter of a fighting nichna, and I heard the warrior in her voice as she asked.

"Pruck."

"I'll take that as a yes. So, let's try a second question. Are your personal problems regarding this subject bigger than, I don't know, the deaths of everyone in Ilari?"

"Probably not." I didn't like her message.

"You don't know me well," she said "but believe me, I grew up in a family quite different from yours. I like yours, to be honest, and mine not so much. But there is one thing I know how to do that your sisters may not. I could die keeping a secret if I had to."

That seemed more dramatic than necessary, but I got the point.

"Let's move away from the market, and I'll show you the reason I asked to see you," I said. "Then I'll explain why it's complicated."

The arrows' extra oomph impressed Joli more than it had me and after a few demonstrations she wanted to try the obvious.

"Next time you shoot, I'll push and we'll see what these arrows can do."

Neither of us was prepared for the effect.

"Hawk scump! I can feel the life in these little pruckers as they fly," she said. "Where in Heli's name did you get them? And yes, they will *absolutely* make a difference. What were you thinking? We can be over four hundred paces away and still hit horses hard enough for the poison to release."

"I thought so."

She shook her head. "There's still pods of old magic in more places than we know. And these do have a power to them. You said you got them from a Scrudite? I've heard stories about the bowls and cups they carve, but I've never heard of them making weapons. Trust me, if they did the Zurians would have heard."

"I don't think they make weapons, normally. Just tools and utensils. But one of them has become uncommonly concerned about this pending invasion."

"Good for him. He sounds like a smarter Scrudite than most."

I winced. "They're not stupid people."

Joli didn't back down. "Nah. Nobody smart lives in a little hut and wears rags." I let it go. She spoke from ignorance.

"So tell me. Why would one of them start making weapons?"

"Could be he's in love with a woman involved in this fight. A woman from another nichna."

Joli caught on.

"Wait … You're not in love with some artist in K'ba, are you? Your whole family has it wrong. You've fallen for a varmin Scrudite!"

I looked at the ground and said nothing.

"Come now. This happens. It can't be that bad."

"Oh, it is." I needed to make her understand the seriousness of my situation. "My mother warned me that if I ever showed signs of developing feelings for an unacceptable man, she'd lock me up till I came to my senses. She didn't say it like she thought it was funny. I think she might do it."

Joli didn't flinch. "I've met your mom. She might. But Ryalgar would never give up your secret."

"Not intentionally. But Joli, there's so many of us. Out it slips to another and then to another and it always makes its way to Mom."

"Not a dynamic I grew up with, but I get it. Okay. I'll be your stone wall."

I must have looked puzzled. "Your barrier," she said. "No fire can pass through me. No secrets either. I'll bring the arrows into the forest and instead of bragging about them to everyone, I'll be vague about their origins, but also make sure we plan for them and use them. By the time they get linked to Scrud there will be no connection to you. You have my word."

Over dinner that night, I told my parents I planned to celebrate Tirga in K'ba. My mother set her goblet back on the table with more force than necessary but said nothing.

"How are your paintings coming along?" my father said. "Is my metallic paint still as popular?"

"Oh yes. I mean sales have dropped but I still have orders I haven't filled."

My mother sensed a way to turn the conversation to her concerns. "And these extra coins you're getting from all those sales? You're saving them?" For years now I'd contributed a small agreed-upon amount of my art income to the household. I never thought my parents would expect a bigger cut if I had success.

"Yes, Mother. Supplies cost money, as does travel. Surely you're aware that I've not asked you to finance my, uh, hobby. I understand we aren't wealthy enough to squander what we have."

She acknowledged my facts with a nod.

"I think what you do is more than a hobby," my father interrupted. "It's a profession. Of course you should keep the extra profits; we'd never expect anything else. Would we, dear?"

"Thanks, Dad. I realize I may not always be able to sell as much as I do now, and yet I can't imagine a life without being able to paint. So I put coins aside to ensure I'll always have the resources to be an artist."

"Sensible," he said.

"Ridiculous," my mother said at the same time. "A woman need not finance her diversions. A good husband provides for his wife's enrichment and entertainment."

"Well, just in case ..." I squirmed in my seat, preparing to stand and make my way out of the room before the conversation went any further downhill. My father beat me to it.

"I almost forgot. I've got to go check on something in the barn," he said, the last words coming over his shoulder as he walked out. Dad knew better than anyone how to avoid a tricky discussion.

Mom waited until he was out of earshot.

"You seem unable to end things with your artist paramour," she said. "Perhaps your parents' insistence you don't travel to K'ba for a while would be the greatest favor we could do for you."

I took my time blowing my breath out through my mouth. "I'm going out to the barn to talk to Dad about the metallic paint he makes for me."

She looked me at hard, with a warning in her eyes. But I didn't stop.

"He's so proud of how *well* his idea for this paint has worked out. I bet he can't wait for me to come back from K'ba with another report on how popular it is."

Mom knew when to change her tactics. "Tell me you're not saving this money so you can do something foolish like marry this artist."

That, at least, was easy to do.

"Mother. I promise you. I am not saving my money to marry an artist from K'ba."

With that, I turned and walked out to the barn. I knew I had to tell her eventually that there was no artist boyfriend. But not tonight. I just wanted to get over to Scrud for the holiday.

Once I arrived in Scrud, Bohdan seemed more interested in my promise to be friendly to his friends than he was in spending time the way I'd hoped. He insisted we go over to the communal hearth as the sun went down. Warm evenings meant the fire was small and ceremonial.

Much as in my own nichna, tidzys and young couples gathered to eat and drink together on the eve of holidays. Tidzys often sought a partner around the fire, while couples enjoyed the chance to be more affectionate in public than custom usually allowed. Bohdan was clearly after the latter.

I suppose after years of sitting alone at such affairs it was understandable he'd want to show off a little, but that sort of playfulness wasn't my style.

Bohdan pulled me onto his lap almost immediately. As I wriggled into place I could feel his eagerness for the finale to the evening. But, ready or not, he wanted to sit with his friends and snuggle me tight against him while they watched. *Look at me. Tonight, I've got one too.*

Meanwhile, I was supposed to become uncharacteristically chatty. Believe me, if you don't find conversation with strangers easy, it does not get easier when your boyfriend keeps fondling you under your skirt while pretending no one can see what he's doing. Especially if you're fairly sure they know varmin well what's going on.

I saw it as juvenile behavior, the sort of silliness new tidzys engage in and outgrow. However, he seemed to find it all cute and funny.

This man has done you so many favors and asked for so little. He gets to do this. The voice in my head had a point. So I tried. I really did. I asked questions of all his friends and gave nice answers to theirs while he discreetly played with me however he wanted. Childish as it was, he looked like he had the time of his life watching me squirm around his deft fingers as I smiled at his friends.

By the time we got to his hut, I'd had it with this game. I started to say so when he came at me with such an explosion of desire that I pulled my clothes out of the way lest he ripped the fabric in his enthusiasm.

I expected our lovemaking to move too fast for me, leaving me even more irritated, but to my surprise, our public foreplay had aroused me as much as it had him. Perhaps more.

We'd hardly begun when I had an explosion of delight beyond anything I'd felt before. I was stunned.

"So, you do have a playful side to you," he murmured as we lay together afterward. "I'll have to take you over to the fire and fondle you in front of my friends on every holiday."

"No," I replied.

He answered with a grin that spoke volumes.

"Okay. Maybe just every so often."

****

An eighth had passed since I'd slipped up and told Magomet's mother that Bohdan was my boyfriend. As far as I knew, Magomet kept quiet about the information, which I appreciated. But he also avoided our group once I arrived in town. If I showed up unexpectedly, he found a reason to leave. The others all noticed.

Only Zoya knew about Bohdan and my mistake with Magomet. The next time I stayed at her parents' inn, she had news for me.

"Magomet came to me an ank ago," she said, "asking me what I thought about your situation. He's not dumb, he knows we tell each other things. I did the best I could. I told you were sincere about the celibacy, and then you met this incredible man from Scrud and you couldn't help being drawn to him. I said you meant to show Magomet the respect of telling him properly, but his mother caught you off-guard and now you don't know how to fix it."

"Wow. That's better than what I could have done. Do you think he believed you?"

"Of course. Why wouldn't he?"

The next morning, I learned he hadn't believed Zoya.

Magomet sent a messenger to my room, summoning me to the marketplace at midday to "discuss my treachery" in a public location. Treachery? Did he mean to him? Or to his parents' cause? Neither was good.

I considered not going, but remembered my resolution about not making enemies. I had to fix this. Important things, things well beyond my feelings, were at stake.

I repeated Zoya's explanation of my behavior over in my head. I'd report the same thing. I'd even beg his forgiveness for having spurned him and then found another. One can't control one's heart, I'd say. Hopefully, if I went on long enough, I'd soothe his pride. Then we'd move forward as awkward friends instead of as silent enemies.

~ 13 ~

Facts for Another Day

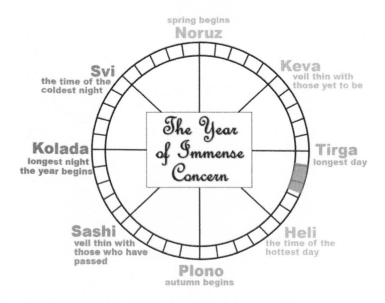

Magomet paced as I tethered my horse and made my way over to him. I saw anger in the clomp of his feet and in the way he held his arms against his chest, but even that didn't prepare me for the hate I saw in his eyes as I approached him.

"We should have talked sooner," I said.

"We should never have met at all," he replied. "I'd be the better off. Why, why did you have to go and do this?"

I assumed he meant falling in love with Bohdan.

"I didn't mean to. It happened. I meant to tell you but..."

"Don't give me that prucking goat scump. Do you think I'm that stupid?" He spat the words at me.

This wasn't going as well as I'd hoped.

"Of course not."

"Yet you've played me for a fool since halfway through our advanced studies. How many of our friends knew you didn't really give up sex? How many of them laughed at me behind my back the whole time?"

Perhaps I had a bigger problem than I realized.

"I think I'll be celibate to help my art." He said it in a high little voice intended to mimic me. "I'm so devoted to my creativity I'm going to walk away from men." Then, in his own loud, deep voice. "Except you didn't, did you, you little pruska? You slept with anyone who'd have you while I pined away for you back in Pilk, filled with my love for you."

"I, I slipped up a few times, it's true."

"I've got testimony from five young men in Vinx who had sex with you, one of them more than once. Tell me, did *that* just happen? Heli, you're more randy than a bitch in heat. How come I never saw that sort of enthusiasm in my bed?"

He'd stopped pacing and stood looking down at me, both hands on his hips.

"I tried to let you know we weren't lovers, Magomet. I *really* tried."

"No, you didn't."

"Yes, I did. But you wouldn't listen, no matter how I said it, and you ignored all the other ways I tried to let you know. Sure, I spoke gently because I didn't want to lose our friendship, and I didn't want to break up our circle of friends. I finally declared myself celibate because I didn't know what else to do."

I saw the hurt under his anger, and I felt bad. But no woman loves a man because she feels bad for him. It doesn't work that way.

"You should have told me directly. Loudly. And often, so I understood. *That* would have been the kindest thing."

Perhaps. Some of my sisters would have handled it like that but I couldn't imagine confronting any man over and over until he finally left me alone. Besides, adamant as Magomet was, I doubted he'd have backed off. I wanted to tell him that and more, but as happened so often, the words didn't come.

"There was no way this could have ended well," I said.

"Yeah? It didn't have to end with my hearing you tell my mother, my *mother,* that you were in love with a prucking Scrudite!"

See? That had been one of the few times I had said what was on my mind and look how it turned out.

"So what happens now?" I asked.

"That's up to you. More than one woman has pleaded for forgiveness and been accepted back into a man's heart, you know."

I felt icicles forming around my own. *No, he couldn't possibly be hoping for that.*

"I could make your life wonderful, Olivine. Acceptance in the top art circles. All the painting you care to do. A husband who adores you and whose family does too. What in Heli more do you want?"

Yes, he could give me the perfect life, with everything I longed for. Except for love.

Pruck my stupid heart. Why hadn't it had the good sense to fall for Magomet to begin with?

"It's too late," I said. "Part of me wishes it wasn't, but I can't ignore the last two years."

"Okay then." He stopped. He looked up at the sky. He looked down at the ground. He looked right at me. "I'll accept your friendship instead and hope you'll accept mine."

Seriously? All that anger, then this?

"Friends respect each other, of course," he added, in a far milder tone than he'd used since I arrived. "Therefore, I will expect your ne'er-do-well boyfriend to remain out of the picture, and certainly out of K'ba, so he is unable to further humiliate me."

"You can't dictate where ..."

"I'm not finished." His voice grew louder, "I will expect that bit of consideration from you at least until the Mongols come to claim their tribute. After that, we'll discuss our future."

"I don't think ...."

"I'm still not done." He spoke louder now, enough to drown me out. "In return, I'll assume your sisterly loyalties to the reckless fools have faded and the wisdom of the Sage Coalition has persuaded you to support the K'basta cause. As it has so many others. I'll not look into your activities nor cause others to do so either."

"I don't need ..."

He didn't pause.

"If you're really good to me, I might even drop hints that locals should stop boycotting your work because of your family. That's so unfair. We're better than that. So what do you think? Would you like to be *friends* or not?

The amount of rage he managed to stuff into the word *friends* astonished me.

Perhaps I should have screamed at him to do his worst, vowing never to spend less time with the man I loved in order to soothe his ego. Perhaps I should have defended my sister's plans and told him what I thought of his frightened Sage Coalition.

But I knew better. If I had to pick one time in my life to spew out all the repressed words from years past, this was not it. I needed to say what I had to say to avoid making an enemy because I knew I was dangerously close to having one.

"We're friends," I said.

"Good," he replied.

I made excuses to the others that I needed to return to Vinx for a longer time than usual. Aside from whatever horrible bargain I'd just made with Magomet, I knew the warm weather of Tirga would be filled with practice sessions amongst the long eyes and the oomrushers and I wanted to attend every one of them as I focused on my part, away from the curious eyes of K'ba.

I made a quick stop in Scrud, long enough for one bout of great sex and the warmest hellos I could manage with my new Scrudite friends. I assured Bohdan that the Velka were delighted with his enhanced arrows.

He sensed my concerns were elsewhere and didn't pry. I appreciated it. Of course I'd tell him about the whole nasty encounter with Magomet later. I just wasn't ready.

When I got home, I couldn't paint. The artist inside of me had crawled into a cave inside my head and she wouldn't come out. I tried to coax her but she wouldn't be dissuaded.

I could shoot, however, and shooting arrows felt good. I placed a larger and softer target on the far side of the barn, to better judge my aim and better protect my arrows. I spent my mornings out there, aiming at imaginary people who looked like Magomet, or like the art dealer in Pilk who'd left my name off of my painting. Sometimes they even bore a vague resemblance to the shopkeeper in K'ba or worse yet to my mother. That last one made me uncomfortable, but I knew imagination couldn't be controlled any more than love could. So I shot at phantoms.

Each day I walked out a little further from the target, yet the arrows clumped closer together as time went on. Also, the walk tired me out less, and my arm stayed strong longer. The practice seemed to agree with me.

I avoided conversations with everyone at the farm. This would have prompted questions if I'd been anyone else, but it was me, so no one noticed. My mother warmed up for some reason, but she took her time telling me why.

On a day when the breeze blew hard, she asked me to start laundering the heavy linens. I didn't think much of it because we always tried to do such on a windy day. But one can't walk away in the middle of hanging up the wet laundry and she knew it. As she headed out to join me at the clothesline, I realized I'd been set up.

"Olivine, dear. Let me give you a hand with those big things. I hardly meant for you to do this all yourself."

We stood together with our bags of clothespins, our day dresses getting soaked as we hung sheets and towels and she told me what was on her mind.

"I've stayed in touch with the mothers of the kids you and Celestine grew up with," she began. "You two had such a nice circle of friends. Do you still hear from any of them?"

I shrugged. Celestine did.

"Kind of."

"Well, the moms all remember you two and how creative you were. So different, and yet both so talented. That's how they describe you."

"Umm."

"A couple of them sought me out to share something they thought I ought to know."

That introduction would have worried me if it wasn't for the conspiratorial grin on Mom's face.

"I wish you'd talked to us more about the artistic community in K'ba." She sighed. "Your dad and I just don't know much about them. But of course some artists have done well for themselves. I should have realized that. They're not all struggling."

"True ..."

"I've learned some are established leaders in the community, with considerable wealth and prestige. I mean, no one ever hears anything about the K'basta Royals except that they are terribly elderly and out of touch. It makes sense that the more successful artists in K'ba would fill that void."

Okay, this was just weird.

"I wish you'd told me." She said it again.

"Told you what?"

"About this boy. Magomet. He's the child of two of K'ba's most famous painters! I'm speaking of the Jaqeli family, of course."

"Yes, that's Magomet's parents. They have a big studio; they've been kind to all of his friends."

"See? You are so lucky to have gotten to know them. Tell me, do they like you?"

"Well enough. Why?"

"Because when I feared you'd given your heart to some young man over there, it never occurred to me he'd be the son of such people." She shook her head. "I should have trusted you more."

She thought Magomet was my artist lover? How had this happened?

"A couple of the mothers told me your boyfriend Magomet was so cute. He rode over here a few anks ago, to learn about the boys you grew up with, making sure, you know, none of your heart was still bound to any of your tidzy trysts back home. He said, being from another nichna and all, he wanted to make sure he did the right thing by you. Now really, how many men are so considerate before they propose marriage?"

So that's how he'd learned of my non-celibate fun.

"He told them he planned to propose marriage?"

"Well it *is* time, dear, and I know you must be sick with worry after everything I've said to you about marrying an artist but I had no idea. His status in his community makes him almost an honorary prince, at least among the K'basta."

Great. Now Magomet was a prince?

"It doesn't matter, Mom. I've already told Magomet 'no.'"

"Why? Because you thought I wouldn't approve? Oh no, dear. Let him know you've reconsidered."

"It won't work, Mom, for a lot of reasons, and honestly your feelings about him aren't the problem."

She looked insulted but said "There's nothing that can't be overcome, daughter. Speak to me."

I don't know what got into me. Maybe I'd held back so much for so long. Whatever the cause, I sat down in the mud made by all the dripping sheets and I burst into tears. She surprised me when she sat down next to me and put her arm around me. She even kept it there while I cried.

"There, there. A woman can change her mind. A man understands that. This can be undone. It can be fixed."

"No." I shook my head. "No. For starters, his family hates us now, Mom. All of us. They're the leaders of this movement in K'ba that thinks we need to give in to the Mongol's demands. Pay the tribute and do whatever else they tell us to." Sobs punctuated my words. "They don't know I'm helping Ryalgar, and they'd never let me set foot in their studio if they did. I have to hide everything I am when I'm over there now."

"Oh. Well. Yes. That *is* a problem." She looked flustered that her ideal plan for me had met such a large snag. "I've heard about this Sage something nonsense. Nobody here thinks it matters worth a bowl of beans but I guess it could be serious over there."

"It is. You've no idea. Magomet and I have no future now." My tears slowed, the emotion spent.

"You poor baby. First Ryalgar with her betrothed prince, then Coral falling for that womanizer. Now this. Why do my beautiful daughters have the worst of luck?" She stood, noticing the mud coating both of our backsides.

"Come. Let's clean up. There will be other, worthy men I promise you." She wrapped her arm around me, somewhat awkwardly, one last time. "I'm so glad you finally talked to me, dear. See? Isn't that much better?"

I supposed it was. I'd shared some truths with her and it had gone okay. That fact that I'd never loved Magomet to begin with, and that I now cared for a Scrudite, well, those were facts for another day.

~ 14 ~

Best When Left Alone

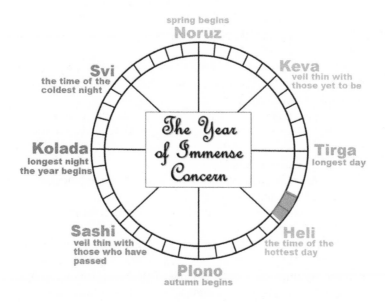

Now that I lived at my parents' farm full-time, Joli and I met often. She needed my help to try out ideas for focusing her oomrush abilities on archery, and I needed her help to figure out how my enhanced eyesight could provide the most precision. Our combined skill was a tricky dance between two people with different sorts of abilities.

I liked working with her and felt proud to have a friendship with my older sister's friend. Families are funny that way. The younger ones look up to the older ones long after the age difference matters.

As Joli and I talked, I learned that her upbringing left her with no understanding of the Sage Coalition's point of view. "To capitulate is to lose one's reason for living," she insisted.

"Word is the Mongols are relatively kind masters," I said. "They expect no conversion to their religion or their ways, and they allow their subjects to govern themselves. All they want is a fixed amount of tribute."

"Right. And no doubt that amount rises every year until the poor farmers revolt or starve. No master stays kind. Humans aren't made that way."

I couldn't argue with her. Nothing in my experience indicated they were, and these stories about the Mongols' treatment of their vassals were only rumors. And perhaps wishful thinking.

She told me of the man she had planned to marry in Zur, years ago, and of her hasty departure to the Velka when he became fearful of her oomrush abilities.

"I'd have thought Zurians would welcome such a skill."

"They welcome skill in areas they understand, like weapons. My people never took to things they weren't accustomed to. My boyfriend certainly didn't."

"But now? No men at all?" After I said it I found the question too bold, but she laughed.

"Occasionally. For fun. Turns out I like men for pleasure but I'm not the pairing up sort. Good thing, I guess."

"I didn't think I was cut out for a relationship either. Not because of the long eye thing, but because my painting leaves little room for the attention a man demands. Then I met Bohdan."

She gave it some thought. "I've heard Scrudites have different, I don't know, social and family arrangements? Might be better suited to a lady like you, though if you want a life with him you're probably going to have to leave the home you grew up in."

"I know. If we survive all this, I want to have my own art studio in K'ba, assuming the K'basta will forgive those of us who fought.

"I can't imagine they won't if we win. So. Will you marry him?"

"Possibly. He wants to remain a carver and says he has to live in Scrud to do that. And I need a studio. Whatever we do, we'll need separate homes."

"That doesn't sound so bad."
"No. It doesn't."

Later in Tirga, Joli organized a massive tryout to decide who would work with whom when the big day came. Nikolo, Arek, and I arrived together and welcomed the other three long eyes as soon as we recognized them. Of all the ones who'd agreed to become competent archers and help us, only these three had followed through.

A large man of my father's age had ridden the furthest, coming from the banks of the Wide River in Kir. I remembered him saying he'd picked up a bow as a child and hadn't put it down since. We thought his size and years of practice would make up for his aging eyesight.

The mother from Lev had the most exceptional vision of any of us, but she'd never tried archery. She had promised to find a teacher and learn. Today we'd discover how far she'd come.

The third recruit taught ancient history at one of the better places of higher learning. She also had strong eyes but had learned archery as part of her fascination with old cultures beyond our realm. She'd claimed to be "not that good" but said she'd get better.

Although there were only six of us, there must have been twenty oomrushers. All Velka, I guessed. They ranged in age from Ryalgar's twenty-five years up to the indeterminate age of my grandmother.

My grandmother? Yes. I'd grown up thinking she'd died years ago, but Ryalgar told me she lived with the Velka instead. I'd met her during my visit and tried to make conversation with her, but despite my efforts, it felt like talking to a stranger. I guess it was. Now, she sat on the bench with the other oomrushers. I had no idea she could do this, too.

Joli impressed me with her organization as the oomrushers auditioned for the honor of being assigned to one of us. We worked with all of them while Joli evaluated the results. She planned to pair us with the best six so that these teams of two could begin training together immediately. Because we had extra oomrushers, Joli also experimented to see if her archer long eyes found a second or third oomrusher helpful.

As she squinted at her notes, ready to make her assignments, she asked a question I'd been wondering about.

"What are we calling this thing, anyway?"

Ryalgar, who'd been too distracted to do more than wave at me, gave me a grin as she answered.

"The Chimera. We're calling the big plan, the entire illusion, the Chimera."

I smiled back. The mythical three-part animal from another realm had fascinated me as a child when big sister Ryalgar brought me stories from her school about this combination of a lion, a goat, and a snake.

"What in name of my great uncle's arse is a come-here-uh?" said one of the Velka.

"Kuh-mere-uh," Ryalgar corrected her

"I've heard of it," Arek spoke up. Of course he had. I'd told him about it when I'd tried to paint the creature using nothing but my imagination. Turns out it's hard to make a picture of something with nothing to look at.

"We're the snakes," my grandma said. "Sneaky and deadly."

"Okay Snakes. Listen up." Joli had made her decisions. "Our best shooting usually happens when two oomrusher friends work with one archer. More oomrushers muck things up. So here are the teams."

I found it cute that Ryalgar's best oomrusher buddy was my grandmother. I found it interesting that Ryalgar was the stronger of the two.

My assignment pleased me. All my practice earned me the title of the second-most proficient archer, behind Nikolo, a former archery coach. Although to be fair, the large older man from Kir came in a close third. My long eye abilities were in the top four. The mother from Lev outdid us all as far as vision went, while Arek, me, and the history teacher tied for second place.

And, of all the archers, I was the only one who didn't get a pair assigned to me. Joli and I made a well-matched pair, outdoing every combination of others, provided no one else tried to help us. It seemed to fit.

I wondered if Joli's practice sessions with me had been deliberate, done in hopes of honing our relationship. Perhaps she'd wanted to work with me. But if so, that was fine.

I tried to catch Ryalgar's eye, to see if she felt disappointed I hadn't been assigned to work with her and Grandma. A family team would have been nice, but if she cared, she hid it well. She even congratulated Joli and me on being the strongest pair.

When Joli called a second practice later in the ank, Ryalgar didn't attend. Coral visited the farm and came into the barn to see how we did. The whole time I practiced she looked at me as if she needed to talk, so I broke away to see what was on her mind.

I expected something serious, but she only wanted to complain about Hana, the Velka who'd been put in charge of Coral's part of the plan. I didn't like Hana either. The woman was pushy, but I thought Coral over-reacted. My sister sometimes did that. I hoped she and Hana would reach an understanding and get along before the Mongols attacked us.

Heli approached. This celebration of the hottest time of the year had never been my favorite holiday. Outdoor picnics and swimming were common activities. So were naps.

Knowing Bohdan wanted us to observe the holiday together, I struggled with what to do. I couldn't invite him to Vinx. I didn't want a repeat of sweating in the heat of dusty Scrud as we sat around a fire with his friends. The worst of summer did nothing for my sociability.

K'ba was my best choice. My savings dwindled but the shopkeeper still owed me for a painting. Those coins would cover lodging anywhere we'd be welcome. Would Bohdan like this idea?

Magomet presented a problem. I knew I'd left him with the impression I'd agreed to his unreasonable demand that Bohdan never visit K'ba. Maybe Bohdan and I could go somewhere on the outskirts along the river? The canyon had several steep footpaths down, used by locals to draw water and bathe but also used by tourists eager for the adventure of splashing around in the fast water as it tumbled down from the mountains.

Crowds would be everywhere on Heli, but I'd seek out a place further away than most, perhaps on the southeast edge of the settlements, on the side closest to Scrud. Better yet, some of the locations excluded children on holidays, allowing adults to swim with little or no clothing. That would solve the problem of Bohdan standing out as a Scrudite and drawing attention to us.

Would he like public skinny dipping? On Heli? I thought so.

I needed more information, and I knew who had it. The reczavy loved skinny dipping. I could leave a day early, go to the reczavy camp, and find Gypsum. She'd know the safest place for Bohdan and me to go.

When I told my parents of my desire to celebrate Heli with my artist friends, neither raised an eyebrow. They had no reason to object. I'd been home for over four anks now, acting pleasant and helping with chores every day. Better yet, Mom no longer feared I hid a relationship with some man she needed to protect me from.

Yes, I *had* snuck over to Scrud twice under the guise of going to the market, but as far as they knew, I'd been a model daughter since Tirga.

"Have fun," my dad said.

"Be careful," my mother added. "You know." I presumed she referred to Magomet and the Sage Coalition.

"Don't worry, I will."

Mentioning I planned to stop off to see Gypsum on the way seemed like a bad idea, so I left it at that.

I'd seen the reczavy camp in the distance plenty of times. The road veered far enough away from it that most people could barely see the tents, but I wasn't most people, at least not regarding eyesight.

I confess. I'd stopped my horse more than once and focused on the bright colors, wondering if I could see one of the infamous naked men standing around a campfire. Wondering if my eyesight would be good enough to make out the details.

I did glimpse nude body parts on occasion but the peep show lost its charm. I suppose the exercise helped me determine the limits of my vision, which was good, and the limits of my curiosity about the nudity of others, which apparently wasn't all that strong.

I probably should have sought Gypsum out sooner, but simply riding into the reczavy camp unannounced intimidated me. Nonetheless, two days before Heli, I did exactly that.

"Got a visitor," a hefty woman with a deep melodic voice called out as I rode up. Then to me, as I got closer. "Welcome.

Lost? In trouble? Curious?" She pointed to a jug of water. "Thirsty?"

"Yes."

Her laugh was as pleasant as her voice.

"Which one?"

"All of them. But mostly I'm looking for my sister. Gypsum."

"Gypsum!" The yell was directed to one of the back tents. "You got *another* sister out here. Haven't seen this one yet. Want her to stay?"

"What's she look like?"

"Skinny. Shorter than the others. Hair like bronze." The woman took a step closer and squinted at me. "Really green eyes."

"Yup. Make her comfortable."

The woman gestured to a nearby rock. "Have a seat. I'll get you some water."

Gypsum came out of the tent, her tall thin body wrapped in a colorful robe that reminded me of the Scrudites clothing, except instead of being woven together, the various rags were stitched together like a quilt. It was pretty in an odd way and it suited her fine light blonde hair blowing loose in the breeze.

"I'm so glad you came."

We hugged. Gypsum had always made sense to me, maybe because we both struggled more with my mother's demands than the others. Or maybe because we each promised ourselves we'd find a way to get out of Vinx and go somewhere that we could be free.

And look at her. She'd gone and done it while I'd only tried and failed. I should have visited her sooner.

I looked around. The camp was shabby but more well-tended than I expected.

"Good for you," I said. I think she knew exactly what I meant.

I spent the night there. She had such little contact with the rest of the family that it seemed safe to confide everything about Bohdan to her, as well as my problems with Magomet and the rest of K'ba. Her life seemed so much tamer than mine, despite the controversial people she lived with and her efforts to help Ryalgar. And as I guessed, she had plenty of information about the best places to skinny-dip in K'ba.

Of all my troubles, Bohdan interested her the most.

"A Scrudite. I think that's more rebellious than running away to join the reczavy." She grinned.

"Not until I actually tell people about it, it isn't."

"You will have to do that, you know."

"I know."

~ 15 ~

What a Long Eye Sees

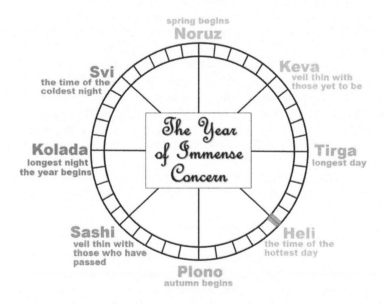

spring begins
Noruz

Svi
the time of the
coldest night

Keva
veil thin with
those yet to be

Kolada
longest night
the year begins

The Year of Immense Concern

Tirga
longest day

Sashi
veil thin with
those who have
passed

Heli
the time of the
hottest day

Piono
autumn begins

Gypsum recommended a small K'basta swimming area located almost on the border with Scrud. We wouldn't need to pay for lodging because none was available.

Bohdan loved my plan. He borrowed a horse and a small tent and we set off on the day before Heli. After a long half a day's ride we got to the Canyon River and found the steep but well-worn dirt path that would take us to the thin crowd of people below. We lead our horses down with care and tethered them in the shadiest spot we could find.

The sun blazed during this hottest part of the afternoon and almost everyone played in the refreshing water rushing around the boulders. After our sweaty ride through the desolation, we didn't hesitate. We stripped off our clothes and joined them.

Once the cold water chilled us down, we ate our picnic dinner under a bright blue sky, donning only enough clothes to protect our most sensitive parts from the sun. Then we set up our tent along the narrow bank far from the others and did all the wonderful things we'd come to do.

I felt brilliant. I'd devised the perfect celebration.

I saw no one I knew, but the next day Bohdan kept running into friends. He told me that Scrudites often came across this border to play on their days off and they made up a lot of the naked revelers. Each one seemed to know and like Bohdan. I'd no idea my beloved was so popular with Scrudites outside of his own clan.

If running into others bothered him, he didn't show it. He greeted each one and introduced me as though we'd met in a tavern fully clothed. I did my best to be equally confident. To my surprise, something about the warmth, the water, and the holiday made it less awkward than I'd have guessed. I even managed to converse at length with three Scrudites, mostly by keeping my eyes on everyone's faces.

I suspected some of the revelers were reczavy, while others were K'basta hoping to have a memorable holiday. The rest must have been tourists with a local contact who'd told them about this alternative. The lack of clothes made it hard to tell who was what, and I supposed that was part of the charm.

We played in the water, napped, and enjoyed ourselves until late Heli afternoon. We planned to camp a second night, then make our way back up the steep canyon and ride to the nearest K'ba settlement to get breakfast before the long ride back to Bohdan's place.

The Canyon River is in a canyon of some size. If I could walk on nothingness the way I walk on the ground, it would take me two hundred paces to get from Ilari's side over to the adjoining realm. The drop from the top of the canyon down to the water is often steep and in many places the river has no bank but rushes along the canyon wall. It would take at least ten men standing on each other's shoulders to reach from the water's edge up to the top of the canyon. So, when one travels down to an area with a shore as we had done, one is essentially trapped.

The water moves fastest in the spring when the snow melts in the mountains, but even at Heli the current is strong. Boulders abound and the rocky river bottom is treacherous. Crossing the Canyon River is dangerous enough that only a show-off tries it, or the most foolhardy of thieves, or those desperate to flee one side or the other.

At least half of the holiday crowd gathered their things to leave as the afternoon turned into a summer evening. These people no doubt lived close by, either in Scrud or in the K'ba settlements. Bohdan waved goodbye to those he knew, wishing them a safe ride home before dark.

Those of us with further to travel, the tourists and the reczavy, prepared to spend the night.

Only faint light remained when I saw the figure standing up on the cliff looking down on us. The large man held his arms tight against his chest in an angry stance I knew well. Had he been anyone else, I'd have ignored him, knowing both the distance and the diminishing light would keep him from recognizing anyone where I stood.

But this man and I shared something. Our eyes could see incredible detail at a distance and in failing light.

I placed my hand on a scrubby bush to steady myself, and then I concentrated hard on his figure. The desert-like twilight around him blurred as Magomet grew larger and came into focus. First I saw his whole body, then, with incredible clarity, his face. He looked into my eyes with a raw fury I had never experienced.

For a single breath, I saw nothing but his two irises, burning into mine with hurt, longing, and most of all with rage. I had dared to set foot in K'ba, his land, with the man I loved.

I stared back, sure he saw my own eyes as well as I saw his. But what emotions did he see in their green depths? Surprise? Fear? Guilt? Or the defiance that grew within me?

I guessed he saw them all, and my fate depended on which emotion he judged to be the strongest.

Bohdan and I made a small fire before complete darkness. Out in the dry lands the temperature drops at night even in the summer, and the fire's light allowed us to stay up and talk. I wanted to discuss my early love life. Most of it had come up already, but given the dangers we faced, Bohdan needed to fully understand my history with Magomet.

No tidzy becomes jealous when speaking of their lover's past. We all have one. Some prefer to hear more details, others less, but I didn't expect anything but sympathy for the predicament I'd landed in. I got it, along with a measure of disgust for what Bohdan termed Magomet's "overly zealous" pursuit of me.

Our conversation turned to the Sage Coalition and its growing hold on K'ba while the rest of the realm remained dismissive of the movement. Bohdan feared for my place in the artistic community, and he feared that the Coalition could harm Ilari's ability to stage an effective defense.

"What a messy time to fall in love, huh?" I said.

He put his arm around me. "Do you suppose most couples think the troubles in their world are so unique, or so compelling, that they face challenges others didn't have? I mean, not to take away from the seriousness of this invasion …"

I understood what he meant, but …. "No, I think we've got more problems than usual."

I steered the conversation back to Magomet because tonight I had to tell Bohdan about the horrible meeting I'd had nearly an eighth ago. When I finished, I saw Bohdan's concern that he hadn't heard of this sooner.

"I know, I know. I just wanted to ignore it for a while. Let my thoughts settle. Please understand. I've hardly seen you for the last four anks … but I knew you had to hear this and I planned to tell you tonight. But now, well, you really need to know."

"He has no way of realizing I'm here."

"That's not true."

"Olivine, even if he rode out to this part of K'ba, he couldn't possibly tell I was down here."

"I saw him up on the ridge tonight after sunset. Standing up there, looking down"

"How could you know it was him?"

"I'm a long eye, remember. His posture and size caught my attention, so I looked closer."

"And what did you see?"

"Him. Furious. Looking closer at me."

Bohdan looked up on the ridge then back into my eyes.

"Wait. Is he a long eye too?"

"Yes. That's the problem! He's as good as I am and I'm certain he saw me and saw you too."

Bohdan shook his head and laughed.

"Then I'm glad you decided to update me. Should we worry he'll attack us while we sleep?"

"No. It would be too dangerous to climb down here in the dark. We need a little light to see."

Bohdan looked at the narrow riverbank on which we camped. Our lack of a place to run was as glaringly obvious to him as it had been to me.

"Were there others with him?" he asked.

"Not that I saw, but ..."

"... but who knows. We need to rise at dawn and get up this varmin cliff. Our best bet is to get over to the village in Scrud along the border. We'll be safe there; I know plenty who will lend us a hand."

I didn't like having to end our holiday in such a panic, but I saw the wisdom in his plan.

A few short hours later, we bundled ourselves against the chilly dawn and led our laden-down horses up the path in the growing light. We saw no sign of Magomet, or anyone else, as we rode across the unmarked border into Scrud. I thought the villager's immediate willingness to help us went beyond mere courtesy and wondered if Bohdan's status as a top carver made him someone important.

Here, the houses looked more like housing elsewhere, achieving a mix between the huts of Bohdan's village and the settlements in K'ba. I noticed other signs of civilization as well, including a tavern, two inns, and several shops. These Scrudites had adopted some of the ways of their neighbors.

But they hadn't lost the sense of community that seemed to define Bohdan's world. They fed us and our horses and gave us fresh water for our journey across the desolation. Several offered to accompany us, but Bohdan insisted we'd be fine.

Although I kept looking over my right shoulder as I rode, no one came towards us from K'ba as we crossed over the bleak terrain. The dusty wind would have made the ride miserable on a nice day, but at the hottest time of the year, it provided a precious bit of cooling against the summer sun.

When I saw Bohdan's little hut by the road in the distance, I let out a whoop of joy.

I planned to spend a few days alone in K'ba after the holiday, getting caught up with Zoya and other friends while avoiding Magomet and his family. I needed to check in with the shopkeeper to collect my payment, and he and I needed to discuss the remaining orders and how I'd fill them.

But now, I just wanted to go back to my parents' farm where no one could bother me. Specifically, I wanted to be in my own room, with the door closed and fluffy down pillows over my head to shut out the noise and turmoil. I knew fatigue and frustration inspired this, but, if I was completely honest, fear played a part too.

I couldn't afford to give in to the fear.

No doubt suspicion about me had grown as my sisters' exploits became better known throughout the realm. People find it easier to distrust, and even hate, those they have no contact with. By making myself scarce in K'ba for the last eighth, I'd allowed misgivings about me to strengthen.

I had to get over there and be seen. I needed to socialize in the taverns and paint out on the streets as the other artists did in the warmth of summer. I needed to smile and, yes, talk to the fine people of K'ba so they had a harder time vilifying me. I had to get over there and fight the damage Magomet wanted to cause.

And perhaps there was another role I needed to play, as well.

The rest of the realm's lack of concern about the Sage Coalition puzzled me. The leaders in K'ba were informed, intelligent and persuasive. They obviously thought they had a way of making Ilari pay the tribute. How did they intend to do this?

If the Velka knew more of what the Sage Coalition planned, then they might take this threat as seriously as they should. They might devise a better way of dealing with it. But the upper echelons of the Coalition would not show their hand anytime soon. Not to anyone they perceived as a threat.

So … could a quiet artist, one anxious to establish herself as loyal to the K'basta, be trusted enough to learn more? You'd think not, but the quiet artist I had in mind hadn't expressed her opinions in public. Good thing she seldom did.

Perhaps the Sage Coalition wanted to think it could win over the heart of a young woman whose family loyalties pointed her elsewhere. I needed to get over there and find out.

~ 16 ~

Involving Deception

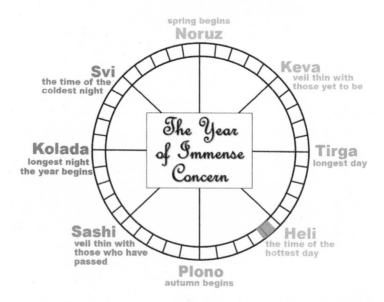

spring begins
Noruz

Svi
the time of the
coldest night

Keva
veil thin with
those yet to be

Kolada
longest night
the year begins

*The Year
of Immense
Concern*

Tirga
longest day

Sashi
veil thin with
those who have
passed

Heli
the time of the
hottest day

Piono
autumn begins

Although I wanted to find Zoya or Arek first, I forced my feet to take me to the shop that sold my work. Best to get one unpleasant thing out of the way.

"Look what the wind blew in," the shopkeeper said, greeting my unexpected arrival. "I'd almost decided to use the funds I owe you to send a messenger to Vinx to see if you were still alive."

"I meant to get back to you sooner. I've been spending more time on my parents' farm," I said. "They needed my help."

"Hmm. Sure it's not your sister that's needing you now?" His tone was skeptical but not hostile.

"Is that what everyone here thinks I've been doing?"

He put down whatever he held in his hands, letting me know I had his full attention.

"I've tried to tell people you're not involved in anything bad and that you can't be blamed for what members of your family do, but the pressure on me has been mounting. I'm sorry, Olivine, but I risk losing too many of my customers, and even some of my suppliers, if I continue to sell your work. It's not a decision I made lightly."

I looked at the wall where he'd hung my best painting after the disastrous Noruz exhibit. It no longer hung there.

"Your friend Magomet has been particularly outspoken about the need to ostracize you from our community. Did you two have a tiff of some sort?" His eyes turned sympathetic. "Some men can be such rantillions once they get rejected. And snubbed for a Scrudite? Ouch. Talk about a blow to a young man's pride."

"You more or less figured it out."

He gave a satisfied smile at hearing his assumptions confirmed.

"I thought as much. You should know that two other young artists I often saw with you have been circulating around echoing everything Magomet says. It hasn't helped your cause."

"Zoya? And Arek?"

"Oh no. I know both of them. This is another girl and a boy that often hung with you."

I'd hadn't given much thought to Delia and Pasha since they'd become a couple over the past year. Yet Delia's parents owned an art supply store and Pasha's parents ran an inn, so both families influenced the community. It sounded like Magomet had wisely enlisted their support.

"That's a shame." I met his guilty gaze. "It's alright; I understand. I can hardly expect you to lose business on my behalf."

"See," he said. "This is *just* what I told people. You may not say much, but when it comes down to it, you are as reasonable as anyone I know."

"Thanks." I had to laugh. "That's what our neighbors used to say about me. Not that I was reasonable, but that I didn't say much."

I didn't mention how I hoped that trait would now enable me to spy on his community.

"I've packed your remaining things up for you. Can you take them all today?"

Oh. So he hoped to remove every trace of me from the store.

"I don't think I can carry it all. I'll take what I can and come back another day."

Now that he knew I'd make no trouble for him, he seemed sad.

"Olivine. You're talented. Don't stop painting. When this is over, and it will be someday ... well, then I'd be honored to sell your work again. Just so you know."

"We part as friends," I said, using a ceremonial farewell from days long gone. I thought it worked well for this occasion.

Zoya and I sat in a corner of her parent's pub, near a boisterous table at which the patrons appeared to be spilling as much as they drank. Their noise covered our conversation while their drunken sloppiness drenched our noses in the smell of ale. Under other circumstances, I'd have moved away, but this afternoon we needed the shield they provided.

Zoya leaned in close to my ear to tell me that Arek had been as scarce in K'ba over the last eighth as me.

"I think he and Nikolo have snuck into town a few times just to, you know, be together, but people here are positive Nikolo is working with your sister, training her archers. So obviously Arek is more suspect than you. This has gotten scary."

She turned her head so I could speak into her ear. "Will being seen with me cause you problems?"

"Some." She saw me wince. "I can handle it."

"Could you handle more? My sister needs scouts. Long eyes will be particularly valuable. I've learned there won't be training ahead of time so you wouldn't have to travel back and forth. Are you interested?"

"Are you kidding? That would be perfect for me. But, um, I may need to stay at your parents' house once I get involved. Just to be safe. Do you think they'd mind?"

It was my turn to say "Are you kidding?" Zoya and her family had given me lodging for years. Plus, my parents had dutifully added a small room for each additional daughter, leaving them in a far too large a house.

"Of course you'd be welcome. Wait until Kolada gets close though. No need to bring on problems sooner than we have to."

She nodded.

The whole timing issue took me to the bigger thing I wanted to ask her. I leaned into her ear again so I could speak softly and still be heard.

"Look, I'm struggling to figure something out. What are the Sage Coalition's plans? I mean, the Royals and the Svadlu both want to resist and they control the country. My sister may annoy the people here, but stopping her won't make the Svadlu lay down their weapons or make the Royals pay the tribute. How do they plan to accomplish that?"

Zoya glanced up at the server approaching us.

"Another afternoon wine for both of us," she told the young woman, raising her voice to be heard over the raucous crowd. "Make sure you water it down more this time."

"Yes, Miss."

Zoya leaned closer to me. "I've been wondering the same thing. My parents have grown sympathetic to the Coalition, but they don't get involved in politics. No matter how often I ask questions, they can't tell me what they don't know. I thought about going to more meetings with them, trying to participate ..."

So. My friend Zoya had been thinking the same thing I had.

"Your friendship with me is well known," I said. "They'd suspect you as a spy."

She looked at me. "Well, if I went to gather information for you, spying *is* what I'd be doing, isn't it?"

True.

"Look. I've been thinking about this too," I said, "and I have a better idea. I think it'd be safer for you if we went together."

"Me and you? Are you crazy? That's worse. You're more suspicious than I am."

"I know. That's the point. We pretend we've had a spat about this. It wouldn't be surprising. You're adamant the Coalition is right and I'm not so sure, because of my family. You bring me along to convince me. They like winning people over, don't they? All I have to do is act like being convinced is a possibility."

"Maybe," she said. "I could tell them you came to learn, to make your own decision apart from your kin."

"Exactly. Would they keep me from entering?"

"I don't think so. Not if we say that."

"Doing this would make me safer here in K'ba, too," I told her. "People would at least back off and give me room to consider the Coalition's position."

"Probably, and it could help me as well. I'd be the good K'basta trying to win over my friend. If nothing else that could give me cover to get more involved after you leave."

We scooted apart and looked at each other.

"How soon can we do this?"

"There's a big meeting every few nights. The next one is the day after tomorrow."

We'd both gotten excited as we talked, the way people do when they make plans in a theoretical way. Picking a night to attend this meeting turned our ideas real.

"I'll have to outright lie. You know I'm actively training to help my sister."

"But you're not training to kill Mongols," she said.

"No, I'm not. I'm training to shoot at their horses, and we're just trying to incapacitate them."

"Okay then. Tell the Coalition you have no intention of killing anyone in this skirmish. That's the truth. You can say it with vehemence. Then ... I know you. You can avoid answering questions better than most."

"I'd still be misleading them."

She seemed amused.

"Spying does involve deception. You understand that, right?"

"Of course I do. It's just ... never mind. We need answers about the Coalition's plans, and I'm the only one in my family that can get them."

"I agree. So stay in K'ba, and everyone in the tavern will see us have spirited discussions over the next two days. Then, we'll go to this meeting. You do your best to seem sincere. I don't think we'll get many answers but it's worth a try."

She was right. We had little to lose and so much to gain and all I had to do was not say much. What could be easier for me?

"Let's do it."

I hadn't painted for anks, but being in K'ba brought back the urge. Zoya and I agreed I shouldn't visit Magomet's parents' studio. Painting on the street alone might be unwise as well as I needed to avoid discussions with anyone.

So, friend that she was, Zoya set me up in a room at her inn with her paints to use while I waited for this meeting. I placed my easel by the window to get as much breeze as I could and then immersed myself in the joy of doing what I loved.

Yet my mind wandered.

Who led this Coalition, anyway? Artists like Magomet's parents? Business people, like friends of the shopkeeper who'd once defended me? The vast majority of the K'basta lived here in the settlements along the Canyon River, so surely the movement was centered here.

The reczavy occupied the other edge of this nichna, with their camps straddling K'ba and the open forest. What did the reczavy think of the Coalition? How about the few K'basta who lived near them?

Almost no one lived in the desolate space between the two edges.

What did the Royals of K'basta think of the Coalition? Surely they sided with the other Royals in believing we had to defend the realm. Who *were* the Royals here? My mother had described them as elderly and out of touch. Wow. If they were elderly and out of touch to her ...

For all the time I'd spent in K'ba, I realized I'd learned little about its leaders. They didn't mingle in society, nor were they influential like Royals in other places. The K'basta seemed embarrassed to have royalty. Or maybe the Royals were embarrassed by their subjects. I'd never thought to ask.

I'd also never been told where their castle was. Castle, of course, was a figurative term for any home belonging to Royals. In Vinx the castle was the grandest residence in the nichna, but it was still a large stone lodge not far from the central market.

I knew a lot about Vinx's Royals, of course, and plenty about those in neighboring Gruen, and everyone knew all about the Royals in Pilk. The ones in Lev and Kir often were the subject of gossip, and even the Royals of Zur, Faroo, and Bisu got commented upon. But now that I thought about it, I knew nothing about the Royals in Eds. Or K'ba. Or Scrud. The dry lands all eschewed the trappings of royalty in ways the other nichnas did not.

Take Scrud for example. Where would they even put a castle? Only days earlier I'd seen all of the small settlement along the Canyon River adjoining K'ba. Nothing there looked as if it could possibly house Royals, even Royals who were Scrudites.

I'd traveled as a child with my father to the other Scrud settlement along the Canyon River, the one adjoining Bisu, as he had business there. No one had mentioned Royals in that settlement, either. If we'd passed a castle, surely he'd have pointed it out to me.

That left the huts of Bohdan's clan. Any castle there would have to be hidden in the forest or I'd have seen it. So that's where it had to be. But why no mention of it, ever? Forget finding out who ran K'ba. Who ran Scrud?

Something uncomfortable squirmed in my brain. It had to do with Bohdan's prolonged wait for a mate, and the complications causing it. Up until now, I'd considered his situation my extreme good fortune because it meant he wasn't married yet. But what if it was more complex?

The only other families I knew where lineage was so closely watched were all Royal.

No. Bohdan couldn't be part of the Scrud royalty. I laughed at the idea. No one who lived in a tiny hut by the side of the road was a Royal. Not even in Scrud.

~ 17 ~

A Border Dispute

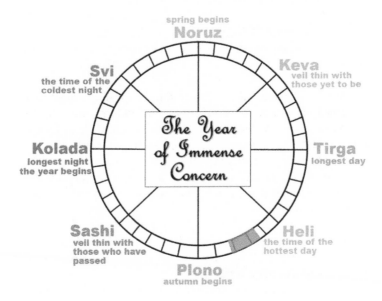

My time in K'ba flew by. I spent half of it in the tavern with Zoya staging our performances of my conversion to the Sage Coalition's point of view. I spent the other half bent over a tiny canvas in my room, enjoying the smell of paint as I created the image of a single rose much like one growing down the street. This miniature called out for a man to buy it for a woman he fancied. Such things brought only a small coin but they sold easily, even at the market in Vinx where I'd be selling it.

I finished it on the afternoon of the meeting, right before Zoya's parents made an excuse not to attend. I suspected they didn't wish to be seen with me. I knew it wasn't personal. By both profession and temperament they avoided controversy, and like it or not, my sister had made me controversial.

Zoya, however, seemed so invigorated by our upcoming deception that I feared her enthusiasm would give us away. When I suggested she try to appear more nonchalant, her response surprised me.

"Of course I'm excited. I've finally persuaded my dear friend to consider the error of her ways. Anything less than giddy would be suspicious, now wouldn't it?"

Oh. She gave this some thought.

"You don't mind if I look hesitant and uncomfortable instead, do you?"

"Of course not. Anything else would be suspicious, too."

"Good thing, because hesitant and uncomfortable is exactly how I feel."

We met at one of the larger indoor theaters where actors performed plays. The two entrances both had long lines of people waiting to get in. A doorman greeted those ahead of us by name and admitted them. When we came to the front, however, he extended his arm to block our path.

"I'm sorry, Zoya," he said. "But tonight is only for those already committed to the cause. We hold other sessions for people seeking information."

"I'm well past seeking," she responded with indignation. "And I've spent days now persuading my best friend to come to listen to the people whom I deem wise. I've *finally* won her over, and now you won't let us in?"

"It's true." A man further back in line spoke up. "I've heard the two of them arguing every day in her parents' tavern for the better part of this ank. Spirited discussions, but the greened-eyed lass seems to have been convinced."

So. All that play-acting hadn't gone unnoticed. I couldn't let Zoya's clever work go to waste.

"Please, sir." I put as much contrition into my eyes as I could. "Don't blame me for my family. I understand you've heard of them and have concerns but I won't cause trouble here. I only want to learn more about the things of which my friend spoke."

The man looked around for someone more important to ask, but no such person appeared.

"Very well." I could hear his sigh. "Please be quiet and don't draw attention to yourself."

"Of course."

If the man only knew how much I hated attention.

After a couple of short and impassioned introductions, one of the K'basta walked the evening's main speaker onto the stage. Much to my surprise, he wore the saffron cape of a Svadlu officer. His rank explained the single layer of loose-knitted cheesecloth draped over his face. The gasps from the audience told me his appearance here was a first.

"I come today to give you first-hand information about the interrogation of the frundle of whom you have all heard," he said in a low monotone voice.

Murmurs all around assured me the crowd had a great interest in this frundle. I winced. Ilarians seldom said the word frundle aloud because direct references to this disease involving a certain amount of emotional instability were considered rude.

My own younger sister was such a person, though Iolite had turned out to be one of the lucky ones. Her appearance was near normal, with only her silver hair and purple eyes confirming her status. She'd had mostly good health since birth and, more importantly, had never experienced the episodes which haunted the lives of most frundles. Iolite was as lovable as a younger sister could be and growing up with her had taught me more sympathy for this condition than most people had.

"This brave young woman," the Svadlu began "continues to supply us with information we'd have no way of knowing otherwise."

Oh. Their frundle was a female, too. I wondered how old she was. Probably not a child, as the episodes seldom began before puberty.

"Deep, deep into her trances, she listens to the Mongols as they talk. She *understands* them."

"Can she ask them questions?" a member of the crowd yelled. One of the doormen moved towards him to silence him, but the Svadlu answered the man anyway.

"No. We know so little about how these episodes work, but she insists she's tried to talk to them and they can neither see her nor hear her. Yet, fear not, she gains much information."

"Like what?" yelled out a woman off to my right. The Svadlu held out the palm of his hand to quiet her.

"She has heard them speak of Ilari! We're an enigma to them, such a small country, so isolated and so untested in the ways of war. They've scouted our land and seen our wealth of crops. The fine foods and drinks we produce from our bounty impressed them a great deal. They're eager to have us as part of their empire and hope we may be wise enough to acquiesce and join them."

Cheers and smatterings of applause erupted from around the room.

"Our frundle knows they do not harm those who submit to their terms. She says they have an uncommon amount of honor for conquerors, and we need never fear their demands will become unreasonable."

Cheering and applause followed this second pronouncement, but I noticed it was more subdued. The idea of demands increasing each year until they became unbearable struck a chord of fear even with those who wished to pay the tribute.

"Ah, but the most important of this young frundle's courageous revelations concern what the Mongols have done to those who chose to fight them instead. Horrible, horrible consequences."

"Like what?" yelled a young man in the back of the room. Someone always wanted to hear details about the worst. I shut out most of what the Svadlu officers said as he described charred children's bodies and babies mercifully sliced in half with a sword so they never had to feel the flames.

"Listen, you fine people of K'ba." The speaker's voice grew more forceful. "You and you alone know these details, for the Svadlu are keeping this young woman's revelations hidden from the population. Their pride compels them to fight. Their ignorance blinds them into thinking they can win. They cannot!"

"That's right!" "Isn't it the truth!" Yells of support came from all around me. The Svadlu officer waited until the room quieted before he went on, and when he spoke again his voice rang out with conviction.

"Over the next many anks, it will be our duty, as patriotic Ilarians, to get this message out to the farmers and herders and shopkeepers and wine makers who have the most to lose. We will, we must, change Ilari's mind. Our lives and lives of our children depend on how well we deliver our message!"

The power in his final words reinforced the crowd's convictions. Strange thing. They convinced me, too. Had I not known of Ryalgar's plans, I'd have joined the Sage Coalition that night.

But I did know of them. Ryalgar offered an alternative to either devastation or servitude. However, Ryalgar only offered a *chance* of surviving while the Coalition offered an almost sure escape from death. They had certainty going for them.

To choose Ryalgar's approach, one had to believe she had a good chance of succeeding. Did she? Up until now, I'd considered her ideas only in opposition to the Svadlu's inevitable defeat. Now, I weighed her plans against the Coalition's promise of life, even if it was a diminished life. Which did I prefer?

The decision was more difficult than I would have guessed.

The next morning I left for Vinx. Only one well-marked road ran through the desolation of K'ba, connecting the settlements along the Canyon River with the smaller area containing the reczavy tents. This main road veered left before the reczavy camp to protect the sensibilities of those who preferred not to get too close. Then it angled towards the Scrud village of carvers along the forest's edge. As I rode along this last part, I watched a tiny figure on the horizon grow larger with every few steps my horse took.

Before long I stared hard and Bohdan came into focus. He grinned at me. Then he made faces. Then he blew kisses. Then he stuck out his tongue. He had no way of seeing my reaction, but I supposed he entertained himself wondering if I and my talented eyes watched him. Yes, he knew I planned to visit him this morning, but didn't he have something better to do than wait in the middle of a dirt road for me? I knew he did.

For all his playfulness, his presence made me wary. Why was he standing in the center of nowhere under a hot summer sun?

A small clump of scraggly trees grew off to his left and he kept glancing toward them. As I neared the unmarked border between the two dry nichnas, I saw movement in those trees. I slowed my horse and focused my gaze. A man hid in the thicket, a large man mounted on a fine horse. Leaves hid his face from me, but it had to be Magomet. Bohdan must have discovered him there somehow, and now he stood in the road to warn me or perhaps to aid me. Nothing else made sense.

If I stayed on the road, I'd pass by Magomet before I reached Bohdan. I could ride through the scrabbly brush instead, but why should I bother? I rode towards Magomet with my head held high.

I looked at Bohdan. As I brought his face into focus, he mouthed the words "Magomet. Be careful" several times. I wished I had a way to reply but I'd be near enough to shout at him soon.

As I passed the trees, Magomet rode out of the small grove towards me.

"What are you doing out here?" I asked.

"I thought this would be a fine place to have a conversation with you."

He turned his horse so he rode alongside me.

"I suppose you think you're clever," he said.

"Why would I think that?"

"Because you went to the meeting of the Coalition last night."

"Yes, I did."

"You put on quite a show of how Zoya convinced you to rethink your loyalties, didn't you? Oh yes, I heard all sorts of people praising you this morning. Amazing how fast people will change their tune."

This wasn't good. Magomet knew me well. Had he figured out what Zoya and I were up to? Did he plan to finger me as a spy? That would give me one of the shortest careers in espionage possible and perhaps put Zoya in danger.

"Well it won't work," he said. "You may think you've removed my power over you, but I have plenty of other ways to hurt you if you embarrass me again."

Oh right. He'd promised to turn the community of artists against me if Bohdan set foot in K'ba. So he'd tried. Did he think I'd gone to the meeting only to keep him from having leverage over me?

I looked at his face. He did. This was all about him. My being driven by higher ideals, or even by a desire to stay alive, didn't fit into his calculation at all.

I hated to play along, but I dared not risk Zoya's safety for the satisfaction of taking him down a peg.

"It seemed worth a try," I said.

We approached Bohdan, and Magomet studied him with interest.

"This is your boyfriend?" He snorted a laugh. "I should have known. My mistake for not looking closer. Scrudites all look alike to me."

"You know Bohdan?"

"I don't know anyone in Scrud, but I do know that any woman from outside ought to go to great lengths to leave this particular one alone."

Bohdan continued to stand in the middle of the road with his hands on his hips, but now we'd moved close enough for him to hear us.

"Scrudite. I say you're five paces into K'ba. Back up five steps before I kick your arse," Magomet bellowed.

Magomet? I couldn't imagine him kicking anyone's arse, but he looked mad enough to try.

"You're quite mistaken. I'm a full six paces inside of Scrud, so I think I'll come forward five."

Bohdan looked like he enjoyed taking those five big steps forward. He'd never struck me as much of a fighter either, and he was smaller than Magomet, but I thought he'd come out ahead if the two of them came to blows.

Should I try to stop this pissing match before it got started? They might both feel better after a fight, but I didn't want anyone hurt and certainly not over me.

"Don't do this. Either of you."

Bohdan didn't take his eyes off of Magomet as he answered me.

"This issue of where I can and cannot go is between me and this overblown artist who had the poor sense to threaten me," Bohdan said. "Please step aside, Olivine, and let me find out if this rantallion can fight."

Magomet didn't take his eyes off of Bohdan as he dismounted.

"Given you people are too poor to have horses, I'll dismount mine. Because I'm a gentleman, not an animal raised in a hut."

Honestly, I thought I heard them both growl as they started to circle each other, fists raised.

In truth, I hoped Bohdan would kick Magomet's oversized arse. However, if either of them looked like they'd seriously injure the other I was ready to throw myself in the middle and beg them both to quit. I trusted Bohdan not to go that far, but I wasn't sure I felt the same generosity of spirit towards Magomet.

"Fine. I'm not watching this nonsense." I remained on my horse, turning to give them a full view of her backside.

I heard a blows landing and several loud grunts, more of them from Magomet. I turned around when the noises stopped. Magomet lay face down in the dirt as Bohdan straddled him, twisting one of his arms high behind his back.

"Don't break it. It's my painting arm. Don't break it," Magomet whimpered.

"Don't ever bother Olivine again," Bohdan answered.

"I'm not involved in this, remember." I gave Bohdan a withering look.

He ignored me. "Don't ever tell me where I can and can't go," he added.

"Believe me, I'm washing my hands of both of you," Magomet said. "Olivine deserves the mess she's made by falling for you."

Bohdan let go, stood up, and dusted himself off. Magomet did the same. Neither said a word as Magomet mounted his horse. I watched him ride away as though nothing had happened.

Men.

"Would you like a ride?" I asked Bohdan. I could tell he considered insisting he would walk, but thought the better of it. He hopped up behind me.

"What was Magomet talking about when he said I deserved the mess I made by falling for you?"

"You know. A girl from a good family like yours falling for a Scrudite."

I didn't believe Bohdan's answer, but I'd seen the damage to his face as he mounted my horse. It looked worse than I expected. Now wasn't the time for a conversation.

~ 18 ~

Helpful or Not

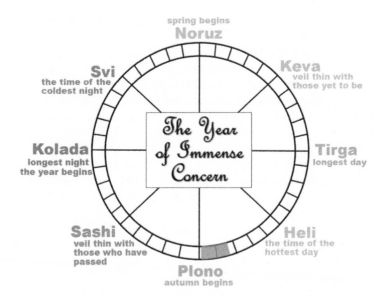

When I finally returned to the farm in late Heli, I'd been gone almost an entire eighth. A lot of family drama transpired in my absence.

Throughout Keva and Tirga I'd watched my parents worry about Iolite as they waited for her to let them know she'd finished school. When no word came, and letters from them began to go unanswered, they'd sent a messenger to speak with her. While I was gone they received word the messenger couldn't find her.

Then they'd done what most parents would do. They hired a carriage and went to her school. At the end of their day-long journey, they learned Iolite had finished her studies earlier than most and been gone for two eighths, despite letters she sent to them claiming otherwise. My parents were understandably frantic.

Then Coral brought word from her military husband that Iolite worked with the army. Days later Iolite confirmed this with a letter insisting she was well. Apparently, her letter worked. My parents calmed down. However, I reached new levels of agitation when I learned of this news.

The Svadlu man at the Sage Coalition meeting told everyone the army had a young female frundle working with them. My missing sister *was* a young female frundle working with them.

Yet, after Zoya and I wormed our way into this meeting, nothing gave me the impression that this young frundle was "perfectly safe."

"Taking great risks on our behalf and being exceptionally brave," were the words I remembered. Not a comforting message if the person being described was your little sister.

My parents needed to know what I knew. Yet, it would upset them and they had no way to help. Did this Svadlu officer who hid his identity tell the truth? He had, after all, been speaking at a political rally.

I decided to tell them the entire story, so they could judge the source of the information for themselves. That turned out to be a huge mistake. I never got to the part about Iolite because they became so upset when they learned I'd been at the rally.

"It was just a meeting," I said in response to their reaction. "Zoya and I snuck in as a lark. No big deal. We thought we could learn more about what this Sage Coalition was planning."

"That would be considered spying by many," my dad said with a sharp stare. "Dangerous game for two young women to play for fun."

"What in the world possessed you girls to behave so irresponsibly," my mother added.

"I'm trying to tell you. We heard a member of the Svadlu speak. He said …"

"What was a Svadlu doing at a Sage Coalition meeting?" Now my dad was more upset. "Did you recognize him? If you did, surely you realize that could put you in more danger."

"He was disguised. He covered his face." This conversation was going nothing like I intended.

"Did he recognize you?" my mother demanded to know.

"No. I'm sure he didn't. And he said nothing important. Don't worry about it. I'm so sorry I brought this up."

Life on the farm grew easier for my father at the end of the summer. The wheat was in storage and the fall oats weren't ready to harvest, so he repaired things and got the farm ready for the cold. This year he behaved as though the coming winter would be like any other. What else could he do?

The day after my botched attempt to tell my parents about Iolite, I tried to have a serious conversation with my dad. He was well-traveled. Why not ask him about the other subject that bothered me?

"Dad? Do you know where the castle is in Scrud?"

He looked up at me, surprised, as he reinforced the bin for holding the hay that fed the horses once the grass was scarce.

"You're developing an interest in geography?"

"No. I've ridden through there so often going to K'ba and I realized the other day that you never hear about the Royals in Scrud, K'ba, or Eds. Are they all recluses?"

He smiled, always pleased to hear any of his daughters curious about anything.

"Each nichna is different, you know. With its own lineage, its own customs. The less isolated places have come to influence each other over the centuries but the places you ask about ... not so much. Understand, the K'basta royalty precedes all these new developments in K'ba by hundreds of years. Their Royals have no tie to art or entertainment and much more in common with the Royals of Eds."

"That's surprising," I said. "Given how much the Edsers hate us, I mean hate the K'basta. But if you think about history, I guess it makes sense. And it explains why the Royals have such little presence there now."

He shrugged. "You'd know more about that part than me."

"So what about Scrud?"

He seemed amused I'd returned to the subject of Scrudites.

"They've always been a different kind of people. Don't know where their customs came from because they're not much like anything else around here. Nice enough, really, but I think other Ilarians don't understand them. Word is long ago they had to be talked into setting up a monarchy, so they could be a proper nichna and represented in the council of the ruling princes."

"They didn't *want* to have a ruling prince?"

"No clear records exist. Some historians say they wanted to be residents of an open prairie, much like the Velka occupy the open forest. Others say they already had a matriarchy and wanted a ruling princess."

"Really?" I'm sure my eyes lit up at this idea. "Why not let them?"

"Oh, come on, dear. That would have caused no end of problems."

"Why?"

Dad winced. "You know I advocate for opportunities for women; no man does so more than me. But, Olivine, if you have women rulers in one nichna, then the women of all the others will want the same. No man will have peace until the women get it. And then what a mess we'd have."

"Why would it be a mess?"

"Succession and heirs would all become chaos. The system would come crashing down. Now, it's clear and sensible and it works for everybody. For the women too. Anyway, historians think the other nichnas insisted Scrud comply with our rules and eventually they did, but not with much enthusiasm. I believe to this day being a Royal in Scrud is little more than a formality. As far as I know, they have no castle except for whatever hut the leader happens to live in."

"You'd think that might have changed over the centuries," I said.

"You would, but they are a stubborn lot. Look at the way they've clung to all their other ways."

"Their poverty is part of the reason for that," I said, feeling defensive for these people I'd come to like.

"Part of it, but they could do more to raise their standard of living and they don't bother." He shrugged. "They're entitled to their ways, I suppose."

He went back to his hammering, then he stopped, "I did meet their ruling prince once, you know. A few years back. Nice enough fellow, a surprisingly older man. One of the wood carvers. Word was he had lots of daughters but only one son and late in life at that. Their particular canons say his son begins his rule once he's suitably married."

"Did you meet the boy?"

"Heli no. Only heard he was slow to wed. I'm sure the issues are resolved and he's happily married by now. Why such curiosity?"

Dad asked me the question, but I think he suspected.

"I ride through there often. Just wondered."

"Olivine, unlike your mom, I have no particular ambitions about who you marry. I mean, I want him to be able to care for you and be kind to you, but as long as you're happy, I'm happy. You know that, right?"

"I do."

"But I also know that people who come from opposite backgrounds seldom find happiness together. It's like, I don't know, when the foundation of a house gets built one way on one side and a contrary way on the other. The whole structure isn't stable. Either way is fine by itself but the two can't combine. Do you follow me?"

"Sort of."

I left it at that. I had enough to think about. The frundle being brave for the Svadlu was *probably* Iolite. And the unmarried son of the wood carving ruling prince was *probably* Bohdan. Yet I needed to be sure before I did anything drastic about either situation.

However, if I was right about Bohdan, this prince thing sure sounded like something he should have mentioned to me by now.

The next day Joli and I planned to practice together. I hated not to show up, so I fought my urge to ride over to Scrud and demand immediate answers. Perhaps some physical exertion would help me calm down. Meanwhile, I fretted over whether to try to tell my parents about Iolite again. They ought to know, but I didn't need them inserting themselves into my and Zoya's scheme.

Joli and I practiced together at least once an ank, with me meeting her at the forest's edge of wherever I was. She brought supplies: a bow for me if I didn't have mine and always a quiver full of what she called "the magic arrows." Then we'd find somewhere safe and out of sight to work.

Often I'd bring fresh arrows given to me by Bohdan for her to take back into the forest. I knew they went to the Velka women called green witches, the ones who'd dedicated their lives to understanding plants. They now worked to perfect the poison tips. Their latest issue had been designing tips to go deep enough into the horses' flesh to release the poison and yet not so deep as to cause internal damage or to leave the animal prone to infection later.

"Have the Velka figured out yet where these special arrows come from?" I asked her as we got ready.

"Those working with the poisons knew right away. The Velka have an impressive understanding of all the old ways, and I couldn't keep them from sensing ..."

"I expected as much. But did they ask *how* the Scrudites got involved?"

"Nope." Then, when I said nothing in reply, she added, "You underestimate how much these ladies value discretion. One remarked about how these arrows possessed unusually strong qualities even for the carvers." She shrugged. "No one asked for details."

"My mother has backed off on the idea of locking me up," I said.

"That's good. She's now okay with you marrying whomever?"

"Hardly. She heard about an old boyfriend of mine, an artist in K'ba with rich parents, and decided I'd been sneaking over to see him. Apparently, he would have met her minimum requirements. I gave her the bad news that we'd parted ways."

"Scrudite man never came up?"

"I didn't see a need to mention him."

Joli looked uncomfortable. "You know you're going to have to tell her someday."

I shrugged. "I used to think so but now, maybe not. Scrudite man and I could have an unsolvable problem as well."

She looked at me closer. "Unsolvable problem? I'd have expected you to be way more upset about that."

"Oh, I'm upset alright, but I have to get the facts from him. I don't want to lose it completely and *then* find out I'm wrong."

"So. What are you doing practicing here with me?"

"Calming down. This is too important for me pruck it up. I'll ride over there in the morning."

"Hey." She walked up to me and hugged me. I suspected a Zurian didn't do that often. "I hope this love thing works out way better for you than it did for me. Okay?"

That night I sat both my parents down and got them to promise they wouldn't say a word until I finished speaking. It was an agreement I'd probably get once in my life, so I didn't want to waste it. I told them of hearing the Svadlu speak of Iolite's contributions at the Coalition rally.

"Both the Svadlu and the Coalition are trying to use Iolite's information for their ends, but Ilari is the stronger for knowing what she knows."

"But, but a frundle's episodes can be extremely draining for them," my father said. "Is she in danger?"

I held a finger up to my lips, but answered him honestly. "I don't know. I certainly couldn't tell from what this unreliable man said. But, she is where she says she is, and she's helping Ilari. I couldn't leave here without telling you that much."

"You're leaving? You just got home!" My mother looked to my dad for support. "She's only been here a few days."

"I know." I held a finger up to my lips again. "I don't want to go, but have something I need to go straighten out with a young man. I'll be back soon and when I am, I'll tell you everything that matters. Okay?"

My dad nodded. I think he was way ahead of Mom regarding the issue I had to address, but he couldn't have known exactly what I planned to do, because I didn't know either.

I left first thing in the morning, with only a few essentials thrown into my saddlebags. I didn't intend to stay anywhere long and I wanted to gallop as much as I could.

Low dark clouds moved in from the south as I rode, and the grey turmoil writhing within them spurred me to go faster. I didn't need a dousing of water before I arrived. When a cold wind followed the clouds, I started to shiver and wished I brought a cloak.

The coming storm had an effect, though. It cooled my temper.

Yes, lovers *should* tell each other everything. I believed that. But if they didn't, should the entire love be thrown away? If someone else asked me for advice, I'd recommend forbearance, at least long enough to find out if the reason for the omission was sound, or even just sincere.

Would I follow my own sage advice? Probably not. People seldom did.

~ 19 ~

I'm the One

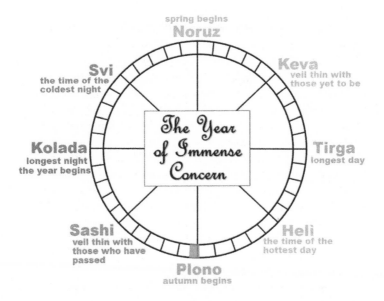

Bohdan saw me coming and met me as I dismounted. He offered a bucket of water to my thirsty animal as heavy pellets of water began to fall. He turned towards me, took one look at my face, and he knew I knew.

"Come inside and get out of the rain."

It fell harder as the wind picked up and he pulled me toward his hut.

"Please. Sit." He offered me a mug of water from his jug. "Will you let me give you some information before you yell at me?"

I put the blanket he offered around my shoulders. "Fine. Talk."

"Let's agree that when we first met neither of us thought we'd come to care for each other like we do now. So we didn't greet each other with much information."

"Of course not. Now, let's agree we've had plenty of wonderful opportunities to talk since then."

"We have."

"And ..." A clap of thunder forced me to pause.

"And I had good reasons for not telling you," he said. "A few of them."

"Explain away."

I sipped water as the rain pounded on the roof. The thunder continued to rumble as he spoke of how royalty worked in the reluctant principality of Scrud. My father had largely been right. The Scrudites hadn't wanted to be a nichna, or at the least had wanted to use their own matrilineal rules. Somewhere in the ancient days of Ilari, they were told no, so they developed a system to pass an almost perfunctory leadership from father to son. No one liked it all that well.

"It worked okay, though, until I came along. When fate left me with no immediate options for a mate in my own clan, and it became clear I was so drawn to being a carver that I wouldn't move away, my family worried the system had finally failed."

"Failed how?"

"They thought I'd grow tired of being single and fall in love with an outsider."

"So what if you did?" Then I got it.

"Wait. I've never heard of anyone marrying a prince from Scrud. Ever. I bet they don't let you marry an outsider. Is that true?"

"No. If it were that simple I'd have told you long ago. Look. We don't have a royal family or a palace. At most, we have two Royals. One is the ruling prince – my dad at the moment – and the other is the crown prince – me, for now. Marriage makes me the ruling prince and I can marry whomever I please, but my wife has obligations."

"Obligations?"

"Yeah. An outsider has to leave her mother to become one of us. Live here full time. Raise her children as Scrudites. This has only worked out a few times in our history; others don't adapt to living here well. At first, I thought it might be possible with you. You seemed so different. Special. I waited to see if my hope was realistic. I wanted it to be."

"Is it?"

He laughed. "Heli, no. You'd be miserable. You need a studio, paints, and people to appreciate the art you create. It took me too long to realize I'd destroy you by asking such a thing of you."

Part of me wanted to tell him he was wrong, that I could and would give up anything for him. But I knew better. He knew better.

"Okay, you've explained why you kept silent for, maybe, half a year, until you figured me out. Then what?"

He gave a helpless shrug and leaned closer to me as if he were about to share a secret. The rain fell more lightly now, but he spoke so softly that I struggled to hear him over its patter on the roof.

"Then, I had to figure me out, too. I'm no prisoner here, I can leave Scrud and live in K'ba with you. I don't have to be the crown prince. Instead, I can be the man married to a famous artist."

"That's the hope I had."

"I know. And I wanted to think it could work. I sought a way to contribute by making frames for your paintings. But it didn't take me long to realize I can't give up being a carver any more than you can give up what you are. I had to accept that the best you and I could have would be a life lived half apart."

"But we figured that out, each in our own way."

"We did. So it surprised me when I balked at the idea of staying part-time in Scrud and *not* being the prince. I know it sounds childish, but please understand. Even as a little boy I knew I'd be the one to live in the hut nearest to the road, serving as a guard and an ambassador for my people like my father did."

"I wondered why you lived out here."

"It's what our crown princes do. And I'd probably be allowed to keep my hut, but could I handle giving up the task I'd been raised to perform?"

Bohdan's confession prompt a new question.

"What happens to Scrud if you don't take the crown? You have no brothers."

"The crown moves. A cousin of mine in the settlement adjoining Bisu is already married to a lovely Scrudite woman. If I choose a life with you outside of Scrud, he becomes our leader."

"Will he be a good one?"

"Eventually."

So many things started to make more sense.

"The carvers are going to hate me, aren't they? I mean, because of me they'll no longer be the clan of the ruling prince. You say Scrudites don't put much value on these things, but everyone puts some."

He nodded his agreement. "We are people, after all. I understand how pursuing my happiness will make them sad."

"They must know it's coming. Don't they ask you about your plans?"

"All the time. I keep telling people I don't know what I'm going to do. That's the real problem, Olivine. Right now the carvers need to believe in me and they need to focus on preparing for this invasion. Any decision of mine only causes trouble we don't need."

"As long as you remain undecided, everyone works hard at making arrows?"

"Yes. And my dad remains our leader. He's good at it and he needs to be the ruling prince through this. So you can see why I tried to put off talking to you until after Kolada. You can be as mad at me as you want, and I don't blame you, but I swear I've been trying to do what was right."

The rain had stopped and I peeked outside. I had to admit Bohdan's approach made some sense, now that I knew the full situation. A bit of blue could be seen off to the south. My anger had left with the storm.

"I could have kept this secret, you know."

He looked at the ground. "I almost told you, a few times, but …

"… but there were too many ways it could have gone wrong."

I finished his sentence for him because I understood him as well as he understood me.

I had mixed feelings that night as I lay with a man who was, at least technically, as much of a prince as Ryalgar's Nevik or as Coral's Davor. I suppose I felt a certain amount of, I don't know, vindication in finding out I could attract a prince, too.

The satisfaction with the situation ended there, though. I didn't want to marry the ruler of any nichna or be constrained by the rules of any royal family. I wanted to live the life I wanted and do the things I was meant to do. Strange as it seemed, this prince wanted those things for me, and he would go to great lengths to see I had them.

This prince loved me.

And on the day he declared his love for me and his intent to leave, he'd be a prince no more.

The next morning I couldn't keep from scrutinizing everyone I saw, wondering how they felt about me. As we sat outside Bohdan's hut on the damp wooden bench, enjoying our lunch, I told him I wanted to go celebrate Plono elsewhere. He agreed but pointed out we didn't have a lot of options.

"What would you think of a visit to the reczavy?" I asked

"I don't think they appreciate people dropping by, especially on holidays. I've heard that's a sore point with them. Tidzys, or worse yet married folks, who want to come to play for a day."

"I can understand that. But my sister ..."

"Right. Your sister was there. Is she still with them?"

"I think she'll be with them for life. She invited me to come back. The timing might be bad but ..."

"It's not that long a ride. I can borrow a horse. Let's go find out."

My showing up suddenly surprised Gypsum but as soon as she understood my predicament of nowhere else to go, she set Bohdan and me up in a guest tent at the edge of the camp and left us be.

We made good use of the privacy, and in more ways than we expected. A foot massage and a chance to share one's worries can be intimate too.

"What if your arrows go *too* fast?" I asked as he braided the hair on the back of my head the next morning. His sisters had taught him the skill well.

"I thought the Velka designed the tips to barely penetrate the horses' hides no matter what," he said.

"They did. But now they're creating even less poisonous tips to shoot at the Mongols we want to capture. Human skin isn't so thick. I'm worried the arrows will kill the people even if the poison doesn't."

"Wait. I thought the herders were going use ropes to capture the Mongols whose horses got shot."

"They're going to try, but this is a backup for the difficult ones. Wait. How did you know about the herders' role?"

"These plans aren't secret. Most of my Scrudite friends who live near Bisu practice with the Bisuite herders. Scrudites want to help capture Mongols, too. A couple of anks ago they talked me into joining them. I'm part of their plan now." I heard the pride in his voice.

"Wait. You're going to be out on the battlefield?"

People could get killed out there.

"Of course I am. Every able-bodied Ilarian will be. You're a little out of touch with how these plans have grown, aren't you."

Maybe I was. I thought I'd be shooting at horses in the dawn all alone. Well, with Joli but she didn't count. I hadn't expected an audience of half of Bisu. Or my lover risking his life after I finished my task.

"At the last practice I got assigned to a special group," he said. "We're the ones with fighting experience." He ignored my harrumph, knowing I remained annoyed about his brawl with Magomet. "We'll handle the particularly dangerous Mongols, so you won't have to shoot at them."

When I didn't say anything, he added "You know, we carvers can work with you. Make arrows specifically for people. Thinner, more fragile. Different looking *and* knowing their job. Would that help?"

"I suppose." I'd stopped worrying about the arrows. My concern was for him. Why did he have to do this? He did enough by making the arrows.

He finished my hair in silence, deftly tying a ribbon around the end. He began to knead my shoulders and upper back with his hands.

"We will all risk our lives on that day," he whispered into my ear. "Our sisters, our parents, our friends. Only the little children, the sick, and the very old who flee to the forest will be safe. And maybe not even them."

"You're right."

I'd just assumed the Scrudites wouldn't be involved that day, because they lived in a world all their own. But no capable man like him could or should hide as we fought for our lives.

"I'm proud of you," I said. I meant it. "Scared, but proud."

He walked around to face me. "I know exactly how you feel."

He and I parted a day later, as much in love as we'd ever been. I sighed as I watched him ride back towards his home, then I sought out Gypsum.

"You've been incredibly hospitable. Can I repay you somehow?"

"Bring wine and treats to share next time," she suggested. She gestured towards Bohdan's silhouette in the distance. "You've got yourself a problem, don't you?"

"I suppose." I looked around the camp she called home. "But so do you."

"Yep. Figure you'll deal with Mom and Dad after Kolada?" she asked.

"Yep. You?"

"Of course."

"It's only two eighths away."

"I know. I've got a lot a life to live in a quarter of a year."

"We all do."

She and I parted with a hug born of both love and fear.

I took a route to Zoya's parents' tavern that avoided the shop which used to sell my paintings, skirted around Delia's parents' art supply store, and missed the center of town where so many artists sat outdoors and painted in the early autumn sun. Lucky for me, Pasha's parents' inn sat on the other side of town, so I didn't have to avoid it too.

Zoya wiped off tables when I came in. She waved to me and gestured to an empty seat. Another server put a mug of ale in front of me before I could speak up.

An older man squinted at me. "You're the one, aren't you?"

"The one what?"

"Leave her alone," the older woman next to him said. "No one wants to talk politics in a tavern. She just wants a drink."

"Fish scump," he replied. "Everyone talks politics in a tavern. Don't they?" he asked me.

I gave him a vague smile, hoping to discourage him.

"You're the sister. Part of that family causing all the trouble."

There wasn't a good response so I made none.

"It's alright," he assured me. "We've heard how you've broken with your family. Have you told them how you feel? If you haven't, no one would blame you for that, you know."

I looked around for an empty chair further away. I didn't want to have this conversation, and certainly not until I talked to Zoya and found out what had happened in my absence. Maybe I could ask his wife where she got her shawl.

I felt a light touch on my shoulder and turned to see Zoya eying my talkative neighbor with concern.

"I could use your help in the kitchen with something," she said. "If you don't mind just bringing your ale ..."

"Of course." I followed her through the kitchen and into the alleyway behind.

"I've so much to tell you," she said. "Don't talk to anybody here. Please."

"Of course I won't. I was trying to get away from him ... It sounds like what we did worked, though."

"Yeah. Maybe too well," she said, looking up and down the alley to see if we could be overheard. "Come. Let's walk."

I nodded. We'd notice anyone following us, trying to stay within earshot.

"The Coalition *loves* the narrative of a lost sister breaking away from her kin because she sees the light of reason. You were right. We played into exactly what they wanted to hear."

"Great. So what's their plan?"

"Well, it *was* to scare the citizens of Ilari into paying the tribute."

"I'm sorry. That isn't really a plan."

"It's all they thought they needed. They believed that our only alternative was to stand by and watch our woefully inept Svadlu lose badly. And then die. Easy choice, right? They've gathered witnesses from other lands to speak, and Svadlu like the one we heard, and after Plono they intended to take to the road and make their case to the Royals and citizens of each nichna. They believed that the people's overwhelming fear would nudge the reluctant Royals. They also believed that if most of the Royals banded together they could prohibit the Svadlu from fighting."

"I wonder if they could?"

"It would have been interesting to see who really runs Ilari, wouldn't it? I mean in a weirdly intellectual way."

I realized where Zoya was headed.

"This explains why they hate Ryalgar so much!" I said. "I kept thinking she shouldn't matter to them, but she does because she messed up their plan by offering another alternative."

"Exactly. She matters because her choice is one the people like. They're out there shoveling dirt and practicing archery and screeching at horses, all the while thinking they can save themselves. Who doesn't want that?"

"So stopping Ryalgar is the one thing they care most about," I said.

"Yeah. Otherwise, they *have* no plan for getting us to pay the tribute. And guess who walked in and offered them their best chance of stopping Ryalgar?"

"Her sister."

"Yeah. And her sister's friend. They want the friend to convince the sister that all of Ilari's fate depends on her spying on the Velka and finding a way to bring Ryalgar down."

~ 20 ~

Both Scared

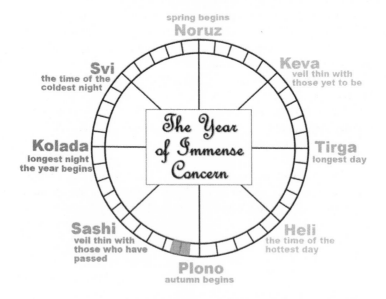

spring begins
Noruz

Svi
the time of the
coldest night

Keva
veil thin with
those yet to be

Kolada
longest night
the year begins

The Year
of Immense
Concern

Tirga
longest day

Sashi
veil thin with
those who have
passed

Heli
the time of the
hottest day

Plono
autumn begins

All the time I spent shooting arrows couldn't change one essential fact. I wasn't a fighter. I was a problem ignorer. A go-along-er. I wanted my issues to disappear so I could do something that mattered. Like painting.

Yet now I had a problem I couldn't pretend away. I supposed I could tell them I hadn't been persuaded well enough to actively work against my family. They might understand and merely ask me to leave K'ba and never come back. But what good would that do? It would leave me on the outside, unable to see my friends or help my sister with her Coalition troubles.

I could alert Ryalgar to the problem, although I felt certain she and the Velka already knew of the situation in K'ba. I mean, didn't the Velka have women in every nichna, spies who doubled as old people selling potions in the marketplace? I doubted I knew anything they didn't.

And what of Zoya? I couldn't abandon her, leaving her to lie to her parents after I left town in disgrace.

And yet if I stayed …

Sometimes when I'm painting I know my work needs fixing, but I can't figure out what to do next. I've learned that if I pick up the brush, don't think, and just do what I do, I often paint what I need. It's eerie, like there's some other part of me that knows more than I do. Yet, it works.

So that's what I did. I told Zoya I needed to go for a walk alone and think things through, and she understood. Then I set off on foot with no plan, rather hoping I'd do something other than walk in a big circle.

I did.

I walked to Magomet's place.

When I realized where I was I stopped, horrified. The last time I saw Magomet, he'd slunk off after losing a fist fight with Bohdan. He'd only sustained temporary injuries but I knew his pride had gotten a permanent blow. Talking to him could be dangerous.

Maybe he wasn't home.

Well, his peace-loving parents wouldn't welcome me either after hearing about my violent boyfriend attacking their son, would they? And I knew Magomet well enough to be sure he'd told the story that way.

"Olivine?"

I heard my name above me and looked up to see Jasia leaning out of the second-story studio window.

"What are you doing here, child?"

"I'm not sure, to be honest."

My answer didn't seem to baffle her.

"Come inside."

She motioned me in, sat me down at her kitchen table, and poured me afternoon wine.

"I'm sorry Magomet got hurt," I said.

"Pfft." She waved her hand dismissively. "He was fine. I love my son, but I suspect he brought those injuries on himself. What did he do – challenge your boyfriend to a fight?"

"More or less. I was angry with Bohdan, too, for participating."

She shook her head. "Men. Entirely too predictable sometimes, aren't they?"

I had to laugh. "Do you think they consider us the same?"

She grinned. "I think more often we puzzle them. We're not naturally so straightforward, or at least a good many of us aren't."

I looked at her. I felt like she was trying to tell me something, but I couldn't figure out what.

"You and I, we're both inclined to less direct solutions, aren't we?" she said. "And because of that, we've gotten ourselves into an unfortunate situation."

"We have?"

"Olivine, everyone else in town may be convinced that you've accepted the Coalition's perspective, but I don't believe it, not for a heartbeat."

Speaking of heartbeats, mine stopped. Magomet's *mother* was going to bring my short career as a spy to a close?

"I've known you since you started your advanced studies, dear. You don't say much about it, but you love your family. Your conversion to a cause opposed to your sisters is so unlike you. Yet I've kept quiet about my doubts, hoping I'd get the chance to ask you in person. What are you trying to do?"

I squirmed and stared into my wine. She deserved an answer. I couldn't think of a better option than the truth.

"I *am* trying to learn more about the Sage Coalition. I want Ilari to survive, and I want it to happen as peacefully as possible. So I thought I could go to a meeting and find out what's going on here and use that information to keep Ryalgar and others from getting hurt. I don't want you people to hurt my sisters."

My voice rose on those last words, and Jasia leaned away from me in surprise.

"No one intends to hurt your family, dear. What makes you think that?"

"The way people talk about Ryalgar. Her only crime is to care deeply about our fate and …."

Jasia held up her hand to stop me.

"So you're scared of us. Just as we're scared of you."

"Yes. I suppose. But we're both scared that our army's best efforts will fail, so at least we have something in common."

"True. And that's quite a lot. Not to mention a mutual desire to avoid a slaughter. Perhaps we *do* need to learn more about each other."

"Exactly. That's all I was trying to do!"

"No. You were trying to learn about us. I think we need to learn more about each other."

I got the distinction.

"What I don't understand," she continued, "is your willingness to risk all of our lives on the hope that your sister's plan will work. It's not a given. You do understand, don't you, that the cost of fighting back *at all* is a death sentence for everyone in Ilari? The anger you hear towards your sister is our resentment at her making that decision for all of us. It's something she has no right to do."

Now it was Jasia's voice that grew louder as she spoke, and I recognized the mutual fear she'd mentioned.

"You misunderstand. No matter how poorly Ryalgar's plan goes, she believes the Mongols will *not* retaliate because of it."

"That makes no sense. They always retaliate for resistance."

"Maybe not if you don't kill any of them."

"I'm sorry, but you can't possibly stage a battle without killing anyone. What is she thinking?"

"You don't know much about her plan, do you? That is exactly what she's trying to do."

And at that instant, the problem made sense to me.

Those involved in Ryalgar's plans had no idea those in K'ba thought the Chimera condemned them to certain death.

Those involved in Sage Coalition had no idea of the pains Ryalgar took to be able to negotiate with the Mongols, no matter what the outcome.

The Coalition and the Chimera needed to talk.

As the afternoon wore on, I did a spectacular job of failing at espionage. Rather than learning new facts about my adversary, which *is* the basic idea of intelligence gathering, I spilled every detail of what my side was doing. At least every detail that I knew.

Yet, I felt good about it.

Jasia listened. She worried Ryalgar's plans could still go awry and result in disaster despite the good intentions. However, she agreed the Chimera was not the death sentence she and others had assumed.

She asked if I would come to speak to the leaders of the Sage Coalition, telling them what I'd told her. They needed to know Zoya and I would be of no help in bringing Ryalgar down, but perhaps we could shepherd in the better alternative of finding common ground.

It was a reasonable request, but it had been one thing to explain all this to Jasia in the comfort of her kitchen. It was quite another to stand in front of a room filled with hostile people and give this information. Yet, if I didn't, the Coalition would proceed with its road show attempting to scare the people of Ilari into inaction. I thought many of the farmers and herders would ignore them, but some wouldn't. Some would abandon their efforts and some would make outright trouble for Ryalgar.

I needed to prevent that if I could.

"I know this is urgent," I said. "But I need a couple of days. Let me ride home, learn the latest about what is happening and try to get word to Ryalgar of what I am doing."

"I suppose I can stall for a day or two," she said.

"Good. Tomorrow I'll ride home. The next day I'm supposed to practice archery with one of the Chimera's leaders and I'll speak to her about this. She talks to Ryalgar all the time. Then the next day I'll ride back."

She winced. "That's three days. Can you speak to the group the night you arrive?"

"I'll be tired, but I suppose."

"Good. I'll set it up for three nights hence."

By the time I left the studio, the sun neared the horizon. Exhaustion overtook me as I walked back to Zoya's inn.

The next morning I stopped to see Bohdan on the way home. Of course.

As we sat on the bench in front of his hut enjoying a cool autumn breeze, I told him of the crazy turn of events in K'ba. He listened, but I felt like I only had part of his attention.

Finally I asked. "So what's on your mind?"

He shrugged. "You know. The usual."

"Usual what?"

"Usual pressures on a prince." He laughed. "I had a few too many ales with my friends and something slipped. I didn't tell anyone anything but they somehow figured out that you'd learned about my situation."

"Oh no. You wanted them to think I didn't know, didn't you?"

"I did. They let me know that I should have told you sooner and they complained that I hadn't asked you to serve as my consort. I've spent the past few days arguing with my friends, telling them that while you are wonderful, you can't be what they want."

"I'm sorry, Bohdan. This is just the sort of nonsense you wanted to avoid." I put my arms around him.

"They know I'm stalling until Kolada passes. I guess it's close enough now that I can get away with it."

"You can. Tell them I'm uncertain about the future, too. That much is the truth."

He raised an eyebrow. "Uncertain about me?"

"Not in the least. Just uncertain about everything else."

Joli shared one trait with my oldest sister. Both she and Ryalgar were driven to understand how things worked. Me, I was happy just knowing they did.

Our recent practices had become dominated by Joli's growing concern that the horses wouldn't be as closely clumped together as we hoped. Then, we'd need to be able to aim well in the dim light and account for changing winds over the abnormally long distance the arrows would travel.

I had the eyesight to focus on the target, and I would be doing the aiming and shooting. All well and good. But once the arrow flew, she powered it, not I. How would she account for an unexpected breeze when she wasn't the one who could see the target, or at least see it as well as I did.

Winds had been light throughout the hot summer days, making it hard to test the extent of this problem. When we met shortly after Plono to practice, we had the swift variable breezes that characterized autumn.

I wanted to talk to Joli about my situation in K'ba, but she wanted to try out an annoying amount of experiments to test her ideas before we took a break.

"Please. We can talk later. The winds might die down," she insisted.

So we tried this and that before we noticed an amazing fact. Nothing we did mattered.

Once I pointed an arrow at my target, and Joli gave it the extra oomph only she could, the arrow went where I sent it regardless of changes in the wind. It even seemed to adjust for a small amount of misaiming on my part, as long as my intent was clear.

"These things self-correct," Joli said, holding a single arrow in her hand and studying it with reverence. "How do those carvers do it? This could revolutionize warfare."

"I'm not sure that's a good idea."

"Of course it is. More accurate arrows mean more victories. Why wouldn't anyone want that?"

"Because soon the other side will have more accurate arrows too and then more people will die. Are you sure want that?"

She laughed. "You have a point. Ideas get out, arrows get stolen. Perhaps we'd be better off making our weapons less effective with every war." She laid down the quiver she'd picked up. "So, wind is no problem. Glad we understand that. Now, what is this thing in K'ba you're so upset about?"

Out came the story of Zoya's plan to spy on the Sage Coalition, the coalition's desire to enlist us to work against Ryalgar, and my conversation with Jasia.

"Well, you have been busy," she said. "On behalf of the Velka, we appreciate your efforts, but honestly no one thinks these people in K'ba are going to cause trouble for us or anyone else."

"I think you underestimate their passion," I said. "And the fear their witnesses could generate. They may not be able to stop the Chimera, but they *can* create problems."

"Then by all means go and convince them to be on our side."

"It's okay? I mean, no one cares if I speak on behalf of the Chimera? It's not like I have any authority."

"Bat scump. You're Ryalgar's sister. But if it makes you feel better, I'll deputize you as … my assistant. I hereby declare you are the top aid to the second in command of the Chimera. How's that?"

"Okay, I guess ... You're sure no one is going to care if I tell them everything we're doing?"

"I can't see how it could hurt anything," she said. "And it might help to have them on our side. Do your best. At our next practice, let me know how it goes."

And with that, I became authorized to speak for the entire civilian resistance to the Mongol invasion.

~ 21 ~

An Honest Woman

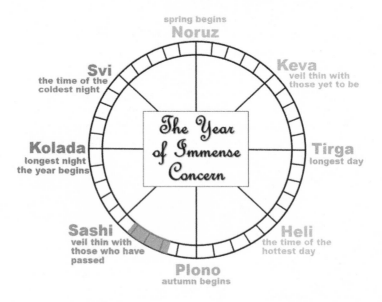

Any of my sisters would have been a better choice than I. I knew that as I looked over the hall packed with K'basta.

Once, I'd been desperate to impress these people. I found them creative, original, and not fettered by the conventions permeating the simple farm folk who'd raised me. I had wanted them to like me and to love my art, and I'd have done almost anything to achieve that end.

Now I sat in front of them, my heart pounding, as they scrutinized me to see what their enemy looked like.

Words had never flowed from my mouth as easily as they did for my sisters. I knew what I meant in my head, but so often the phrases became tangled before they made it to my throat.

Could this have been worse? I thought not, as the people whose admiration I craved most stared at me with hostility, about to hear me in my worst ineptness.

A panel of three of K'ba's leaders sat at a table slanted towards me, prepared to ask me questions and to maintain order. Jasia was one of the three. I saw Magomet's father in the audience, but not Magomet. That, at least, was some small blessing.

"Today we have a different sort of guest," the older of the two men at the table stood and spoke. "Rather than one who tells us why we must fear the coming invasion, this one brings a unique message."

Rumbles of conversation began.

"Quiet. Please. K'ba prides itself on being the most informed nichna in the realm. If we wish to claim this mantle, we must listen to others. So hear this young woman. She wishes to tell us of her sister Ryalgar's plans."

He gestured to me to speak.

I knew simple facts would serve me best. I took a deep breath and exhaled, as though I were about to shoot an arrow.

"Those others, the ones you have heard speak before today. They have told you the truth," I said.

Murmurs of surprise followed.

"Just, well, not the whole truth. Their stories of the havoc the Mongols wreak on those who oppose them are accurate by all the accounts we have heard, too. Your desire to avoid such a fate? It is sensible."

The murmurs grew louder.

"Quiet. Please," the older man said. "Let her continue."

I tried to speak with more force, so my voice would carry.

"What you haven't heard is that these invaders have their own code of honor. It's not the same as ours, obviously, as we don't ride into the realms of others and demand tribute."

I got a little laughter for that remark.

"Nonetheless, my sister has learned that the leader of this horde places an uncommon value on the lives of his fighters. He overwhelms his enemies in part because he wishes to not lose the life of a single one of his soldiers. In fact, he prefers not to lose the life of a single horse."

I had their attention now.

"My sister also learned the Mongolian culture places a high value on cleverness and the ability to do things. They'd rather learn from others than kill them. Because of this, it is possible to be allowed to live if one gains their respect."

I saw puzzled looks on much of my audience as they considered whether to believe me or not. Though the sun had set, a watered-down afternoon wine sat on my table. I took a small sip.

"This fact led her to design a resistance that was both smart and nonviolent. I know that sounds impossible, but she's a Velka, and she's turned to many of their old tricks. I also know you don't put much faith in their ways, but some of the Velka's abilities, like how they can manipulate plants to grow, well, those are without dispute."

I got a few nods. Magic or not, the Velka could do unusual things.

"She's also sought out other odd talents in the realm, some of which have turned out to be surprisingly strong."

"And suppose we don't believe in those either?" someone from the back of the room shouted.

"Yeah. There is no such thing as luski!" a woman up front yelled.

The older man stood to demand order. I kept talking.

"You don't have to believe in them. You just have to know that, fail or succeed, my sister has devised ways to deter the invaders while hopefully sparing every one of their lives. She believes they will therefore spare us if we fail."

"In other words, K'ba's plan could still be implemented after your sister's?" the man at the table asked me.

"Absolutely. Her idea doesn't exclude yours. She's designed a first response. If it succeeds, we still have to negotiate to keep them from returning and doing this all again. If she fails, our approach can be, and probably should be, to acquiesce, just as you wish."

Three people stood up and each one shouted a question. All three needed answers.

"How do you stop an invasion without killing anyone?"

"What are you doing to keep the Svadlu out of this?"

"What if she's wrong, and they butcher us for her efforts?"

I held up my hands to hush them all.

I spoke to the first woman.

"Listen. She plans on tranquilizing some of their horses while they sleep. Then frightening more horses into throwing their riders. Then using smoke and illusions to drive much of the remainder into the Wide River. The Svadlu gave her soldiers to train the farmers and herders of the eastern nichnas, so they can capture some invaders and hold them prisoner, one to a household. Fighters and horses will be released as a condition of the Mongols leaving our realm and never returning."

I saw a few scattered nods of approval. I had reached a few.

To the man who spoke second, I said, "The Svadlu gave their word they would let us try our way first, and the Royals have made it clear to our soldiers that their job is to stand behind us and look fierce as we negotiate. Your task has not changed. You will need to persuade the Royals to pay the tribute if Ryalgar fails. I think you can do that."

Then I turned to the young man who'd asked the third question. I knew my answer to him was the most important part of my message.

"What if!"

I barked it out as loud as I could. People hushed when they heard the quiet woman yell.

"What if the Svadlu don't do as the Royals command? What if our careful efforts to save the lives of the invaders go unrewarded? What if the Mongols won't negotiate with us? What if they won't even accept our surrender? What if they never would have accepted our surrender no matter what we did? What if all they want to do is ride in and kill us all? What if?"

I stared at the man. Then I looked at my audience.

Jasia stood. "I can answer that question," she said.

I knew she could. She and I had already had this conversion.

"If any of those are the case," she said, "we've been totally prucked all along."

The room erupted with conversation.

"Quiet!" Jasia shouted it with a power I didn't know she had. "I propose this to K'ba. We intended to persuade the realm to agree with us but we delayed to hold this meeting. Now, I propose the leaders of K'ba spend the rest of this eighth learning more about this Chimera, as they call it, and looking into ways we could compliment it. If by Sashi we aren't satisfied with what we've learned, we'll return to our original plan. There will still be time to persuade the Royals. On the other hand, if we *can* work with this, this thing, then perhaps that will be better for all."

One voice rang out above the others. It was Magomet, standing in the back of the room.

"By leaders of K'ba, who exactly do you mean? Our Royals? They're not even here. So by whose authority do *you* speak?"

Jasia gave her son a withering glance. The older man at the table replied.

"Please, now. We know the royal family of K'ba ages without a suitable heir. Long ago they disengaged from the day-to-day workings of our nichna."

"Yes," Magomet said. "As have the Royals of Eds and Scrud. All three of the dry nichnas are plagued by useless Royals hiding as we face our most troubling times."

Was he trying to make trouble for Bohdan and his family?

"We do not meddle in the leadership of our neighbors," the younger man at the table said, giving Magomet a sharp look. "As to our Royals, there are issues to which all here are not privy. The royalty of K'ba deserves our sympathy, not our impatience. You K'basta have chosen us three to lead the Sage Coalition, and we will spearhead this investigation into the Chimera." He looked at his two cohorts for approval. They both nodded.

"Many of you will be asked to aid us in our inquiry," the older man added. "We will reconvene here two days before Sashi to render our recommendation."

As people stood up to leave, Jasia walked over to me.

"For a woman who doesn't say much, you did incredibly well." She smiled.

I blew out a puff of air, relieved the whole ordeal was over.

"I'll do all I can to get you the answers you need and help you with your decision."

"I'm counting on it."

"What was Magomet getting at?" I couldn't help asking her.

"I'm not sure," she said. "But I intend to find out."

For the next few anks my life settled into a simple pattern. I'd arrive at the farm to help Mom and Dad with chores and to exchange information with them and any sister I could find. I'd practice with Joli and sometimes others, telling Joli all that had happened since I last saw her so she could pass the word on to Ryalgar.

Then I'd ride to K'ba, but of course I'd stop to see Bohdan on the way.

In K'ba, I'd confer with Zoya first. She had leveled with her parents and they now welcomed me because I not only caused no trouble but worked with the Coalition's leaders. Then I'd go to Jasia's art studio to answer her latest questions and bring her whatever information she had requested. I'd ignore Magomet if he glared at me from a distance.

In K'ba, I'd also paint something small and simple to calm my mind. Then I'd ride back to Scrud, spend time with Bohdan, then ride on to the farm to do it all again.

The ank before Sashi, Jasia waited for me in Zoya's parent's tavern. She'd never done that before and her solemn face worried me as I entered. Zoya looked up as I walked in and I motioned for her to join us.

"Something bad?" I asked Jasia.

"Something difficult," she replied. "We've finished our review of your plans. So many people helped. The Velka we spoke with, the members of your father's road crew, your Svadlu sister. She is a force, isn't she?"

"Sulphur? Yes." I had to smile. "She's impressive. You got the information you needed? From her and others?"

"From so many. We never actually got to speak with Ryalgar or your grandmother but everyone else filled in the gaps for us. We understand the plan and we *will* recommend cooperation with you as a first choice, with the caveat that we must do all we can to get the Royals to pay the tribute if the Chimera fails."

"That's the best news you could give me! What's the problem?"

Jasia looked directly at me. "My misguided son has spent all his time with the younger K'basta, festering a hatred of you beyond anything I thought him capable of."

Magomet again. Why wouldn't this man leave me alone?

"Don't worry," I said. " He has no way to hurt me."

"He's doing something worse. He risks hurting the entire realm because of you."

I'm sure I looked baffled.

"He, and two of your old friends …"

"Delia and Pasha …." Zoya said.

"Right. The three of them have spread rumors about how you can't be trusted. He's developed some crazy theory about how you're secretly working with the Royals of Scrud, K'ba, and Eds, who he's decided are all conspiring to deceive the people. He's using your relationship with Bohdan to substantiate this."

"Oh for pruck's sake …"

"We know it's nonsense, but he's worked up a lot of anger among the young people of K'ba, tapping into their considerable impatience with our Royals to generate a disturbing amount of agitation. Now, the leaders of the Coalition fear that without the support of your generation, any alliance with Ryalgar is doomed."

"This is absurd. Can't somebody reason with him?"

She closed her eyes for a heartbeat. "Maybe. I'm ashamed to tell you my son has declared that if you will meet with him, he'll tell you how you can persuade him that his ideas are false."

"Don't do it," Zoya said.

"I have to, don't I?"

We all knew I did.

Magomet and I arranged to meet in a small park with benches where people ate their lunches. He sat at one end of a bench. I sat down at the other.

He laughed derisively. "Don't flatter yourself. I've no desire to sit close to you."

"Good. So why are you destroying my reputation?"

"You've none to destroy. You're already a proven liar and a pruska."

I sucked in my breath at the insult but didn't reply.

"A pruska," he repeated. "One who sleeps with any lowlife beggar who will have her but *not* the man who loves her. But you can't help that about yourself, can you?"

I wanted to slap him, but instead I looked at him with as little expression as I could manage. This conversation had to go well.

"However, I am an unusually generous man. If you will behave like an honest woman for once, then I will tell others you are one."

"How do you think an honest woman behaves?" I answered in a soft monotone.

"She stops cuddling with dirt bag Scrudites and devotes herself to saving the realm she claims to care so much about."

"You want me to stop seeing Bohdan?"

"Not exactly. You may speak with him but you may not touch, kiss, or pruck the man, now or ever. Starting today, you will be as celibate as you once claimed. *That* will make you an honest woman. Any reports to the contrary, and I swear I will scump up this alliance between the Coalition and your Chimera."

"Wait. You would actually mess with our realm's survival just to keep me celibate? For pruck's sake, what is wrong with you?"

He made a loud and angry noise I supposed was a laugh.

"You believe your own lies, don't you?" he said. "None of this is going to work. We're all going to die no matter how we deal with the Mongols, so I'm not scumping up anything. But, I do intend to die with the satisfaction of knowing that in the end, he didn't get you either. It's not much, but I'll take what I can get."

I stared at him in disbelief. He was serious.

What choice did I have?

I promised him I'd do it. Kolada was six anks away. Bohdan and I could stay away from each other for that long.

~ 22 ~

The Wrong Direction

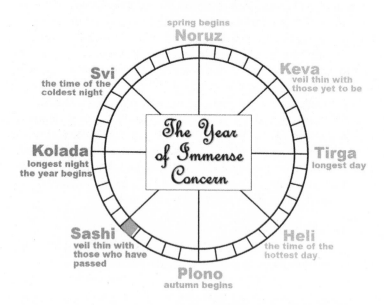

Magomet took me at my word, knowing he had one big advantage. He thought everyone in Ilari would die no matter what. All he wanted was to prevent me from having love or joy before then.

Meanwhile, hope cursed me. I thought there'd be a tomorrow if we played our cards right, and that our odds went up if I didn't have an angry spurned lover determined to hurt me.

Not that I was that vital to the war effort, although my role as a long eye had worth. No, it was more that I sat at the nexus of important groups and was close to critical people. Want to make me really, really sorry I didn't keep my promise? Magomet had multiple ways, and his ways had dire consequences.

I told Zoya and Jasia of my promise to him, and of how I'd made my peace with it until after the invasion. I wasn't quite sure what I'd tell Bohdan, but that was a problem for later.

Word spread fast that Magomet had met with me and new information had been revealed. He'd decided he'd been wrong about my intentions. Passions cooled. The Sage Coalition rolled out its plans to support the Chimera along with its plans to convince the Royals of the need to choose capitulation as the backup plan. As far as I was concerned, I wasn't involved in that second decision.

A few days before Sashi I prepared to leave K'ba to deliver my news to Bohdan. I wavered between the two obvious options. I preferred to tell Bohdan the entire truth and ask him to join me in the five ank charade that I'd spurned him. Once the invasion was over, we'd set things right. Simple and easy.

But I worried Bohdan wouldn't play along. Even if he intended to, I feared he'd decide a man of Scrud didn't put up with being threatened. Then he'd charge over to K'ba and confront Magomet and this time something worse than a fistfight would ensue. However the confrontation ended, the chaos caused inside K'ba by a clash between the despised prince of Scrud and the popular local artist would likely destroy the fragile alliance Jasia and I'd created.

Ryalgar might not know it, but the destruction of that alliance could ruin any hope she had of succeeding.

So, I leaned toward showing up in Scrud and making a great show of publicly dumping Bohdan.

Before I left, Jasia insisted on walking with me over to the shop that used to sell my artwork. I knew she wanted to make things right for me, given the sacrifice I'd been forced into by her son.

"I know. I heard." The shopkeeper threw his hands in the air as soon as I walked in the door. At least he seemed happy about the news. "You're no longer suspected of siding with your sister because we're all siding with her now."

"True."

"Better yet, the young people of K'ba have decided you're not part of some secret force protecting our unpopular Royals. But you never were that, were you?"

"No."

"The stories people create. Did that one come about because your young man turned out to be the crown prince of Scrud?"

"Maybe."

"I couldn't believe it when I heard it. To think he was in my shop, looking just like any other Scrudite." The shopkeeper shook his head. "You just never know."

"I came to ask a favor of you," Jasia interrupted. "I want to make sure you'll carry Olivine's art once all this blows over. She's turned out to be an amazing asset to the K'basta and it would pain me to think she might not be welcome in this community."

"Of course I'll sell her work." He looked genuinely surprised at any implication he'd do otherwise. "She still has unfilled orders. I bet I can get twice as much for them now." He turned and winked at me. "Better for you, better for me, right?"

Well, at least some things were back to normal.

I had one other errand to complete in K'ba. I took Zoya with me to the market, hoping to talk to the Velka about Zoya using her long eyes to serve as a scout. The Velka had been absent the last time I'd been there, the sides of their small tent flapping in the dusty breeze. But word of K'ba's changing mood should have reached the forest by now.

It had. Today two Velka greeted those who passed by, signaling that their presence was more about outreach than sales. A small crowd had formed around their tent by the time Zoya and I arrived, so we stood in line behind the newly curious K'basta chatting with the women of the forest.

"Olivine!" One of them recognized me and called out. I suppose I'd met her a year ago when I visited Ryalgar, but I didn't remember her. She motioned to Zoya and me to come into the tent where we could talk in private.

When I told her of my intent to get Zoya involved in the scouting efforts, the woman squealed with delight.

"It's why we sought *you* out! We knew you preferred not to speak with us here, but, well, now things have changed. Thank the Goddess, right?"

"Uh, yes."

"Ryalgar says she's secured a house out on the cliffs of Vinx. Lookouts will be headquartered there. She knows you have practices to attend and you need to be in place in Bisu days before Kolada, but she hoped you could spend time at this house first, using your peculiar talents to help them get started. And of course, we'd love it if your long eyed friend here …"

The Velka paused and looked at Zoya closer. "You look like the young girl whose injuries we tended to for many anks…. perhaps ten years ago …."

Zoya looked down. "It was me. You were all so kind, and I did heal. Finally."

"Horrible thing. Did they ever find the man …"

"No. He was a traveler staying at the inn, and he fled the realm."

The Velka shook her head. "We thought there was something special about your fighting spirit. I know our scouts would be honored to have you among them now."

I'd never seen Zoya blush before, but she did then.

"How soon could you make your way to the outpost?" the Velka asked Zoya.

"I need to help my parents a while longer, but I can come two anks before Kolada."

"That's perfect. And you, Olivine? What can I tell your sister?"

The Velka had made me a better offer than she realized. I didn't want lingering good-byes with my family or friends and this avoided all of them. Plus, I'd be in Vinx where I could focus on my archery. Best of all, the odds of successfully misleading Bohdan grew if I could avoid him. I'd stage a showy farewell to him over the next few days, then disappear from Scrud until all this passed. It was perfect.

"I'll be at the outpost a few days after Sashi if you like."

I planned to ride into Scrud and tell Bohdan, loudly and in earshot of others, that he wouldn't see me until after Kolada. Then I'd ride to my parent's farm and say goodbye to my family, explaining that needs elsewhere would make me scarce until after the attack. Then I'd gather up my archery equipment and go up to the house on the cliffs and give the Chimera my all for five anks.

It was a good plan.

Then I rode into Scrud, and it changed.

At first, I thought the man riding out to meet me was Bohdan. He looked like him, but more tired. Was Bohdan ill? As I got closer, I recognized my mistake. This was Bohdan's father, a man I'd only spoken to twice. I'd never picked up the warmth Bohdan's mother and sisters had shown me, but I now knew his situation was different.

Once the crown passed to the next generation, Bohdan's father stopped being a Royal and any remaining status came only from having sired the necessary heir. If the crown passed to a cousin instead, his status dropped considerably.

Honestly, everyone's convoluted rules of succession struck me as barbaric, but given those rules, I didn't expect this would be a congenial conversation.

"You came to celebrate the holiday with my son?" he said as he approached. "May I speak with you as you ride?"

"Of course." *Say more. Something friendly.* "I regret we haven't had the opportunity to get to know each other better."

He smiled. "I've kept my distance knowing our interests don't align well. I wish for my son to accept his crown. You stand in his way."

Right to the point, this one.

"You may assume I'm selfish," he continued, "but I'm not. It is my people I am concerned for."

I shouldn't have argued with him, but the idea that Bohdan didn't care about the needs of Scrud offended me.

"Bohdan tells me his cousin will make an admirable ruler. Perhaps better than he would."

"Snake scump." The older man spat into the dirt. "The people love Bohdan, his dedication to the nichna, his skill as a carver. He stands for the best we are. This cousin he speaks of, the child of my wife's sister, he hires himself out to the Bisuites to herd their cows."

I suspected a little bias had colored his assessment. Then I realized Bohdan's father offered me the one thing I lacked and desperately needed – a motive. He offered me an understandable reason to tell his son, the man I loved, to go away. I needed to thank this man, not argue with him.

"Please. Tell me more about why you think this cousin won't rule as well."

I did my best to listen and ask concerned questions.

His father and I rode to Bohdan's hut together. We passed through most of the carvers' village on our way, and others followed along, sensing that a visit to Bohdan from both his father and his outsider girlfriend would produce news. I intended to not disappoint.

Bohdan saw us coming and greeted us outside.

"I hoped you'd make it here before Sashi." He grinned at me with a you-know-why twinkle in his eyes. Sheep scump, this was going to be hard to do.

"Father." He nodded a greeting to his parent. "To what do I owe this pleasure?"

"Your girlfriend and I have had a lengthy conversation. I'm sorry it didn't happen sooner. She's a thoughtful and intelligent woman, son, and I can see why you find her attractive."

"I'm glad you two got along." I heard the edge in Bohdan's voice; I could tell this conversation concerned him.

"She and I have reached an unfortunate conclusion. I believe she wants to share it with you."

The man turned to me. It was my show now.

I looked around at the gathering crowd. I'd needed this conversation to be overheard and make its way to Magomet's ears, but I'd have preferred a few people, not this throng. Yet there was no sending them away now.

"I'm sorry this has to be so public." I looked at the ground, gathering my courage. "Your father told me much about you and what your leadership means to Scrud. It seems you've been far too modest, and I've not given enough thought to what a crucial time this is."

"Olivine, don't be absurd. We need each other now!"

"I know. We do. But your father has convinced me that others need you more. I don't know ..." I faltered. "I *do* know that you need to give Scrud your full attention. Please, promise your people that you will reconsider marriage to me and move forward with a plan to be their ruler instead."

"I will do no such thing. They don't need me that bad." He glared at his father. "This is ridiculous."

"No, Bohdan, he speaks the truth," I said. "All of Ilari needs you to do what's right."

I admit I looked into his eyes begging him to find greater meaning in my words.

"Being with the person one loves is always the right thing to do," he said.

"You'd think. But not this time. So I'm going to make it easy for you." I took a look around. I had everyone's attention now. *Here goes nothing.*

"Consider our relationship over."

People began to whisper as my eyes watered up.

"It is ended. Done. If I must ride through here again, I won't stop. Please don't make me. I … I'll always think of you with love." Tears started running down my face with those last words, and I wiped at them with my sleeve. I gave an unladylike sniff.

Then I turned around and I galloped away as hard as I could.

It was the best of all possible exits except for one mistake. I *had* intended to ride on to Vinx, spend Sashi with my family, and then go out to the cliffs. But, I'd galloped in the wrong direction and now I raced towards K'ba as everyone watched.

I wasn't much of a performer, but even I knew that stopping my horse, yelling "oops," and turning around would mar my exit. So I did the only thing I could. I rode back to K'ba instead.

~ 23 ~

Beyond the Cows

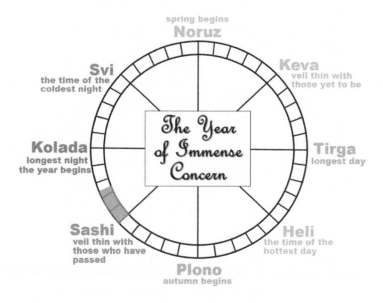

spring begins
Noruz

Svi
the time of the
coldest night

Keva
veil thin with
those yet to be

Kolada
longest night
the year begins

*The Year
of Immense
Concern*

Tirga
longest day

Sashi
veil thin with
those who have
passed

Heli
the time of the
hottest day

Plono
autumn begins

"What are you doing back here?"

It was the first thing Zoya said as I walked through the door of her family's tavern.

"Don't ask."

She knew I didn't mean it. She whispered something to one of the servers then shepherded me towards one of the small corner tables, bringing a mug of something for each of us.

"Did you break up with Bohdan?"

"Oh yes. With a style that would have impressed you."

After two long thirsty rides, my ale went down fast. As it did, out came the full tale. Soon we were laughing and crying as I told of my flawed dramatic exit from Scrud.

I had a sense of the tavern filling up as we talked, then I remembered. This was the Eve of Sashi, a night known for its revelry. Days ago I'd intended to spend it having a party for two with Bohdan. When I left this morning, I'd planned instead to celebrate it quietly with whoever was home on the farm.

But now I was in a tavern in K'ba and things would get rowdy.

"Zoya! Olivine!" I picked out Arek's familiar voice in the growing din.

"We heard we were welcome here again, so we came over to celebrate Sashi together," Nikolo said.

They walked over arm in arm, the way no one would notice here but everyone would stare at back in Gruen. I was glad they'd made the trip

"Thought we'd start our celebration at your place, Zoya. Are you off tonight?"

"I told my parents I'd help, but they've got plenty of others. I can go have a drink with you. It's been so long since we've been together."

She stopped. It had been, but "we" had once included Magomet, Pasha, and Delia, none of whom we wanted to see tonight. It also hadn't included Nikolo, who I thought was a welcome addition.

She disappeared to check in with her folks and grab her cloak.

"Did the Velka ask you to work with the scouts out on the cliffs?" Nikolo said.

"Yes, I'll be spending most of my time there until Kolada."

"Good. We'll be there sometimes too. We can practice together when we are."

Arek looked around the room. "The party is getting started early," he said.

We stopped to listen.

"Five prucking anks left. Five anks!" A large man flung his empty mug onto the floor. No one moved to pick up the shards.

"But it could be our last Sashi together," a woman at a small table said to her lover, wiping tears from her eyes.

"To my dead ancestors!" yelled a skinny young man at the end of the bar. "May I not be joining you varmin for many years!"

He got everyone's attention. Sashi was, according to our teachings, the day on which we honored those who had passed. In truth, people acknowledged their joy in being alive on Sashi while drowning their fears of meeting their ancestors in ale.

This year, Sashi would likely involve more of that than usual.

"Want to go somewhere quieter?" Zoya asked.

"Is there going to be such a place tonight?"

She motioned for us to follow. We picked up our drinks and walked single-file into a private courtyard reserved for her family's use. There, huddled together in blankets under the light of a nearly full moon, the four of us talked of old times and favorite dreams and theories about how the world worked.

We'd barely begun when we noticed the first light of dawn in the eastern sky. How had that happened?

When I left the following day, I rode through Scrud at a fast trot and saw no one as I passed the village of carvers. I was both relieved and disappointed.

I stopped at the farm, hoping to stay overnight on my way to the lookout spot on the cliffs. My parents had expected me home days earlier and wanted me to stay longer but I was anxious to learn what being a temporary look-out would entail. I also didn't want to share the mess my personal life had become.

I told them of the Sage Coalition making peace with Ryalgar's Chimera and how my paintings and I would be welcome in K'ba after the invasion.

"That much is good, right?" my father asked. He seemed preoccupied with his problems but looked up at me with concern. I suspected he sensed that more was wrong than I wanted to admit.

"Yes," I replied. "That much is good. And the work you're doing with the roads? It goes well?"

"Yes," he said. "Well."

I left it at that.

My mother seemed melancholy. Because she was the only one available to take Coral's baby to safety, she'd accepted the inevitable and gone as far as agreeing to shelter with the Velka until the troubles passed. She had to be dreading it. I promised her I'd come back for a visit before she went into the forest.

The next morning I left for the cliffs.

Children in Vinx love to visit the cliffs. Most look to the right first, staring across the wide expanse of the Southeast Lake and looking at the thick marsh around it. Straight ahead they see the grasslands of Bisu, rocky and drier than Vinx and mostly used for grazing. Cows live there, and cows are exciting because few of our farms keep cattle. Then off to the left, they can barely make out the canyon holding the rushing waters of the Canyon River.

The most amazing thing out there is the entrance to Ilari. Everyone knows that somewhere between the marsh and the Canyon River, and beyond all those cows, another land begins. Children are fascinated by this. So are the adults.

Forty-two days before Kolada, I stared out towards that border after I arrived at the stone cottage that would house the lookouts. The little structure had been constructed as payment to a former captive of the Mongols, who'd asked for a home here in return for teaching our fighters as much of their language as he could remember. He and his family had left for the safety of Pilk, and now the scouts would use his home.

A woman dressed in the soft grey wools and leathers worn by advanced teachers came out to greet me. Her features and coloring told me her ancestors came from elsewhere. Such wasn't uncommon; wanderers and refugees had made their way into Ilari throughout our history. But when she spoke, her accent told me she was born in another land as well.

"You're the sister who is a long eye, aren't you?" She studied me with a gentle gaze. "I'm so glad you could help me set up. Your abilities will be so useful." Her dark brown eyes were as kind as her words, and I liked her.

We spoke as we stood on the cliff, looking at the spot where Ilari ended. She shared her plans for the teams of lookouts and told me of the various systems she and Celestine had devised for communicating back to the rest of Ilari. As she spoke about the two of them, I knew.

Maybe I heard the love in her voice as she said my sister's name. Maybe I knew Celestine would only be drawn to one who was gentle and this woman conveyed tenderness with her every word.

My surprise faded. Celestine *had* enjoyed the company of girls early on. Many did, so I hadn't thought much of it, though it hadn't appealed to me. Boys, on the other hand, never seemed to please her. I just thought she was particularly picky.

Then she'd become usually closed-mouthed about her new lover, more so than me. Who does one have to keep quieter about than a Scrudite?

The answer stood next to me.

"You're close to my sister Celestine, aren't you?"

The woman gave me a fearful look. "She told you?"

"No, she's never spoken of you, though I wish she had. Don't worry, I'll say nothing to anyone."

The woman looked at the ground, choosing her words with care. "I think that's wise. But how do you know?"

I shrugged. "I can't help it. I'm her twin."

More people arrived over the next few days and the little house grew crowded. Firuza showed others how to use her extraordinary invention for seeing far away and then she and I devised a schedule that would have either a long eye or a person with her device observing the horizon day and night.

She'd set a limit of eight people living in the house. Some, like me, would leave after a few anks and be replaced by those with no role to play in the fighting. Others would come and go between keeping watch here and performing the more strenuous work of climbing poles and using flags to convey messages elsewhere.

I began taking shifts early on, spending a part of the day, or sometimes the middle of the night, bundled against the increasingly colder wind as I stared out to the east, scanning for anything beyond the cows. While I felt glad to use my talents, this job had a downside. It provided me with far too much time to think.

Mostly, I thought about Bohdan and how much I loved him and missed him and hoped he'd accepted my rejection but somehow kept his love for me alive. If he held on to the hope that all would change after this threat passed, it would.

Sometimes I worried about Magomet. Would his hurt pride lead him to do something else destructive in my absence? I had to hope my total removal from K'ba was the best thing for that situation.

Sometimes I felt bad for Bohdan's family. Sometimes I worried about mine. Sometimes I worried about everything and how this was all going to go. If I couldn't get my mind to move on, I'd ask for the next person to start their shift early. Then I'd go for a walk, find a low spot I could crawl into for shelter, and I'd pull out charcoal and my precious paper. Over the anks I spent there, I drew hundreds of tiny scared angry plants and at least as many little animals that shouted out my fright in their shapes and their expressions.

I dared not scream out my terror, but I learned how to let my art scream for me.

I liked the days that held distractions. When I'd been there about an ank, a messenger summoned me to the residence of Vinx's Royals to attend a feast held in Sulphur's honor. I had to borrow a suitable dress from Firuza, but when I got there I was glad I'd bothered. Sulphur glowed as our home nichna gave her the appreciation she should have received back at her Mozdolo. Celestine sang a beautiful song for her, and my parents looked suitably proud. I got to sleep in a soft feather bed in a palace guestroom before I headed back to my duties the next morning.

On several days I met Joli for practice, and those were good days because I had less time to think. Twice Arek and Nikolo rode out to help us keep watch and we practiced together, too. They brought word that Zoya still planned to come to the cottage two anks before Kolada to fill in for those leaving to do other things. I asked them to let her know I'd be visiting with my parents then, but we'd overlap for many days before I had to get in position with the other long eyes.

Get in position.

With the other long eyes.

I felt a gray mass of dread in my stomach every time I thought of that day.

Twenty-two days before Kolada, I rode to my parents' farm to wish them well before the battle. I'd hope to cross paths with one or more sisters, too, but I found Mom and Dad alone, going through the sad motions of securing the farm for, under the best of circumstances, their short absence. Dad would remain for days after Mom left, joining his road crew along the edge of Zur right before Kolada.

Mom prepared one of my favorite meals, which I found thoughtful, and I helped my dad build a feed container for the chickens that he hoped would release a small amount of grain each day so they wouldn't starve.

As we sat together for the meal, I studied them. They both looked older than I remembered and for some reason that brought tears to my eyes. I wondered how we'd gotten to this point with them old, me in love with a man I couldn't tell them about, and the whole world falling apart.

I tried to say something but instead, the tears came.

"Are you okay, Olivine?" Dad asked.

"She's fine," Mom answered. "Probably worn out. Archery. Scouting. Riding back and forth across the realm all the time ..."

"No. I am *not* fine." There. I said it. "I'm in love with a man you'd hate so I couldn't tell you about him and now we've broken up and might never get back together." The words came out between sobs but I think they heard me well enough.

"Are you talking about Magomet, dear?"

"No!" I shouted it at her with anger she didn't deserve. "I hate Magomet. He's a selfish spoiled rantallion who prucked my life up just because he couldn't have me!"

"I see," Mom said.

Dad surprised me by asking in the softest of tones "Who *are* you in love with?" His question reminded me that he'd surmised more about my love life than Mom had.

"Actually..." my sobs stopped but the laugh that followed had a disturbing edge to it. "He's a prince. A real prince, only I was too stupid to know it."

"That's wonderful dear. How could that happen?"

"He's a Scrudite, Mom."

"A what?"

"You heard me. Even *they* have Royals, though you can't tell them from the others."

"I see," she said again. She looked to my father for confirmation. "You knew about this?"

"He didn't," I said, "but I think he guessed it because I kept asking him questions about Scrud."

Dad shrugged and gave her a nod.

"This happened with all that riding back and forth?" she asked.

"Yes. Only now he loses his throne if he's with me but he doesn't care, and his father is upset and I can't be with him because Magomet will completely pruck up the peace agreement between Ryalgar and the Coalition if I am, and he doesn't even recognize the trouble they could cause and so I told him I never wanted to see him again ..."

"Hold on," my mother said. "You love this man? And you told him you never wanted to see him again?"

"Yes. I thought you'd be glad. I'm not going to marry a man from Scrud."

"The man who would no longer be a prince if he married you?"

"Yes. That's what I said."

"Get yourself over to Scrud and tell that man you didn't mean it."

Mom???

"I don't care what he is, dear. Actually, I do care, but it doesn't matter. If you love him that much, what else do you plan to do? Spend the rest of your life crying? How many dinners are you going to interrupt?"

She smiled a little at the last words.

"But Magomet's going to cause all kinds of problems if ..."

"He doesn't need to know."

"Bohdan's dad is not going to accept me..."

"Of course he will. It could take him a while, but he will."

The next question just popped out of my mouth.

"Would you *really* have locked me in the root cellar if I'd told you about him sooner?"

She laughed.

"Yes, but probably only for a few hours, hoping you'd think twice about whatever foolish thing you were contemplating. Sound like you are well past thinking things through, however."

"You think I should go talk to him? Tonight?"

"Obviously not in the dark, dear. I meant tomorrow."

"Perhaps secretly?" Dad suggested. "You know. All the other problem people could hear about this later ..."

"What, what if he thought I really didn't love him? What if he won't take me back?"

My parents looked at each other and they both laughed.

"I wouldn't worry about that," Dad said.

"Now please, finish your dinner," Mom added. "I spent all afternoon on it, the least you can do is enjoy it while it's still warm. Tomorrow will come soon enough.

~ 24 ~

The Right Direction

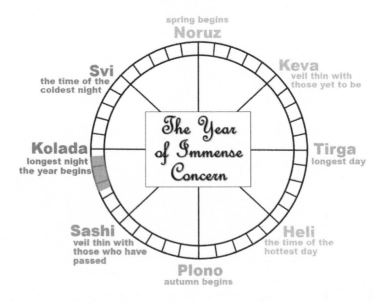

"I left early the next morning, after thanking my parents for their understanding. Mom insisted on packing a lunch for me and including a couple of pastries for Bohdan after I confessed I'd been sneaking her baked goods off to him for the past year. She and I both stayed dry-eyed as we exchanged the longest hug of my life, but Dad wiped his face with his sleeve more than once as he watched.

Then, I rode hard. When I got close enough to see the carvers' village with my long eyes, I saw a lavish campsite across the road from Bohdan's hut. It didn't belong to a Scrudite, yet no one from anywhere else camped in Scrud. Ever.

As I rode closer, I recognized Delia, fellow artist and ex-friend, standing outside the tent. A woman I didn't know stood with her.

"Hello!" I called out as I approached.

"Passing through?" she asked in a pleasant voice.

"No. I come to speak with someone."

"With whom?"

"Why would you care, Delia?"

"Because I'm part of a team of young artists donating our time to ensuring that you've spoken the truth to the people of K'ba and don't conspire in secret with our despised Royals."

Perhaps a private conversation with Bohdan was out of the question. I had another idea.

"I do not conspire with anyone. I bring a message to the current crown prince of Scrud from two other Vinxites. I believe I am allowed to deliver a message to him from a distance."

They looked at each other and shrugged. "As far as we know, you are. Provided it is done in public."

Bohdan stepped out of his hut and gave us all an irritated glare.

"How often do I have to tell you people that we have no connection, at all, with the Royals in K'ba?" he said to Delia. Then he turned to me.

"Last I heard, you never wanted to see me again. I'm sure there is no one else in Vinx interested in sending me a message, so be gone."

"You're wrong," I said. "My mother sends you these pastries and begs me to give you her regards along with them."

"Your mother? She doesn't know of me."

"She does now." I handed him the honey cakes she'd wrapped in cheesecloth, taking care not to touch his hands.

Delia and her companion looked at each other. Was I violating Magomet's decree by doing this? They seemed unsure.

"My father also sends his regards."

"Your father, too?" A bit of a smile began around the corners of his lips.

"Indeed. He has reminded me that the world will be quite different after Kolada and asks me to tell you that he hopes to make your acquaintance then."

"Yes, it will be quite different." He gave me a look that said *you're just not going to make this easy, are you?*

"My mother believes people can always find a way, sooner or later, to do what matters to them," I said.

"Does she now? Is this the same mother that has a thing about royalty?"

"Yes, but she seems to be more flexible than I realized."

We looked at each other, both unsure of what to do next. I wanted to jump off my horse and throw myself into his arms. He looked as if he held similar ideas, but the presence of our two unwanted chaperones gave us both pause.

"You're on your way to K'ba?" he asked.

I wasn't. I'd planned to simply turn around and ride back to the farm but now I felt foolish doing that. I needed a better exit.

"No. I ride to visit my sister."

"Gypsum? Please give her my regards and tell her I hope to see her again soon. Perhaps after Kolada."

We understood each other.

"Yes. After Kolada."

And once again I rode off in the opposite direction of the one I intended.

By the time I reached the reczavy camp, I decided I *did* want to visit with Gypsum. I had a couple of days off from my scouting duties and my parents expected me to stay in Scrud. I couldn't, yet I didn't want to be back with them answering questions. At least they'd agreed to my pleas to keep my situation from my sisters, so the opinions wouldn't be forthcoming from every direction.

But Gypsum already knew about Bohdan, making this visit easy. Maybe I could learn more about her life, and about what the reczavy were planning.

That turned out not to be the case. I'd surprised her again. She greeted me with warmth and told me she was glad to learn my situation with Bohdan had improved, but her camp now faced exceptionally delicate situations and could not deal with a stranger. Would I stay out in the guest tent where I'd stayed before?

Of course I would. I should have realized a good time for me wasn't necessarily a good time for her.

So I settled in amongst the furs and realized how exhausted I'd become. I took a cozy day-long nap during which I stopped thinking about Bohdan, Magomet, art, and archery. I woke the next morning and left feeling stronger than I had in a long time.

I stopped at the farm on my way back and discovered I'd just missed Ryalgar and my mother's departure. I stayed the night to make my father dinner, hoping it would ease his coming loneliness. When I rode out to the cottage on the cliffs the next day, I discovered I'd just missed Ryalgar again. She'd come to give us a pep talk. Good thing all the Snakes met in eight days. She and I would see each other then.

Zoya had arrived in my absence and settled into our routine, as had one of the long eyes I'd originally recruited. The mother from Lev with exceptional vision hadn't become a strong enough archer, but Firuza now utilized her considerable abilities. She, Zoya, and I spent much of our free time together.

I noticed shifts now had at least two on watch at all times and others rotated assignments helping the communications people who counted on our skills. Celestine came and went and we always talked, but she kept her distance from Firuza and never mentioned their love.

None of the other four archers helped out full-time like I did, although Arek and Nikolo came by. The large older man from Kir and the ancient history teacher from Pilk couldn't ride the length of the realm to help us, so I hadn't seen either of them since the large group practice. I looked forward to all five long eyed archers comparing notes at our upcoming group gathering.

As of one ank before Kolada, we had yet to see anything suspicious enough to cause us to raise the something-of-concern-is-happening flag. The Snake met the following day so each archer and oomrusher combination could learn of their assigned position. I waved to Joli when I saw her in the crowd. She gave me a wave back then turned to answer the questions of others.

Ryalgar stood to one side with a sheaf of notes, lost in her planning.

"Hey, Sis," I yelled as I walked up to her. She jumped.

"Sorry. You startled me."

"We keep missing each other everywhere we go." She gave me a puzzled look and I realized she had no way of knowing I'd shown twice right after she left.

"I heard you handled that Sage Coalition nonsense out in K'ba," she said. "Who'd have thought a movement like that could gain traction, huh?"

I felt defensive for the K'basta. "They aren't so far off base. They want to negotiate as much as you do."

"Yes, but I heard they're in Pilk now, trying to convince the Royals to pay the tribute if I, if we, if the Chimera fails."

"You don't think that's wise?"

"I'd rather see us fight for our freedom. Wouldn't you?"

"Let's hope the Chimera succeeds."

"Absolutely."

Joli interrupted us as she quieted the crowd. She stood in front of a large map of Bisu, painted on a big cloth and hung from a clothesline. She used it to show us the location of the flat ground and lush grass designed to attract the Mongols. I made my way over to greet Arek and Nikolo as Joli told us of the thick fog the low-level oomrushers would produce while hiding on barges in the marsh.

Joli showed us how she'd placed four teams in safe spots where they could hit horses from a distance too far away to be suspected. She'd arranged hiding places for each team once their work was done and allowed for ways we could move further to safety. Her precautions eased some of my fears.

Then she told us who was where and I realized the team of Ryalgar, Nikolo, and Grandma had no assignment. Was Joli protecting Ryalgar and Grandma? Nikolo was going to be mad as Heli about that.

"I've trained for this!" my grandmother stood and yelled. "I will not be sidelined because of my age or my position. Nor will I allow you to waste the talents of Ryalgar and Nikolo because of me."

Ryalgar still stood where I'd left her. She dropped her sheaf of notes and she shouted. "If you're sidelining my team because of *me*, you should know better. I'm a soldier ready to do her job."

"I agree," Joli said. "You both have an assignment." She hung a second map showing the hills of Eds.

"You told me to plan for everything, so I did. We have a risk of more Mongols entering through northern Eds. The only defense we will have against them is you three, who will take down as many as possible should this occur."

"This is outrageous." Ryalgar was angry now. I could see the two little bright red splotches she got on her face when she was furious. "They won't come in that way. We'll be sitting there idle, while you handle everything without us. You need us in Bisu."

"I need you where I put you. Am I in charge of this or not?"

I knew how Ryalgar struggled to give the answer she must, but she managed it.

"Yes. You're in charge of this."

"Very well. Then you three should prepare to go to Eds."

Nikolo stood near me. He was absolutely our best archer and now he'd spent all those days of practice for nothing. He blew out a long breath of air.

"Not what I signed up for," he said loud enough for everyone to hear.

I felt so sorry for him I couldn't even look at Joli as we left.

The next day Nikolo came out to the cliffs without Arek. I could tell he remained upset.

"Do you want me to try to talk to Joli about this? She and I have grown close with all our practices, yet she never brought this up. I'm not sure she's thinking clearly."

"No, don't," Nikolo said. "I got word from Ryalgar. She and Aliz have decided to go along with Joli's decision and they've asked me to go to Eds with them. Out of respect for *them*, I'll do so."

"That's too bad."

I started to say "be safe" when I realized it was a particularly insensitive comment under the circumstances.

"Stay vigilant," I said instead.

"Don't worry. I will."

I was glad to go back to the cottage on the cliffs and be away from Joli. Other lookouts had heard what happened, and they muttered sympathetic things to me about Nikolo, who they'd spent time with, and about Ryalgar, who'd impressed them during her brief visit while I napped at Gypsum's place.

Seven days before Kolada Joli and I had planned to practice but she sent word she couldn't make it. Then five days before Kolada, she canceled that practice as well. I guessed she was no more anxious to see me than I was to see her, but it didn't bode well for us working together.

Three days before Kolada I planned to leave to get in place with the others. I'd begun to gather my things when another messenger arrived at the door. He and his horse appeared exhausted from a hard ride.

Did Joli send word not to come? Surely she wouldn't sideline me as well. She needed me!

But no, this messenger came at the behest of another. Once he ascertained he'd located Olivine Renata Glonti, he moved his left hand down in front of his face to indicate he donned the mask of the person for whom he spoke.

"I, Bohdan Avtandil Ukleba of Scrud, humbly request that you make haste to the carver village for the purpose of becoming my wife. Urgent circumstances have arisen and only you can save me. Speed is vital. Please come now."

I stared at him dumbfounded as he moved his right hand upward in front of his face to indicate he now spoke as himself.

"That's all he said?"

"Yes madam. The Scrudite gentleman paid me the extra coins to rush and he appeared quite desperate, in my opinion, if that's what you're asking."

It wasn't but it helped nonetheless. Zoya stood with me so I asked her to tell Firuza, and Joli if necessary, that I'd been called away on a sudden emergency I didn't understand. I grabbed a few supplies and then I rode to Scrud as fast as I could.

The day was cold, clear, and still, so no dust obscured my vision. From far off I saw Bohdan in the road, a speck in the distance. Three Svadlu officers in saffron capes surrounded him. As I came closer I could make out Delia and Magomet near Delia's camp. Several others stood with them. Across the road I saw most of Bohdan's family. I couldn't imagine what sort of confrontation awaited me.

One of his sisters took my poor exhausted horse when I arrived, and Bohdan gave me a look of immense gratitude.

"Will you be my wife?"

I scanned the faces on both sides of the road for a clue. I found none.

"Is this a trick question?"

"No. I am sincere."

"Then yes, I will. But why now? Why here?"

"Because if I am the crown prince at noon today, I have been commanded to go with these Svadlu to be placed somewhere for safekeeping."

"Safekeeping? That's what one does with a ham."

I got a few chuckles.

One of the Svadlu spoke. "The council of Royals has decreed that each crown prince or recently crowned prince must accompany us into the forest to preserve the continuity of leadership in the realm. It *is* important, although not a single prince has been happy about it."

Then I got it.

"You want to marry me so you won't be a prince? Why not just abdicate?"

"He tried," his father said. "My son didn't realize we have no such thing in our canons. A man of Scrud does not abdicate."

"Please help me," Bohdan said. "I need to be out there with you."

"No, you don't. No offense but we have plenty of trained herders ready to fight. Your absence won't matter. Go with these guys and be safe and we can sort out this marriage thing later."

"You don't understand. The arrows. They work well because of how we made them but they will work better if I touch them and talk to them before you use them. I can make a difference, and it's one no one else can make."

I found this last claim a little dubious, but I saw two of the Svadlu look up at the sky. Noon approached. Bohdan and I didn't have time for a discussion of how a carver's magic worked.

"Who will you take if not Bohdan?" I asked one of the Svadlu.

"My nephew rode here haste, as you did," Bohdan's mother spoke. "He has no such role to play in our defense, and he will become our ruler and go with them if he must."

"That works for you?" I asked the Svadlu. They nodded.

I turned to Magomet and his friends.

"This effort to ensure the Chimera is at its most effective will not violate our agreement?"

"I said you were never to touch him," Magomet replied.

"I don't intend to touch him. I'm just going to marry him, and then I'm going to ride back to Vinx. Do you have a problem with that?"

He shrugged. "It's just words. Go ahead."

Bohdan's mother stepped forward, glancing up at the sun in the sky.

"None of us would choose such a way to do this but..."

She reached out to join our hands, then stopped when she saw Magomet's smirk.

"Reach your hands towards each other," she commanded. We did. "As of now, I declare the two of you bound, wife and husband, as long as you both are alive."

Bohdan exhaled.

"We can get this undone later," Magomet said.

"No, we can't," Bohdan replied. "A man of Scrud doesn't divorce." He smiled at me. "Should I have mentioned that sooner?"

I smiled back. "It's okay. I don't think it will matter."

I turned to Bohdan's family, searching for some of those flowery words that always eluded me. If ever there was a time to speak with eloquence, to reach out for acceptance, it was now. But before I could find the phrases I needed, his mother threw her arms around me.

"Welcome, artist daughter," she said. "We'll sort everything else out later."

"Thank you. Thank you all. I, uh, I hate to get married and rush off but I need to get back to the cliffs, gather my equipment, and ride to Bisu. I was supposed to be there by noon today."

"I don't think you can make it by nightfall," Bohdan said.

"Then I'll arrive first thing tomorrow. They'll understand."

I mounted my horse for a slower ride back. I didn't know what to say, so I just sort of waved at everyone. Most of them waved back, even the Svadlu and Delia. Only Magomet glared.

Then I turned and rode off, but at least this time I went in the right direction.

~ 25 ~

In a Fog

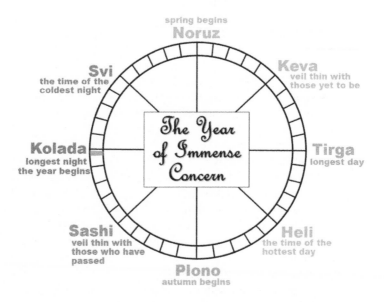

spring begins
Noruz

Svi
the time of the
coldest night

Keva
veil thin with
those yet to be

*The Year
of Immense
Concern*

Kolada
longest night
the year begins

Tirga
longest day

Sashi
veil thin with
those who have
passed

Heli
the time of the
hottest day

Plono
autumn begins

Firuza knew the schedule. When I arrived back at the cottage on the cliff around sunset, she understood I needed to spend the night. That meant tomorrow, two days before Kolada, I'd be a day late getting into position.

"I hope whatever it is you did today warranted this," she said. Her brow wrinkled with concern.

I wanted to tell someone. Anyone would do, but Firuza would do better than most.

"It did. I got married today."

That earned a short laugh. "Well then. Congratulations. But tomorrow at first light, you best get your gear out to Bisu. I'm sure they're worried."

I knew they were. I got little sleep and when I woke we had another problem.

In the late dawn of winter, all the other long eyes stood out on the cliff's edge staring at the pink mist along the horizon. Firuza studied the southeast through the device she called her moon glass.

"You're right. It's them," she said. "Raise the red square flag. The horde *has* been sighted in the distance."

With that new urgency, I bid Zoya and the others farewell and rode to the meeting spot in Bisu with all the speed I could coax out of my still-tired mare.

As I arrived, Sulphur, Joli, and Issa addressed the large crowd using one of Ryalgar's big wooden cones to amplify their voices. Many of our herders-turned-fighters looked like they'd camped here for days, awaiting news. Surely Bohdan would arrive soon, and he'd be as late as I was.

"What is the stupidest thing any one of you could do?" Sulphur shouted to the crowd. She ignored their many creative answers. "Fight with each other," she yelled. "I don't care how scared you are, or how *right* you are. Just for today, do not fight with your neighbor. About anything. At all. If you want to live."

I saw Joli standing next to her and our eyes met. Although a bit of defiance remained in Joli's face, her eyes pleaded with mine for understanding.

Very well. My sister's words were meant for all, but they struck an important chord with me. I'd do my best to put aside my anger with Joli so we could become the dangerous duo we'd trained to be.

"Two days from now, you'll have the luxury of caring about something other than your immediate survival. Do? You? Understand?" Sulphur finished her speech to yells of agreement.

I saw her scan the faces and as she looked in my direction I waved at her from the edge of the crowd. She pushed her way towards me.

"Where've you been? Joli is so worried."

"It's a long story, but I'm fine and here."

"Varmin shame about Ryalgar being sent off to Eds. I don't understand it. Are you and Joli going to be able to do what you need to?" she asked

"Of course we will. Sulphur?" Of the hundred things I wanted to say to her, only one came out of my mouth. "Good luck."

"Yeah. You too. See you when this is over?"

"Right. We'll drink wine together then."

Next, I walked over to Joli, because I knew I had to.

"We need to put this aside," I said.

"I honestly did what I thought was best," she said at the same time.

We stopped and looked at each other.

"I don't think we should talk about it," I said.

"We *have* to talk about this," she said at the same time.

Then we both laughed.

"Okay. Say what you need to," I offered.

"Look. I know everyone is mad at me, and I don't blame them. It's almost why I didn't send your sister to Eds. Then, I don't know, I talked it through with other Velka leaders. They counseled me not to worry about hurt feelings but to do what I thought was right."

I saw her point but the decision bothered me. "What leaders did you talk to? Obviously not Ryalgar or my grandmother."

"No. There's this woman Hana ..."

"Oh, I've heard of her ..."

"Look, I know she's not fond of Ryalgar," Joli said, "but they put her in charge of part of the Chimera, so they must trust her. Anyway, Hana and her friend, a singer named Ura, they had a long talk with me about handling responsibility, and I decided they were right."

"Ura?" I'd met a lot of singers working with Celestine and I'd never heard of an Ura.

"Yeah. Young singer, from Pilk. Nice girl."

I knew what nagged at me. "I don't think Ura is a singer. Could she be a luski?"

"No... that's absurd. No Velka would influence another using a luski." Joli sounded sincere but her face told me she considered the possibility.

"Would you have sent Ryalgar and Aliz to Eds without that conversation?

"Maybe not. But I think sending them *was* the right to do."

Well even if it wasn't, there was no fixing it now.

"Okay then," I said. "Let's move on to doing the right thing here."

Joli and I walked far enough away to leave the stench of unwashed bodies and half-spoiled food behind and found a spot where we could practice in safety. We worked to regain the symbiosis we'd once had. It didn't take long. Our combined sense of urgency got us there.

"Let's not wear out your eyes or your arm," she said before much time passed. "I think you need rest more than practice."

"Does what you do tire you out too?" She'd never mentioned it if it did.

"Absolutely. It takes a lot of concentration." She laughed. "Okay, I admit it, I could use the rest too. Plus, while your sister Sulphur is doing a fine job of keeping this crowd calm, I suspect she could use my help."

"Then I'm going to wander around and say hi to people I know."

"There's room for you at the house I share with Sulphur and the other Svadlu. Want to join us there tonight?"

"Maybe. But if I'm not there, don't worry. I could, uh, have accommodations elsewhere. If so, I'll see you at the house right after I wake up."

"Suit yourself. We get in position in the morning." She looked worried.

"I'll be there. I promise."

As soon as Joli turned to go, I made my way towards the various ragtag camps of herders from Bisu and Scrud. These men and women were grouped into teams of six and had trained for half a year so they could capture one warrior per group. Bohdan wasn't on such a team. Rather, he and others more adept at fighting formed a group of rovers tasked with entering any skirmish that went poorly.

I wondered if he'd be with the Scrudite teams or hanging out with these more elite fighters. I checked both places and didn't find him in either so I returned to the Scrudites' camping area, concerned. Several assured me they'd seen him today. He was here, but they didn't know where.

"Hey, aren't you the lady he just married?" one asked.

"Yeah," another said. "He did it yesterday so he wouldn't have to go hide with the other princes."

"That's me." I studied their faces for traces of resentment and saw none.

"Glad you could help him out," one said.

"Uh, I'm more than a helpful stranger. He and I, we love each other."

"Oh, everyone knows that," the other said. "But good thing you got there in time. He had to be able to get over here to tend to those arrows."

The arrows. Of course. *That's* where Bohdan was. Talking to the arrows, giving them his final instructions or something. I took off to find Joli to learn the location of the arrows.

Two Svadlu stood guard as various Velka added the poison tips which would knock out but not kill horses. This potential horse-saving had been wildly popular with most Ilarians. We needed healthy horses and people hated the idea of animal carcasses strewn around our grazing lands. However, some felt we'd unnecessarily complicated things. War should be straightforward. Kill all you can.

Bohdan sat in the middle of the piles of arrows, picking up each one as a Velka finished it. He studied it, then stroked it and murmured to it, then he added it to another pile. To one of four piles, to be precise. I knew one of those four piles was meant for me.

The Velka seemed undisturbed by his presence and his behavior. I watched until he noticed me.

"Some say this last step is unnecessary," he said, "and we didn't get to do it with Nikolo's arrows. But I've always found the wood does better if it gets encouragement after it's altered like this. Adding something like a poison tip can confuse it a little."

"This is why you wanted to be here today." It wasn't a question. Watching him, I understood.

One of the guards spoke up.

"I'm sorry, madam, but we've been told not to allow anyone here who isn't him or a Velka. These arrows are precious and irreplaceable."

One of the Velka laughed. "Do you know who this woman is?"

The guard shook her head.

"She's one of the four long eyed archers who will use these. This pile on my right is for her."

"She's also Ryalgar's sister," another said.

"And," Bohdan added "she's also my wife." He grinned at me and I grinned back. Two of the Velka raised their eyebrows but they all kept working.

"When you're done here, can we talk?" I asked him

He nodded. "This will take some time. I have a tent set up with the other roving fighters. They asked me to camp with them so we could talk tonight. Go on over; they'll show you to my spot. You can rest there."

I could feel how little I'd slept last night and how hard I'd ridden during the past two days.

"I'd like that."

"May I come in?"

The early dusk of Kolada had come and I'd dozed off in the wool blankets lining the floor of Bohdan's tent.

He entered without waiting for an answer. "Have you had supper?"

"Yes, your campmates offered me some. They're very kind. They ... they don't seem to mind your being a Scrudite."

He laughed. "We've trained often as a group. Perhaps the idea of dying brings people together."

"Perhaps. I don't think my parents would have been as understanding about you without the worry that they were saying farewell to me for the last time."

"And I suspect I'd have faced more resistance about my decision from the people of Scrud under normal circumstances, too. You and I – we were just lucky enough to fall in love while facing annihilation together, huh?"

"Not funny. But maybe true."

He sat down next to me and scooted closer.

"There is no way your Magomet has eyes on us, is there?"

"I can't imagine how, but if he does, I don't care." Bohdan's smell had overtaken me. I intended to enjoy this last night with him in ways I'd been kept from for far too long. "His threats no longer matter. There isn't enough time left for him to do anything."

"Do you know if the Sage Coalition persuaded the Royals to surrender if we fail?"

"No. I never heard. I'm not thinking about us failing."

"Me neither." He'd started to kiss my neck. Any further conversation could wait.

Once we removed enough clothes to enjoy the feel of each other's skin, he stopped.

"What's wrong."

"We're married!"

"Yes? Married people have sex, too, you know. It's okay."

"You bet it is."

It was the last thing he said for quite a while.

When the morning light woke me, I lay alone in the tent. Even huddled under the blankets I felt the cold. I pulled back the tent flap. The fog had moved in.

I took care of my personal needs and accepted a cup of gruel from one of the fighters. He told me scouts had confirmed the horde would arrive at our border by mid-day. Those of us who had to be well hidden needed to get into place soon.

I noticed everyone helped each other, with no need for please or thank you. Most people barely spoke.

A tall man tapped me on the shoulder and pointed. I nodded my understanding. He indicated where Bohdan had gone, so I could say goodbye to him.

My new husband and I exchanged a long silent hug.

"I'll find you when this is over," he promised. "We'll solve all of our problems then."

I nodded, numb. Then I hurried off to find Joli and the two guides assigned to accompany us, carry our supplies and bring back our horses.

In near silence, the four of us headed to the spot they'd prepared for us, a place tucked back against the rugged cliffs of Vinx. Our location gave us a slight height advantage and faced us towards the entrance to the realm. Tomorrow morning, our southeast orientation would enable me to use the first glimmers of light from the winter dawn.

The fog thickened as we rode. I knew I should be glad; it not only hid us but would slow the attackers down and keep my homeland moist and difficult to burn. But it also made it hard for us to find our way. If our guides hadn't been well versed in finding this spot, I'm afraid Joli and I would have wandered around all day seeking it.

Workers had designed our shelter to protect us from the wind and drizzle as we hid. The guides reverently placed the arrows in the deepest part of the hollow that concealed us.

Fifty. I was to wound fifty sleeping horses if I could. I'd been given a hundred magic poisoned arrows with which to do it. Joli looked down at the pile. Then up at me.

"We can do this," she said.

"Of course we can."

But first we had to sit there, silent and still, through the rest of one long, cold, damp day. By late morning I knew the hardest part of the battle wouldn't be the fight, it would be the wait.

~ 26 ~

Shooting the Arrows

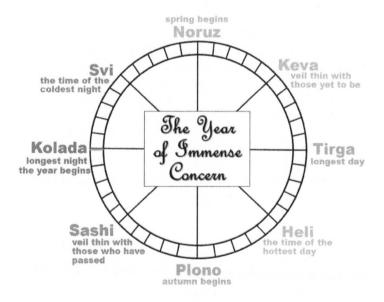

spring begins
Noruz

Keva
veil thin with
those yet to be

Svi
the time of the
coldest night

Kolada
longest night
the year begins

*The Year
of Immense
Concern*

Tirga
longest day

Sashi
veil thin with
those who have
passed

Heli
the time of the
hottest day

Plono
autumn begins

By noon we could hear them. The ground trembled from their horses' hooves, and soon their voices carried across the open grassland. They talked more as the fog grew thicker and they sounded confused. Then angry. I knew the fence that marked our border had been removed. Perhaps they were baffled they hadn't reached it.

Then much of the noise of hoofs stopped. Had they found the first clumps of the lush grass to the southeast of us? Some voices coaxed on the horses, while others argued. The dispute intensified, went on for a while, then it stopped.

The next sounds we heard were those of clanging pots. They were setting up camp. I blew out a sigh of relief as Joli and I exchanged silent gestures of joy. This camping for the night was crucial. Without it, we could do little more than listen as the horde rode by.

I tried to use the sounds to figure out the distance of the nearest the camps and how close to each camp the horses were kept. Perhaps this information would be useful in the morning. Perhaps not.

Tones turned more jovial as darkness edged out the hazy light and I knew Joli and I were safe for now. No one was inclined to look for an unseen enemy in the foggy dark.

She and I agreed to take turns sleeping, to ensure we'd be awake when the time came to do what had to be done. She insisted I rest first, promising to call me once she became drowsy.

I sat on the ground, my back against the damp earth with my knees up against my chest. I pulled our blankets over me, put my head on my knees, and tried to rest. I must have fallen asleep for longer than I expected because when Joli tapped me on the shoulder to wake me, stars sparkled in the black sky.

I nodded and gave her the blankets in silence. Once she settled into the spot for sitting, I listened to the sound of distant snoring as I studied the night sky and tried not to think about the morning.

It felt as if two days had passed and yet morning still hadn't come. I shook my left leg ten times. Then my right. I did the same with my left arm. Then my right. I blew out ten breaths as hard as I could. I rolled my head in a circle ten times one way and ten times the other.

Then I did it again. Anything to stay awake. Anything to stay warm.

Finally, I saw it. The faintest bit of light in the southeast. I shook Joli awake.

"You're crazy. It's still pitch black. Let me sleep," she whispered.

"No. It's not. I can see light even if you can't. Now is when we strike, before the Mongols even know dawn comes.

"You can't see horses in this."

I squinted out over the grass, as shapes came into focus. Grey, everything was grey, but they were there.

"I see them. It's time. Now."

"What if the others don't start?"

"It doesn't matter. The sooner anyone of us begins the better. Facing this direction, we have to be done before the sun gets near the horizon. Or before they wake up and discover what is happening. Whichever comes first."

Joli stood and sighed, accepting that I couldn't be reasoned with.

"I don't see the Mongol horde as a bunch of late sleepers. So if you can see, we start." She picked up one of the arrows and touched it with reverence. "I'll push, and we'll hope these little pruckers are smarter than they look."

I steadied myself and picked up my bow. It had spent the night next to me, ready to use. Joli handed me the first arrow. I stepped out on the small ledge the construction group had prepared for me and I tapped my foot up and down, relieved to feel the ground firm under my feet.

I nocked the arrow, then placed the butt of my left hand against the grip of the bow and curled the upper knuckles of my right hand around the string. I raised the bow as I raised my right elbow. My draw was slow and careful, using the firmness of my arms, the solidity of my bones, to keep the bow taut. My muscles would have enough other work to do.

Without thought, my right hand rested on my chin. The string rested against my nose. My shoulder blades pulled together as I aimed at the nearest grey shape of an animal. It was nearly four hundred paces away, far outside of my range without Joli or without Bohdan's magic. With both of them, though, this horse should be easy pickings. I might as well start with a sure thing.

When Joli and I first worked together, at this point I'd say "push" even though the act of speaking distracted me. Now, I no longer need to say it. She'd seen me do this hundreds of times; she knew what to do when.

The arrow flew, fast and strong, into the gloom until even I could no longer see it. I waited, watching and listening.

"Did you hit it?" she whispered.

"I guess. I didn't hear anything. It's too far away to hear."

"Did the horse react?"

"No, but it's sleeping."

We hadn't given a lot of thought to this. I assumed I'd be able to follow the arrow and see it hit, which I could do in more light. But not yet.

I also assumed the horse would react somehow. I don't know. Twitch. But this one hadn't shifted at all.

"I can't believe I'd miss a target that big, especially one holding still. But I might have. It didn't react at all."

"Well, shoot another arrow at it."

"We can't afford to waste them."

"Just one. You have to at least be able to hit the closest horses, right?"

"Right. Let's do it again."

I repeated the process. Nock the arrow, pull back the bowstring, aim, and shoot. This arrow flew as well as the other. Again, the horse didn't budge.

"Maybe it's dead already," Joli said.

"What? You think it picked tonight to die in its sleep?" My whispers were getting louder.

"Maybe the group next to us started sooner and they got this clump already."

Scump. This was a problem we hadn't considered. At group practices, we'd known exactly where each other stood and what each one of us shot at.

I squinted into the gloom. "Our closest shooter is to our left. There's another group of horses to our right. Maybe we should start on them."

"I think you should pick another horse in this closer clump first. I mean, maybe you hit the first one twice and he's just a sound sleeper. If you did, he's doubly poisoned now. That means he's dead, right?"

"Yeah. If I keep shooting them twice I'll kill them all."

"And if you keep missing them twice, we'll run out of arrows."

I glared at her.

"I'll try another."

I nocked, I pulled, I aimed, I shot. The light had improved a little and this time I focused harder on the result. The horse gave the slightest of shudders when the arrow hit.

"I got this one. I probably got the first as well. Let's keep going."

Joli said nothing as she handed me another arrow.

I looked at the clump and realized I had a second problem I hadn't considered. In this dim light, at this distance, the horses all looked identical.

"I'm going to have trouble remembering which ones I've hit."

"Start on one side and work your way over?"

"Yeah. Some of them are blocking others though so I'll never get them all. Once they figure out which horses look dead, it's going to be obvious where the shots came from."

"Except we're much further away than they think. And we'll be much better hidden by the time they come looking."

I felt shaky and appreciated the calm Joli exuded. I wondered if she was that calm inside.

"Can you count for me? How may I've hit?"

"Sure, but why does it matter? I thought everybody agreed we'd use all the arrows we could until either daylight or camp activity forced us to stop."

"I don't know. It matters to me."

She smiled and handed me a fourth arrow. "Horse number three," she said.

After eight horses, I'd hit every one I had a clear shot at in the small nearby clump. The sky now held a trace of dark blue in the southeast that would allow anyone to know dawn came.

"We need to go faster."

I turned to the clump of animals sleeping to my right. It was larger and better distributed for my vantage point. I could get more of them.

Joli handed me the next arrow. Nock. Pull bowstring. Aim and shoot. Nock. Pull bowstring. Aim and shoot.

After seventeen more horses, I'd done all I could with this group.

The increasing light allowed my eyes to work better. A bigger group of horses slept in the distance, off to our left. Was the archer to my left shooting at this group already? I knew the older man from Kir hid in that direction. He was a terrific shot with great stamina, but he had the worst eyesight of the five of us. I didn't think he'd go for something so far away, at least not in the dimmest light.

"Can we get to that group?" I asked Joli.

"It's pushing it," she said. "But that's got to be over a hundred of them, and we've got a better shot at them than anyone. Let's try."

She handed me an arrow. Scump. My arm had tired already. Why? I'd taken many more shots than this in practice. Maybe the uncomfortable half-night's sleep and the cold had combined to erode my stamina.

Then I realized I'd been skipping something. From the beginning, I'd been taught to take a deep breath and relax right before I fired a shot. It had become such a habit that I no longer thought about it.

But I was fairly sure I hadn't taken a deep breath since I started.

I *had* to be able to get at least twenty-five more horses subdued. I needed to relax before I released every arrow.

Joli handed me my next one. "Horse twenty-six."

And that's when the gusts of wind picked up from the southwest.

"Pruck," she whispered. "Wind is the one thing I can't adjust for because I can't see my target. What do we do now?"

Fatigue had introduced a certain calm into my demeanor.

"You don't have to see. You only need to will it to go. I'll keep an eye on the destination, and we'll trust Bohdan's conjuring to do the rest."

She gave me a dubious look.

"I'm getting tired," she said.

"I'm sure you are. I'm exhausted. But we're not quitting now, are we?"

"No. We're not."

After that, I stopped thinking. Joli stopped counting. I confess, I even stopped working so hard to make sure I didn't shoot the same horse twice. I just aimed, relaxed, and shot. Aimed, relaxed, and shot. Aimed, relaxed, and shot.

I'm guessing I fired at another fifty of them, but who knows. The wind came and went. Joli did better on some shots than others. Sometimes the horse reacted and sometimes it didn't. A few times my body spasmed as I shot, throwing the arrow off so bad it didn't come close. Maybe I hit thirty of them, but at least I got another twenty-five, making the quota we'd planned for.

My arm felt on fire. I turned to Joli to ask if we could stop for a few breaths and I saw tears of exhaustion running down her face.

We're done," I said.

"Yeah," she replied. "Shh. Listen."

I heard the pots clanging. Joli was right. They'd woken, even though the sun lay below the horizon.

I saw a few of them walk towards the horses and I sucked in my breath. We had to hide.

Then I heard one of the horses give a happy whinny to greet the human it liked best, and I remembered that even if two hundred horses couldn't respond, eight hundred of them were fine and those eight hundred were closer to the camps. It would take time for them to discover the damage we'd done. Time we needed.

"Let's get out of here," Joli said.

Although we'd been told about our escape options several times, our guides had left us a cloth with a hand-painted map showing them in relation to the perch we'd shot from. Good thing. I barely remembered my name much less where Joli and I were supposed to go.

She studied the cloth. "Here. This one is the best. A little cave further up the cliff with plenty of shrubs to hide us on the way. I'll bring the arrows. Can you carry your bow?"

I nodded.

"Good. Let's get there before all Heli breaks loose in that camp, and they come looking for us. We have no idea how an army from a place we can't imagine will react when they discover what we've done."

~ 27 ~

Something Else As Well

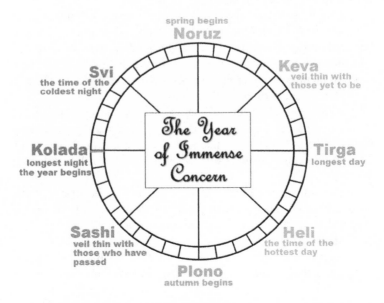

spring begins
Noruz

Svi
the time of the
coldest night

Keva
veil thin with
those yet to be

The Year
of Immense
Concern

Kolada
longest night
the year begins

Tirga
longest day

Sashi
veil thin with
those who have
passed

Heli
the time of the
hottest day

Plono
autumn begins

The waking Mongols tended to their breakfast and personal needs just as an army of Ilarians would.

So different and yet so alike.

I forced my mind to focus on my feet. I couldn't afford to stumble as I followed Joli to the small cave. We kept low. I'd already see many of the invaders looking up at the cliffs. How different would it have been if they'd had long eyes of their own, or even one of Firuza's moon glasses to scan the irregular rock face of these bluffs?

I knew the other long eyes and oomrushers hid as we did. Our enemy showed no signs of noticing of us, but they weren't looking for us. They merely looked around with no reason to be suspicious. Not yet.

The sun peeked over the southeast horizon as we reached the cave. Joli crawled in first then I hid in its mouth so I could serve as our lookout. The rising sun shone so brightly in the cold crisp air that I had to avert my eyes.

One man below who wandered off from his camp to check on his horse gave a loud call of distress. Others ran to him. Once their shouts rang out, men from various smaller camps went to check on their horses. Several picked our arrows up off the ground and waved them in the air for the others to see. Soon their gestures indicated they had figured out that the horses closest to the cliffs had been struck by archers in the night. Several examined the arrows' tips. I felt sure they determined that the animals had been poisoned as well.

The men tried to revive their horses. I had no idea how many slept and how many were dead, but the poison had caused many of the poor creatures to vomit or defecate, discouraging close examination.

The wails that came from the invaders told me these horses had been loved. Perhaps sparing the animals' lives was as wise as Ryalgar thought.

Then the wailing stopped and an ominous silence followed. A thousand angry men turned towards the Cliffs of Vinx and stared. As one, they began walking towards us, moving about two arms length from each other, each inspecting the ground in front of them. Their expressions were clear. The killers of their beloved animals would be found and would die.

I barely breathed as the wall of men covered the first hundred paces, moving quickly at first because they expected the culprits to be two or three hundred paces away. They flowed like water around the small clumps of bushes and the occasional scraggly tree. They moved further from each other as they walked, instinctively expanding their search. Would they stop once they'd come further than any normal arrow would go? If they didn't, they'd find us all hidden in the lower parts of the cliffs.

At about three hundred paces, they paused and discussion ensued. A few of the men had moved towards the middle, and they shouted instructions to the others. The ones in charge. Every army had them.

A large bald man argued with a younger, wiry one who wore his shiny black hair in two short ponytails on top of his head. Big and Bald kept pointing to the top of the cliffs which were at least as tall as twenty stacked men at this place. He thought we'd shot from up there? Perhaps the height advantage would have made that possible.

Two Ponytails shook his head and pointed to the scraggly vegetation between him and the cliffs. He was sure we were hidden down here somewhere. He won the argument. The horde continued to move towards us.

Joli whispered to me that she was going to crawl back and see how far the cave went. I sent my bow and arrows with her, to be tucked into the furthest corner. Possibly we could convince the Mongols we were only scared farm women, hiding in a cave. Perhaps they'd spare our lives.

Then several of them shouted as a man rode his horse out from behind one of the larger groups of bushes off to the right where the marsh lay. His clothing made it clear to me he was a Scrudite, and he held a bow in one hand and quiver of arrows in the other. He stretched both arms out in a universal sign of surrender.

I thought Bohdan was doing something incredibly stupid to save my life and I was furious. But Bohdan was nowhere near here. He and the other trained fighters were secured a distance away, having been given horses to ride in on once most of the horde moved on.

I looked closer. Yes, the man resembled Bohdan, and I'd made this mistake once before. He stooped a bit and had grey in his hair. Bohdan's father had no experience as an archer and no reason to be here. What did he hope to accomplish?

He pointed to their dead horses in the distance and gave an exaggerated nod. *Yes, I did it.*

He dropped his bow and arrows to the ground and slowly dismounted. They watched him and a few of the nearest drew knives and held them ready. He knelt on the ground before them. A universal plea for mercy.

I figured they'd kill him right away, but Big and Bald held up the palm of his hand and barked something at the men with knives.

I jumped at the sound of Joli's whisper in my ear. "The cave doesn't go back far at all," she said.

"I don't think it matters. Look," I whispered as I made room for her at the entrance.

"Who the pruck is that?" she asked.

"Not one of our archers. It'd Bohdan's father, and I can't imagine what he thinks he's doing."

She chuckled in my ear.

"My guess? He thinks he's saving the life of the woman his son loves."

"That's ridiculous. The man hates me."

"Possibly, but I'd say he loves his son more. Could Bohdan have told him how all this was supposed to work?"

"Of course. He probably did."

"Then I think dad here decided to be a contingency plan if the Mongols got too close to finding you. It looks like it's working."

"Heli, they're going to kill him."

But Big and Bald continued to order back the men with knives. Others produced rope and secured Bohdan's dad, gesturing for him to walk back to the camp.

"That's surprising," Joli said.

"Not really. If he *had* shot the horses, he'd have managed it from over four hundred paces. Ryalgar said anytime the Mongols find someone who impresses them, they don't kill them. They study them."

"You mean they're capturing this man because they want to figure out how he can shoot so far?"

"I think so, yes."

"This could be a problem for him."

"I know. Let's hope they save the questioning for later."

As a group of underlings started escorting Bohdan's dad back to the camp, Big and Bald resumed his discussion with Two Ponytails.

He pointed to the top of the cliffs, gesturing with emphasis. I took it to mean *we need to get up there.* But Two Ponytails worried there was more to the problem. He waved at the number of horses who had been hit. He gestured towards the camp. I'd heard Sulphur had taken great pains to have large rocks and big logs placed where she hoped the Mongols would stop. It had largely worked. Even in the fog, people had tended to camp where nature provided places to sit.

Two Ponytails jabbed his index finger at the convenient seats, and then at the tuffs of rich grass the remaining horses chomped on as the men spoke. I got what he meant. This was all a little too convenient. Two Ponytails wanted to get the Heli out of Ilari.

If it meant leaving and never coming back, I'd have been all for it. But I understood that wouldn't be the case. We'd face this threat again, and next time they'd be smarter and more prepared for our tricks. Ilari's best hope lay in Big and Bald winning this argument.

He appeared to be succeeding when two people on horses rode out from behind an abandoned old stone barn off to my left, along the path leading to Scrud and up into Vinx.

"What is this? Prucking Parade Day?" Joli muttered.

I stared and brought the two unexpected visitors into focus. It was a man and a woman, riding together. I thought the slightly-built female in the back was Delia. I knew the large male in front was Magomet.

"It's the absolute last person on earth I'd want here."

"Oh, him. You never described him as terribly courageous. What's he doing out here."

Big and Bald and Two Ponytails must have wondered the same thing because they stopped their discussion and stared. Magomet and Delia slowed their horse and held their arms out, palms up, signaling they meant no harm. I noticed many Mongols had walked back to camp, and now most of them rode out armed with their bows. Several nocked their arrows and aimed at the two on horseback.

Big and Bald held up his hand once again. *Wait. Let's see what they want.*

Magomet and Delia trotted forward, encouraged by the fact that no one had shot at them yet. Once they got within talking range, Magomet bellowed out the information he'd come to convey.

I heard him loud and clear.

"This is a trap! Get out! We Ilarians will take care of our own fools here who think they can outsmart you. Come back another day and you will find the tribute awaiting you!"

Joli stared in horror.

I laughed out loud.

Big and Bald and Two Ponytails both shrugged while most of their men looked confused.

"Magomet thinks the Mongols understand Ilarian," I said. "He has no way of conveying such a complicated message. What is he thinking? And why is he doing this?"

"The last one's easy to guess. He wants to save his people instead of you."

"Maybe he thinks what he's doing is best for the realm ..."

"Maybe," she agreed "but I don't think this guy rides out in front of an army just to do what's right. He's trying to get even with you. That's what drives him."

"Good thing he's got no way of succeeding."

Magomet and Delia had almost reached Big and Bald when the Mongol leader turned to a man behind him and gave some kind of instruction. The man nodded and took off running back to the camp.

"Where's he going?"

"Scump," Joli said. "I bet they sent him to get the translator."

"What translator? No one speaks Ilarian."

"Come on, plenty of traders and travelers have learned some. I heard the Mongol envoys who delivered the ultimatum at Noruz had a translator with them. If you were going to attack us, wouldn't you bring that guy along? Of course you would."

Now we had a problem.

"We've got to stop Magomet," I said to Joli, but she was gone. "Where'd you go?"

"To get your bow," she called from the back of the cave. "And those thin poison arrows with the weird tips. The ones they gave you to use on any Mongol fighter that our cow herders couldn't subdue."

My heart sank. I knew she was right.

"I need to shoot Magomet, don't I?"

"You may have to shoot both of your friends. That or the translator, but then we have to hope they don't have another one. Or we can hope the translator doesn't understand what Magomet says. Are you willing to bet the realm on any of those?"

I wasn't. "The Scrudites designed these arrows not to kill. The Velka made the tips with that in mind. And Bohdan somehow gave them special instructions. Right?"

"That's my understanding."

"Okay then."

One Mongolian fighter on horseback trotted out of the camp towards his army. Behind him sat a man who looked different. Dressed differently. Wasn't a fighter. Joli had to be right.

The wind had quieted. My right arm hurt, but it had rested enough that I could raise it. I hadn't practiced much with these arrows, but Magomet was less than three hundred paces from me and I had a clear shot.

Nock the arrow. Place the butt of the left hand on the grip. Curl the top right knuckles around the bowstring. Raise the bow. Raise the right elbow.

I hesitated.

What if the Velka had calculated the dosage wrong? I couldn't kill Jasia's son, no matter what he'd done.

Draw the bowstring back. Hold the tension with my bones, not my muscles.

The translator dismounted and he said something to Magomet.

I anchored my right thumb against my chin. The bowstring found its familiar spot against my nose.

I couldn't do anything about the dosage now. I had to operate with what I knew.

I drew my shoulder blades together. I exhaled and relaxed.

Of course there was something I could do. I could not shoot.

Magomet opened his mouth to speak and I fired the arrow.

Joli helped. It flew fast and true and hit him on the side of his upper arm before he'd said more than a word or two. It barely pierced his skin, as planned, and he pulled it out himself and looked at it in puzzlement. Then he doubled over, as a thousand faces turned towards the cliffs looking for the source of the arrow.

We stepped back into the cave, barely breathing.

After a few heartbeats, I peeked outside. Magomet was on all fours, vomiting but conscious. Hadn't the Velka said that dosage was a function of size? Weren't these arrows calculated for the average man?

If so, my problem was the opposite of what I'd worried about. The oversized man retching on the ground below was too large for the poison to put him to sleep.

"He needs a second dose," Joli said.

"I can't do that. It could be too much."

"As soon as he stops throwing up, he's going to start talking."

I didn't reply but I knew she was right. I took the second arrow she handed me. Nock. Move hands into position. Draw bowstring. No hesitation. Aim at Magomet on all fours. Exhale. Shoot.

As I shot, Two Ponytails stepped forward with a flask of something, to offer Magomet a drink. A simple courtesy, but as he did so, he put himself in the direct path of my arrow. Would the arrow know it was meant for Magomet and alter its path? Or would it hit the stranger? What had Bohdan told it? I had no idea.

It flew true, and it hit Two Ponytails in the back of his upper leg. He turned around in alarm, pulled the arrow out, and stared at it before he crumpled forward, unconscious.

Big and Bald turned to face me and howled a scream of anger like nothing I'd ever heard. My first thought was that the thousand of them would resume their march to the cliffs, and nothing would deter them from finding me and Joli and killing us in the worst way they could think of. They'd find the others too and all would be lost. I'd prucked up everything, and there was nothing I could do to remedy it.

But as I watched, I saw I'd misunderstood the target of his fury. This leader wasn't just angry at me, the archer he didn't know and couldn't see. No, he was furious with all of Ilari, the realm he thought had now killed his second in command. I knew this because he gestured wildly around him, as though cursing this entire place. Then he motioned to his men.

Mount your horses. We ride on. Let's go beat the living scump out of these people.

The men mounted and pointed their horses towards the road up to Scrud, towards the road leading ultimately to Pilk. Those with no horses yelled questions. Answers came. They were easy to figure out.

Stay put. We'll be back to get you, and it won't take long. We've had it with these people.

Big and Bald rode by Magomet, who struggled to get out words to warn him, but this leader was too angry to care about anything Magomet had to say.

I scanned the landscape, counting. We'd hoped to have two hundred horseless riders left behind. How many did we have? I couldn't say for sure, but two hundred was a close guess.

I crumpled into a seat on the ground as I watched most of the horde ride on.

We'd done it. We'd done a wonderful thing. A smaller army, one of only eight hundred, rode to Vinx where the Lion waited to reduce them further.

But we'd done something else as well. We'd sent the Lion eight hundred invaders who were far more pissed now than they'd been when they arrived.

Would it matter?

~ 28 ~

Instead of Saying Happy Kolada

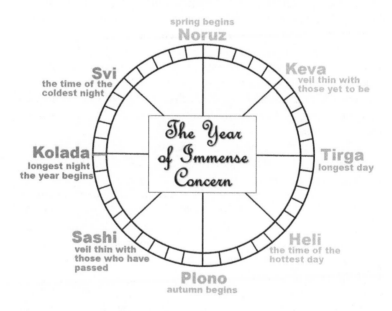

We watched the horde ride on towards Vinx, fearing for those they'd encounter next. I'd never seen humans as intimidating as these eight hundred mounted fighters riding to avenge the loss of one of their own. Joli and I sighed with relief as they disappeared into the distance.

Then we looked closer at the men they'd left behind.

Two hundred scared, angry men scattered across the grasslands looked around for something useful to do. I knew Sulphur planned to bring her people out once those left behind relaxed. She hoped our herders could catch them unawares.

Thanks to the appearance of Bohdan's father, and then Magomet and Delia, these men had no intention of relaxing. Who else lurked in the bushes and hid behind distant buildings? They were restless and suspicious. If they started wandering off and exploring, they'd uncover those we'd carefully concealed.

Had Sulphur and her friend Issa monitored the events of the morning? They must have, for as I fretted, an entire clump of bushes on the side towards The Canyon River rose high into the air. The Mongols stared in disbelief.

Then the shrubs fell to the side as tens of unarmed, mud-covered people crawled up out of some underground shelter Ilarians had dug. Tired and miserable-looking, they held their hands out in apparent surrender as they walked toward the Mongols.

After the first two surprises, the invaders didn't reach immediately for their weapons. I suppose they expected these people were more locals begging for mercy. As the mix of men and women, old and young, both physically fit and less so came towards them, blinking in the bright sunlight, I doubted the invaders saw them as a threat.

Several of them, mostly women, carried heavy bags slung over their shoulders. It looked as though they held their families' most precious possessions, brought along as they fled.

Another similar group poured out of the little abandoned stone building Magomet and Delia had hidden behind. They must have been concealed underground as well, given so many people could never have fit inside. The fifty or so of them began to cover the ground on foot, again unarmed, with dazed and frightened faces and their hands outstretched.

After a third such group rose out of the ground, and then a fourth, the Ilarians numbered as many as the Mongols and our invaders looked more alarmed. A few of them pulled out knives and several picked up their bows.

Joli and I watched in silence. She held the special arrows, the ones designed to tranquilize a human. She'd hand them to me if I saw the need to begin shooting.

When the first group of fifty made it within throwing distance of the closest invaders, they stopped. I turned my long eyes upon them, scanning their faces. I saw real fear, even terror, in their eyes. Not one of these people had ever done anything like what they were about to do. Who would begin? Would anyone?

A young girl on the outskirts stood up straighter. She reached into her bag, as though checking on something, but her hand emerged with a rock in her palm. No one else noticed. Her arm stretched back and the rock flew hard into the stomach of the nearest invader. He doubled over with shock on his face.

I recognized her team members because the five of them moved immediately while the rest stayed still. Half a year of repetition overcame their fears. Without thought, they performed the simple choreography they'd practiced hundreds of times. More rocks flew at the man from his other side, then two nimble youngsters dove for his legs. A large woman pushed him forward from behind and sat on his back while a man pulled a rope from inside his jacket and secured him.

Once the first team acted, motion became as contagious as the immobilizing fear had been. The initial rock throwers picked their targets. Almost without exception, the rest of the group responded with the same precision as the first.

By now about six hundred Ilarians had emerged from a dozen constructed hiding places and the Mongols knew varmin well they had a problem. Those off to the side, not yet under immediate threat of capture, did what we expected and what we would have done. They grabbed their bows and their swords and prepared to put a stop to this nonsense.

This was where we'd lose lives. We'd known that all along.

It fell upon me and my fellow long eyes to keep that loss to a minimum. I stepped fully out of the cave, knowing I stood outside the range of their archers and that they lacked the recourses to seek me out now. I took an arrow from Joli and took down the archer of theirs most poised to shoot. Then the next one. And the next.

I saw others fall, knowing my fellow long eyes – Arek, the history teacher from Pilk, and the big older man from Kir – were doing their part too. But it wasn't enough.

The crowd of Ilarians had grown, and many of the Mongols had been captured. Yet fifty others had grabbed swords and bows and now fought for their lives. They fought exceedingly well. Blood, the blood of Ilarians, covered parts of the ground, and the sight made me nauseous.

Three other things happened as I aimed at more of their archers.

The first involved about twenty fighters on horseback riding in from the direction of Scrud. This group of better-trained locals had hand-made weapons, mostly flails, and they charged into the clumps of Mongol fighters who'd evaded capture by banding together. They separated them, to make them vulnerable to the tactics used by the cow-herder groups of six.

Yes, I knew Bohdan was one of those twenty, riding to evade the swords, knives, and arrows of others as he fought to make our plan effective. I wanted to watch him, to protect him above all others, but I knew my eyes were desperately needed elsewhere.

The second commotion involved my sister Sulphur and her friend Issa, both of whom entered the melee with their swords drawn, looking to engage the Mongols on foot who were doing the worst of the damage with their own swords. I'd been told they'd aim to capture not kill, but Sulphur had warned me that in the unpredictability of a sword fight, lives could be lost. The one time I saw her, she fought three others at once and held her own, moving with the grace of a wildcat.

An invader came at her from behind and nearly got the best of her before Issa stepped in between them. After that, Sulphur and Issa fought back to back, holding off many. I managed to get two with my arrows but I think they subdued all the rest.

The third event began as the quietest of the three, but in the end, it mattered the most.

"Stop fighting. You will be returned to your Khan." Every Ilarian out there had been made to repeat these phrases in Mongolian over and over. Now, they made these foreign sounds to their prisoners. They said them to those yet to be captured. They chanted them together.

I knew they were saying "we will not kill you" even though I heard what sounded like "you guys char may all."

The Mongols ignored them at first. I guessed they weren't inclined to converse while at war and I might never have known otherwise if my long eyes hadn't happened to be trained on a face of one of them when he made the realization.

I saw it in his eyes.

These people, these barbarian foreigners, are attempting to speak my language!

He looked at the six herders surrounding him like they'd each grown a second head. He said something back. They didn't understand him, of course, but they all repeated the little they knew.

"Stop fighting."

"We will not kill you."

"We will return you to your Khan."

The Mongol laughed out loud. He yelled to the others, repeating the words and phrases with the sureness of a native speaker.

Many of them stopped fighting and listened. Some nodded, agreeing with him. Yes, perhaps these barbarians were trying to speak, as horrible as their pronunciation was.

The fighting paused everywhere except for in a few far-flung corners.

Then one of our more linguistically able took it a step further. He made the sounds to convey "They are not dead. Only sleeping."

This must have been a phrase offered in the advanced class because only a few others of ours knew it. Those few began to chant it, loudly, gesturing for more to join in.

Ted. Duck. He. Guy." Over and over. "They. Are. Not. Dead."

Some of ours pointed to the horses. Others to the men felled by my poison darts. The invaders looked skeptical until one of them turned back to the main camp. Two Ponytails stood, unsteady, as two of his men supported him.

"Ted duck he guy," we yelled.

"Ted duck he guy" they yelled back.

It wasn't much, but we had finally communicated.

The part I played in saving Ilari ended as some of the Mongols' horses began to wake and everyone joyously greeted each other with "Ted duck he guy," the way we would have said "Happy Kolada" to each other in another year. Perhaps the way we'd say it to each other a year from now.

Yes, blood was spilled. I saw several mangled bodies, both Mongol and Ilarian, and guessed about ten of each had died. I knew none of them, and one is always thankful for that, despite knowing strangers will be mourned by their loved ones as surely I would mourn my own.

I was asked to write my story and it ends here, but bear with me for a few more words, please, for I must add two more things before I stop.

One concerns my sister Sulphur. I watched her fight, her sword blazing with reflected sunlight as it moved with a speed I wouldn't have believed possible. She's so modest she doesn't understand how remarkable she is. So when she writes her story, just know that she was a woman far fiercer than she will admit. That way, you will better understand how Ilari survived.

The other is about me because I think if you read this far you should know.

By the time I walked from the cliffs into the main Mongol camp, Delia had gotten Magomet on their horse and they had ridden away. I don't know what went through his mind after that because we never spoke again. I think it shows that if you're persistent enough, some problems really will go away. That's something worth knowing.

Bohdan waited for me in the camp, having unbound his father. He gave the man some water as I approached.

"So," his dad said to me. "Better you alive and him happy than me listening to him mourn you for the rest of my life, right?"

What does one say to that? "Thanks for saving my life," didn't seem to fit, but for once the words I wanted came to me.

"Does that mean you'll visit us when he's over in K'ba? Better to have you around, you know, than for me to have to listen to him complain that you never come over, right?"

The man grinned. "Very good. I'll visit a time or two."

As Bohdan put his arm around me, he seemed the happiest of all with our exchange.

Sulphur walked towards us, her eyebrow arching at the sight of me being so affectionate with anyone, much less with a man from Scrud.

"Who's this?" she asked me.

It was time for the truth.

"My new husband."

"Well then." She gave Bohdan a smile filled with sunshine. "Welcome to the family."

She turned to me. "Another hundred or so Bisuites are riding in. Some will help escort the prisoners to individual homes and others will get the horses to safety now that they are waking up. Our invaders seem downright cheery knowing their horses are okay. Issa says she can handle things from here."

I saw how calm the group had become and I had to agree. Elsewhere in the realm, the battle probably raged, but it was over here in Bisu.

"You going somewhere?" I asked.

"I'm not ready to call it a day. If I hurry I'll make it to Vinx before everything ends. If they have the same sort of trouble with the captives we had here, I can help."

Joli came up behind her.

"Then Olivine and I could help, too."

I wasn't sure I wanted to go. I was exhausted.

"I should go alone," Sulphur said. "Faster that way."

"No, the four of us will go," Bohdan said.

"No one invited you," I replied. Varmin. He'd survived one battle. Did he have to do another?

"Did you see me out there with this mace? I'm experienced at separating them for capture."

"Maybe you ought to bring everyone who fought here? For reinforcements," Joli suggested.

"No." Sulphur shook her head. "Most of them are exhausted, and Issa needs the help of those who aren't. This is family only. The four of us will go."

Joli and Bohdan both got the message. "Let's go, family." Joli winked at Bohdan and gave him a friendly nudge.

I had another idea.

"We should make it five."

"No. Why?"

I pointed to Two Ponytails. "Bring him. He's proof without words that we hope to negotiate, not kill."

"He could be trouble," Joli said.

"I know. Put him on the horse with Bohdan." I turned to my husband. "You can handle him, right?"

Bohdan agreed. "The sight of him alive could be what saves the realm."

We gathered our horses and supplies and sat Two Ponytails in front of Bohdan with his hands tied together. Sulphur asked Joli to lead, so she and I could flank our prisoner. I rode with a meant-for-humans arrow ready to shoot while Sulphur kept one hand on her sword. Two Ponytails looked at us both with narrowed eyes, but he didn't seem inclined to put up a fight.

"You up for this?" Bohdan yelled back to me.

"I am. Let's go see if we can't help the next group save Ilari too!"

Thank you for reading my story of how I saved my entire world from oblivion
—Olivine Renata Glonti

What's Next?

The War Stories of the Seven Troublesome Sisters consists of seven short companion novels. Each tells the personal story and perspective of one of seven radically different sisters in the 1200s as they prepare for an invasion of their realm.

Which sister do you think saves Ilari? That will depend on whose story you are reading. For while each of these historical fantasy/alternate history books can be enjoyed as stand-alone novels, together they tell the full story of how Ilari survived. The last three books also describe the rest of the battle and its in many ways surprising outcome.

Want to make sure you don't miss a release? Go to my landing page at https://mailchi.mp/11db23804c68/tell-me-about-new-books to be notified when each book is ready for purchase. I promise you'll only get notifications about the release of these books.

If you enjoyed this story, please leave a review somewhere. If you enjoyed it a lot, please leave a review in several places.

Olivine's Older Sisters

She's the One Who Thinks Too Much

Ryalgar, a spinster farm girl and the oldest of seven sisters, has always preferred her studies to flirtation. Yet even she finally meets her prince. Or so she thinks. She's devastated to discover he's already betrothed and only wanted a little fun. Embarrassed, she flees her family's farm to join the Velka, the mysterious women of the forest known for their magical powers and for living apart from men.

As a Velka, she develops her special brand of telekinesis and learns she has a talent for analyzing and organizing information. Both are going to come in handy.

When this prince keeps meeting her at the forest's edge for more good times, she wonders if being his mistress isn't such a bad deal after all. Then she learns more about his princely assignment.

He's tasked with training the army of Ilari to repel the feared Mongol horsemen who have been moving westward, killing all in their path. And, her prince is willing to sacrifice the outer farmlands where she grew up to these invaders if he must. Ryalgar isn't about to let that happen.

She's got the Velka behind her, as well as a multitude of university intellectuals, a family of tough farmers, and six sisters each with her unique personality and talents.

Can Ryalgar organize all that into a resistance that will stop the invasion?

She's the One Who Thinks Too Much has been available in eBook and paperback since November 2020.

She's the One Who Cares Too Much

Coral, the second of the sisters, has been hiding her affair with the perfect man until Ryalgar can get her life together. But the perfect man is getting impatient, and now she's gotten pregnant. Coral decides it's time to consider her own happiness.

But what does she want? The perfect husband turns out to be less than ideal. She adores the small children she teaches but the idea of being a mother fills her with joy. Meanwhile, her homeland is gripped by fear of a Mongol invasion, and she can't stop crying about everything now that she's with child.

Then a friend suggests the ever-caring Coral has a power well beyond what she or anyone else imagines. Does she? And why is the idea so appealing?

When Ryalgar loses faith in the army and decides to craft a way to use magic to save Ilari, she decides Coral's formidable talent is what the realm needs. Can Coral raise a baby, placate an absent military husband who thinks he's stopping the invasion, and help her sister save her homeland?

She's the One Who Cares Too Much has been available in eBook and paperback since February 2021.

She's the One Who Gets in Fights

Sulphur, the third of seven sisters, is glad the older two have been slow to wed. It's given her the freedom to train as a fighter, in hopes of fulfilling her lifelong dream of joining Ilari's army. Then, within a matter of days, both sisters announce plans and now Sulphur is expected to find a man to marry.

Is it Sulphur's good fortune her homeland is gripped by fear of a pending Mongol invasion? And the army is going door to door encouraging recruits? Sulphur thinks it is. But once she's forced to kill in a small skirmish, she's ready to rethink her career decision. Too bad it's too late. The invasion is coming, and Ilari needs every good soldier it has.

Once Sulphur learns Ilari's army has made the strategic decision to not defend certain parts of the realm, including the one where her family lives, she has to re-evaluate her loyalty. Is it with the military she's always admired? Or is it with her sisters, who are hatching a plan to defend their homeland with magic?
Everywhere she turns, someone is counting on her to fight for what's right. But what is?

She's the One Who Gets in Fights has been available in eBook and paperback format since May 2021.

Olivine's Younger Sisters

She's the One Who Can't Keep Quiet

Celestine, the other twin, is the most social daughter in the family. She loves her music and pretty clothes and the crowds in the taverns who adore her and her singing. Yet, she's been hiding a secret all her life.

As a beauty with a lyrical voice, she's always been Mother's best hope for getting a prince as a son-in-law. When a liaison with a prince never happens, everyone assumes Celestine is being so picky because she can be.

But even in somewhat tolerant Ilari, a daughter hates to disappoint those she loves. How can she tell her family she's fallen in love with a princess instead?

Lucky for Celestine, all six of her sisters and her parents appear to be obsessed with an invading army headed to their realm. Celestine would rather ignore the threat, and enjoy the freedom their lack of attention gives her. Then she discovers her voice can unlock a power that may help save the realm and that the woman she adores wants to join the fight against the invaders.

Celestine knows she can inspire the citizens of Ilari to defend themselves, while her family, for all their talents, seem clueless about how to motivate the masses.

Is it time to put her inhibitions aside and use her voice to save those she cares about? Can she do it and still be true to who she is? And to who she loves?

She's the One Who Can't Keep Quiet will be available in eBook and paperback January 2022.

What About the Youngest Two Sisters?

Look for more information about **Gypsum** and **Iolite** in the next book.

About the Author

Sherrie Cronin is the author of a collection of six speculative fiction novels known as 46. Ascending and is now publishing a historical fantasy series called The War Stories of the Seven Troublesome Sisters. A quick look at the synopses of her books makes it obvious she is fascinated by people achieving the astonishing by developing abilities they barely knew they had.

She's made a lot of stops along the way to writing these novels. She's lived in seven cities, visited forty-six countries, and worked as a waitress, technical writer, and geophysicist. Now she answers a hot-line. Along the way, she's lost several cats but acquired a husband who still loves her and three kids who've grown up fine, both despite how eccentric she is.

All her life she has wanted to either tell these kinds of stories or be Chief Science Officer on the Starship Enterprise. She now lives and writes in the mountains of Western North Carolina, where she admits to occasionally checking her phone for a message from Captain Picard, just in case.

Find her at:
Facebook: facebook.com/46Ascending
Goodreads: goodreads.com/author/show/5805814.Sherrie_Cronin
Amazon: amazon.com/Sherrie-Cronin/e/B007FRMO9Q
Twitter: twitter.com/cinnabar01
Author Blog: sherriecronin.xyz/
Book Series Blog: troublesome7sisters.xyz/

Information About Ilari

Words Used by Ilarians

Ank: Nine days. Business is conducted during the first six days while the last three are intended for family life and leisure.

Heli: The hottest time of the year, but sometimes used as a cussword.

Luski: A feared, possibly imaginary creature who can control others with her voice.

Mozdol: A member of the Svadlu who has been made into an honorary prince due to brave actions defending the realm.

Nichna: One of the twelve principalities of Ilari. Each has its own royal family and is ruled by a prince. All twelve coordinate as regards the Svadlu and other matters of the common good. There is no king, therefore Ilari is not a kingdom.

Oomrush: telekinesis.

Pruck: An extremely rude word sometimes referring to copulation and other times merely expressing disgust or dismay.

Pruska: An extremely rude word referring to a female having any number of undesirable qualities.

Rantallion: A man who is being disagreeable, dishonest, or disgusting.

Reczavy: a group of free-spirited people living in the open forest who choose to continue and extend the sexual freedom allowed to tidzys.

Scump: a rude word referring to excrement.

Svadlu: The Ilarian army and police force. A member of the Svadlu is called a Svadlu.

Tidzy: A young adult who is searching for a mate and is allowed a great deal of sexual freedom around holidays.

Velka: A group of women who live in the open forest, possibly performing magic. A member of the Velka is called a Velka.

The Ilarian Calendar

A year in Ilari is divided into eight parts based on the seasons. Each eighth lasts for 45 days and is named for the holiday at its start.

Each eighth is subdivided into five anks. An ank is nine days long. Businesses and schools are open during the first six days of an ank while the last three, called the ank-break, are intended for family life and relaxation.

Every year astronomers consult the stars to decide which of the holidays will be inside their eighth and which will be treated as extra days. Most years, five or six are ruled to be extra days.

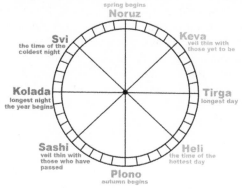

Holidays Marking the Beginning of Each Eighth

Kolada: The winter solstice, the shortest day of the year, and the start of a new year.

Svi: The coldest time of the year, halfway between the winter solstice and the spring equinox.

Noruz: The spring equinox, the start of spring.

Keva: A celebration of those yet to be, held halfway between the spring equinox and the summer solstice. More babies are conceived at Keva than at any other time of the year.

Tirga: The summer solstice, the longest day of the year, the halfway point of a year.

Heli: The hottest time of the year, halfway between the summer solstice and the autumn equinox. Ilarians are not fond of the heat and sometimes use "Heli" as a cussword.

Plono: The autumn equinox, the start of autumn.

Sashi: A celebration of those who have passed, held halfway between the fall equinox and the winter solstice.

The Twelve Nichnas

Ilari is a small hidden land consisting of twelve principalities.

The Entrance

Bisu: These low grasslands at the eastern edge of Ilari supply coveted beef and cows' milk to Ilarians.

The Dry Lands

Scrud: Rain-deprived Scrud is the poorest and least populated of the nichnas and the most lacking in natural resources. Most Scrudites survive by taking menial jobs in adjoining Bisu or K'ba.

K'ba: This drought-stricken nichna has survived by becoming home to artists, entertainers, and those seeking more freedom of choice. It is also a playground for the richest Ilarians and boasts a densely populated area known for its spectacular food and lodging.

Eds: These dry hills leading up to the mountains are sparsely populated with independent-minded goat herders.

The Mountains

Tolo: Home to the highest mountains in Ilari, independent Tolovians mine for ore, produce lumber, and serve as a gateway to the even higher mountains to the north.

The Farmlands

Lev: This nichna is home to the realm's famed vineyards and supplies Ilarians with wine, their most important beverage. It also leads the fashion scene and sparks trends within the realm.

Kir: Ilari's oldest farming region nestles between Pilk and Lev and grows specialty items for the connoisseurs in both of its neighboring nichnas.

Gruen: The fertile soil along the river makes for easy farming of fruits and vegetables and makes Gruen home to one of the two more densely populated areas outside of Pilk.

Vinx: With incredibly flat land sitting above cliffs, the high plains of Vinx provide the wheat, oats, rye, and barley that are the staples of an Ilarian's diet.

The Wet Lands

Faroo: This flood-prone nichna in the rivers bend struggles during heavy rains, but is known for fishing and the boating prowess of its residents.

Pilk: As the informal capital of Ilari, Pilk is home to the Svadlu headquarters, most of the institutes of higher learning, and much of the commerce in the realm. The ruling prince of Pilk coordinates cooperation among the twelve ruling princes. The Pilk Palace outshines any other building in Ilari.

The Forest

Zur: As the only nichna inside of Ilari's large central forest, Zur shares the woods with occupants of the Open Forest including the Velka, the reczavy, and scrounger Scrudites.

Map of Ilari

Meet the Ilarians in this Book

Aliz: Olivine's grandmother
Arek: Long eyed artist from Gruen, Olivine's friend
Bohdan: Woodcarver from Scrud
Celestine: Olivine's twin, a musician
Coral: Olivine's older sister, a luski
Delia: Artist from K'ba, Olivine's friend
Gypsum: Olivine's younger sister, part of the reczavy
Iolite: Olivine's youngest sister, a frundle
Jasia: Artist from K'ba, Magomet's mother
Joli: a Velka oomrusher, Olivine's friend
Magomet: Artist from K'ba, a man enamored with Olivine
Markita: Olivine's mother
Nikolo: Archery coach from Gruen, Arek's boyfriend
Olivine: Fourth child of Markita and Yasen, an artist who doesn't say much
Pasha: Artist from K'ba, Olivine's friend
Ryalgar: Olivine's oldest sister, a member of the Velka
Sulphur: Olivine's older sister, a member of the Svadlu
Yasen: Sulphur's father
Zoya: Artist from K'ba, Olivine's closest friend